CW01501600

For my parents, Juliette and Martin

THE WANDERING QUEEN

Claire Heywood is a scholar of the ancient world, having gained a 1st Class BA in Classical Civilisation and an MA with Distinction in Ancient Visual and Material Culture, along with two academic prizes, from the University of Warwick. Her writing is inspired by her love of mythology, her knowledge of ancient cultures and her fascination with women's forgotten voices. Originally from Coventry, she now lives and writes in Bristol, UK.

Also by Claire Heywood
Daughters of Sparta
The Shadow of Perseus

THE WANDERING QUEEN

CLAIRE HEYWOOD

HODDER &
STOUGHTON

First published in Great Britain in 2026 by Hodder & Stoughton Limited
An Hachette UK company

The authorised representative in the EEA is Hachette Ireland, 8 Castlecourt Centre,
Dublin 15, D15 XTP3, Ireland (email: info@hbgi.ie)

1

Copyright © Claire Heywood 2026

The right of Claire Heywood to be identified as the Author of the Work has been
asserted by her in accordance with the Copyright, Designs and Patents Act 1988.

All rights reserved. No part of this publication may be reproduced, stored
in a retrieval system, or transmitted, in any form or by any means without
the prior written permission of the publisher, nor be otherwise circulated
in any form of binding or cover other than that in which it is published and
without a similar condition being imposed on the subsequent purchaser.

All characters in this publication are fictitious and any resemblance to real persons,
living or dead, is purely coincidental.

A CIP catalogue record for this title is available from the British Library

Hardback ISBN 978 1 399 73025 9
Trade Paperback ISBN 978 1 399 73026 6
ebook ISBN 978 1 399 73028 0

Typeset in Sabon MT Std by Manipal Technologies Limited

Printed and bound in Great Britain by Clays Ltd, Elcograf S.p.A.

Hodder & Stoughton policy is to use papers that are natural, renewable
and recyclable products and made from wood grown in sustainable forests.
The logging and manufacturing processes are expected to conform
to the environmental regulations of the country of origin.

Hodder & Stoughton Limited
Carmelite House
50 Victoria Embankment
London EC4Y 0DZ

www.hodder.co.uk

'*But the queen had long since been suffering from love's deadly wound, feeding it with her blood and being consumed by its hidden fire.*'

Virgil, *The Aeneid* 4.1–2 (trans. David West)

Chapter 1

TYRE

Elissa rolled the dice sticks between her palms. She liked the crackle they made, that woody clatter she could produce with just a glide of her hand.

'Are you going to roll, Little Jackal?'

Her father's voice was impatient, but she could see the smile in his lips. She warmed at the sound of her new nickname. Her father had begun using it these past months, but only here. Only in the quiet, incense-filled air of his chamber. Only when it was just the two of them – as if it were their secret.

Elissa had to share so much of her father. She had to share him with the whole city. The people needed his love, his protection, his warm and wise words, just as much as she did. Every day, they came to the palace demanding these things. But he always saved a little of himself just for her. When she was younger, he had told her stories by lamplight, or picked flowers with her in the garden, or held her hand as she stepped across the rocks at the shore.

Now they played games. He enjoyed teaching her, and she enjoyed learning – for the most part.

Let it be a five, she thought, with eyelids pressed shut. She threw the sticks, and when she looked down, only two had their white bellies showing. Elissa let out a sigh and studied the board. The ivory heads of her jackal pieces stood alert, ears pricked.

'I needed a five,' she muttered. 'To get this piece to the end.'

'And you have a two. That is the way of it. Now, what will you do?' Her father looked at her with a familiar attention. The one that made her feel pleased and annoyed at the same time. He was testing her, and all she wanted was to impress him. For Elissa, there was nothing worse than being made to feel a fool.

'Which piece would you move?' she asked tentatively.

Her father was silent, as if he hadn't heard her, his bearded chin resting on his fist. 'Don't let yourself be trapped, Little Jackal,' he said eventually. 'You must be wily. Put yourself into the mind of your opponent. Know when to guard yourself, and when to act boldly.'

The same advice he had been giving since he'd started teaching her this game. A few months ago, he might have touched one of her jackals, or at least given her a meaningful look, but now he sat still as a stone.

Elissa studied the board once more. 'There are no safe moves!' she complained.

'Then you must make a dangerous one. There is no standing still.'

She glanced between her white jackal heads, and finally lifted one from its hole, placing it down again two holes further along.

Her father's face revealed nothing as he rolled the dice sticks. A four. He picked up one of his own hound-headed pieces and removed hers from the board. Elissa felt her cheeks burn and sullenly rolled the sticks. She would never win now.

'Well done, Little Jackal,' her father said when he had brought his last piece inevitably home.

'I lost,' Elissa grumbled, avoiding his eyes as she put the dice sticks roughly back into their box.

'But you played well.' When she looked up, he was smiling. 'You sharpen yourself with every game. You are so very clever, my Little Jackal.'

She couldn't help beaming at that, though her brow did not fully unfold. 'You always win.'

'Not always.'

'Usually,' she insisted.

'I have played a great many more games than you. You are young yet, my daughter. Do you think I was born with the wits of a king?' He held her gaze in a curious way then, which somehow dampened the burn of her defeat. He looked as if he would say more, and she waited for it. But instead, he pushed himself up from his seat. 'Kiss your brother goodnight before you go to bed.'

The baby had already been laid down when Elissa's clacking steps reached the chamber. She softened them, creeping towards the cradle with a penitent smile that made Barce, the nurse, chuckle.

'He is sound asleep. Don't worry yourself,' she whispered, moving aside so that Elissa could look down into the cot.

Her brother was swaddled in soft wool, and perfectly still apart from the occasional wrinkle of his nose. She studied his face, trying to find something of her father's features there, but it was still too early to tell. Perhaps he would take after his mother, with her high forehead and her flat little nose. Elissa hoped not. She wanted to share something with her brother, a resemblance that would make people smile and say, 'There go the children of the king.' They already admired her arched nose. 'A daughter of King Mattan and no mistake,' they would say. And every time she would beam, holding her chin just a little higher as if to display her inheritance.

She did not remember her own mother's face, not as anything more than a warm smile framed in dark curls. She could not know which parts of her were owed to that woman; if there were any, nobody seemed to speak of them. Nobody seemed to speak of her mother at all. Her father was the anchor of her life, and her identity. He was what joined her unbreakably to that soft, dreaming face in the cradle. She liked to feel that connection, branching out from her in two directions now, instead of one.

'May I kiss him goodnight? Father said I should.'

'Go on, then,' said Barce. 'But don't fuss him.'

Elissa leaned down and brushed her lips against his downy forehead. 'I'm here, little brother,' she whispered. 'I'll keep you safe. I won't let anything happen to you. Not ever.'

She knew he was not her full brother, not her mother's son. But Pygmalion was the only sibling she had ever known, and she loved him fiercely.

When she straightened up, Barce was smiling. 'He is lucky to have you for a sister.' She put an arm around Elissa's shoulder and squeezed her. 'You have ten more years of life than him. He will need you and that clever mind of yours. Even if he does not know it yet.'

Elissa felt her cheeks glow from the nurse's praise.

'And especially with that fool mother of his . . . ' Barce sucked her teeth, then shook her head. 'Asherah, forgive me. I shouldn't say such things. Not of the queen.' And yet as her tongue slid over that word, she seemed to find it distasteful.

Elissa remained quiet, enjoying the feeling of the woman's arm around her. She had spent less time with Barce since Pygmalion was born. She knew her brother had more need of a nurse than she did, but that did not stop her feeling a little abandoned.

They stood like that for a while, watching Pygmalion's sleeping face.

When Barce spoke again her words were slow, as if carefully chosen. 'It is good for you, too, Elissa, to treat your brother well. To make sure that he cares for you, as you care for him.'

Elissa felt the nurse look down at her, but she kept her eyes on the cradle. Why shouldn't her brother care for her? Father always spoke affectionately of his sisters, recounting the mischief they had made together in their youth, before they had gone away to be married.

'He will have great power one day,' her nurse continued. 'Power over Tyre, and over you. Your father rules your life now. He makes decisions for you, and he keeps you safe. One day he will be gone – Melqart preserve him – and you will look to your brother instead. Do you hear me, Elissa?' The nurse moved her hand along the cradle edge, pressing it over the young fingers that were gripped there. 'You'll do well to be sweet to him. A brother's love is a valuable protection, for any woman.'

Elissa's face wrinkled and she tugged her hand away. She already loved her brother. She did not want to be *told* to do so. And she didn't like Barce's talk of a future without her father in it.

'I'm going to bed now,' she said simply, turning her back on the cradle. She felt the nurse's hand brush her dress sleeve, but knew she would not follow. Barce had a more important charge now, and Elissa was too old and too clever to be lectured to as if she were a know-nothing fool.

Chapter 2

CARTHAGE

Loss had become a part of Dido. It was a hole that filled her with its emptiness, pressing up against her insides. After so many years the feeling had joined with the rhythm of her body, like the slow sucking of air into her chest, the uncommanded beating of her heart. So natural as to feel unconscious, and yet so conscious, when remembered, as to consume her.

It had not always been that way. At first, her loss had torn and seared, howling like a beast. Then it had sat like a jagged thing within her, possible to ignore if she kept herself still enough, until an unexpected movement would send a jolt of agony and a thunderous message from her own soul: *Do not let yourself forget.* It was her penance, she told herself, to let the loss reside within her, even after all this time. She could not banish or forget the pain of it. Not entirely. And when she felt it receding, when its edges began to lose the last of their sharpness, she would reshape them. Just enough to know that it was still there, still pressing against her, still keeping her company. To not feel the loss at all would be a new bereavement, a fresh guilt. It would be a betrayal.

The grove was where Dido came to remember. There was a quiet to the place, away from the city. A solitude. And yet the rustling sighs that came from the leaves overhead were enough to remind her that she was not alone. There was a piece of him here. Not a body, and not even ashes. The earth was as untouched as when she had found it. But of all the places that made her kingdom, Dido knew this was where his spirit would choose to be.

'I thought I might find you here.'

Dido did not like to be disturbed when she came to the grove, but she smiled to hear Iarbas's voice.

'If you'd rather be left alone, I'll go,' he said, holding up his palms and taking half a step back.

'No. No, stay,' she said. 'The sun is getting low. I should be returning to the city anyway.' Dido looked up at the blushing sky. 'I hardly realised how long I'd been here.'

He nodded respectfully. The black locks of his hair were braided, as usual, falling past his ears and almost touching the dark, smooth skin of his shoulders. 'Shall I walk with you, then?' he asked, letting a little of his habitual smile fill his cheeks. 'Even Queen Dido may need an escort when the hyenas start to roam.'

She scoffed. 'Cowardly creatures. A fierce stare and they go on their way.'

Iarbas laughed. 'A stare from you?' He pretended to shudder. 'I don't blame them. Well, then, perhaps it is you who should escort me.'

He put out an arm, bare apart from its tattoos, and Dido linked her own around it.

'Hyenas or not, I shall be glad of the company.'

They fell into a familiar step, smoothed by years of friendship. The silhouette of the city lay ahead, a huddled crowd of roofs and towers. Dido knew every line of it.

'What is that new building there, on the east side?' Iarbas asked.

'A granary,' she said. 'We needed another, now that the fields are producing better.'

'Producing well, I should say.'

Dido smiled to hear how impressed he was.

'You know, when you first arrived, I thought you a little mad,' he said.

'You have told me so. More than once.' She squeezed his arm playfully.

'And you may still be mad,' he carried on. 'But I cannot deny what you have built here. Your husband would be proud.'

Dido felt herself stiffen, and Iarbas must have felt it too, for he fell quiet. For a while they walked in silence, their elbows suddenly jostling with one another in a way they hadn't before.

'And are you . . . happy?' Iarbas's voice was thin, hesitant. So unlike his usual rich timbre. He kept his eyes on the city ahead.

'My people are thriving,' she replied.

'That's not what I asked.' He stopped, and Dido had no choice but to stop with him. She unlinked herself from his arm and turned to look at him, to prove to him – or perhaps to herself – that she was not afraid to meet his gaze.

'I know what you are going to say,' she said shortly. 'You have said it so many times, even though you know my answer. You'll say that I should remarry. That I cannot mourn forever. That I should marry you.' She thrust her hands on to her hips, ignoring his step forward. 'You know why I cannot. I have made a vow, Iarbas, to my husband and to myself.'

'I know,' he said softly. The regret in his voice took some of the tension from her arms. 'I'm sorry. Please. I should not have said anything. Come, let us go on as we were before.'

She considered him for a moment, while the evening breeze whipped strands of black hair across her cheeks. She should be flattered, she knew. Iarbas was handsome, well-respected, a leader among his people. She had known him for as long as she had been in Libya, since before the first stone of her city had been laid. Over those years, she had appreciated his friendship, and – more than once – his advice. But his talk of marriage only made her feel guilty. Guilty that he had not taken another woman as his wife. He must have had opportunities. Did he hold back because of her? And guilty, too, that she might ever have entertained the idea of saying yes to him. That she might still entertain it. If not for his own happiness, she wished for her sake that he would marry someone else.

'It is forgotten,' she said, forcing a smile. He smiled too, and though she saw genuine relief cross his face, there was a shadow of sadness behind it.

Eventually, they regained some of their usual ease, and by the time they reached the city, Dido's chest was feeling light once more.

'Will you join me for dinner?' she asked.

'I cannot,' Iarbas replied with a dip of his head. 'My tribe must begin the journey south tomorrow. We go to Lake Triton for the winter.'

Dido felt something within her sink. She ought to have expected his departure. The Auseans only ever brought their flocks as far as Carthage during the summer months. Now that they were finished grazing and trading, she would not see Iarbas again until the spring. She wondered, though, whether he had brought forward their day of departure due to her sharp words.

'Carthage will miss you,' she said, swallowing her regret.

'And I shall miss her,' he said, with a smile.

Chapter 3

TYRE

Pygmalion's nose did not grow to be arched like his father's. The prince was now nine years old, and in almost every regard he resembled his mother. Elissa wondered that she had heard no whisperings about his legitimacy, but then again she doubted anyone at the palace would believe such rumours, even in idle speculation. Pygmalion's mother was only a few years older than Elissa herself, brought to Tyre from Egypt as a wide-eyed child. At the time Elissa could not understand why her father should choose such a bride, but now she understood that the queen had brought much wealth with her, through trade and through gifts. And she had produced a son. What other purpose was there for a queen? She had played her part and earned her title, but the idea that she might have had the gall to conduct an affair was laughable. Even now, as a grown woman, she seemed to do little but nod her perfumed head and smile her vacant smile.

It was not her fault, Elissa had to remind herself. Queen Meret had been taught to recite pretty verses, and to play the flute sweetly, but little else. She had been sent off to her husband without the time to form a sense of herself. It made Elissa grateful to be not yet married. With no children to mind, nor a husband to mind her, she spent her days as she pleased. She could pass a morning in the palace archive reading tales and histories, an afternoon browsing the markets with Barce. And she still played Hounds and Jackals with her father – he insisted on it – whenever he could spare an evening.

She sat in on his audiences, too, not only because he liked her to, but because they were the best way to know what was happening in the city and in the world beyond Tyre. Every petitioner brought a new story, a new puzzle to be solved. She had watched her father give so many rulings that she often knew what his answer would be before he had given it. She made a game of it.

That helped on days like this one, when the air of the petition hall sat thick and still, and the summer heat made Elissa's chin, slick with sweat, slide from her hand each time she propped it up. Despite the soporific mood of the chamber, Elissa remained alert, studying each petitioner, listening with attention to the details of their case. She studied her father's face too, his wrinkles of concern, the puff of his cheeks when he grew frustrated. But she had learned not to be misled by these signs. Feeling and rightness were cousins, not twins.

The man who stood before her father now had a voice that droned like a fly you have given up hope of swatting. Its volume rose and fell, punctuated by a laboured clearing of the throat, and just when Elissa thought his speech had ended, it would begin again.

' . . . and you surely know, King Mattan, that my family has provided grain for the city for three generations – good grain, and always without pests or rot – and that we have always been fair in our dealings, even when disasters strike us or when Tyre's need has been great. We have behaved with all honour under the gods. And I know that the gods have granted you a fair mind – praise be to you and to Melqart who preserves you – and that you, King Mattan, will not allow such injustice to take place in the noble city of Tyre, when my family has—'

Her father waved a hand for silence. Elissa had been watching as his bearded jaw grew stiff with impatience – something the petitioner seemed not to notice. Now the man stood open-mouthed, held in suspense as he wrung a crumpled hat between his hands.

'You shall have the compensation you ask for,' said King Mattan curtly. 'Speak with the harbour master. He will see to it.'

The man blinked with astonishment, before rushing a clumsy bow. 'I thank you seven times and seven times more . . . '

'Once will be enough,' said the king.

As he was led away and the next petitioner was brought forward, Elissa smiled to herself. She had known her father would grant the man what he had asked for, even if he had done himself little favour in the asking. Words could be sweet or stale, but truth was truth and fair was fair. If there was one thing she had learned through all her hours in the petition hall, it was that a citizen's charm was not equal to his need.

The latest supplicant – a thin woman with a babe in arms – had begun to speak, but Elissa's attention was dragged away to her right as Pygmalion let out a loud sigh.

'Another one?' he whined. 'I thought we were going to go and see the ships. Mother said I could see the ships today.'

'Hush, now,' Barce whispered, as eyes were drawn in their direction.

Elissa saw her father frown as he tried to hear the thin woman's petition. Between her own fussing child and the dissatisfied huffs of Pygmalion, the woman's words had been lost.

'I will take you to see the ships later,' Elissa murmured, keeping her face forward so as not to bring further attention to the disruption. 'First we must listen to father and his visitors.'

'Why must we?' Pygmalion grumbled.

'Because he has asked us to. Because you must learn how things are done, for when you are king.'

'When I am King of Tyre, I shall do nothing I do not want to do. I will send all these people away.'

He waved a flamboyant hand in the air, but Elissa snatched it and pulled it down by his side.

'Ow!' Pygmalion cried out, though she knew she had not hurt him.

All eyes were upon them now, including her father's. They looked darker than usual, shaded under his heavy brow. Elissa cringed under the weight of his displeasure.

King Mattan rose to his feet and clasped his elegant hands together. He swayed a little as he stood before the throne, and there were beads of sweat on his forehead. He must be as tired of the stifling hall as they all were, Elissa thought, but her father was ever dutiful to the needs of his people. It was one of the things she admired most in him.

'My apologies,' he said, addressing the thin woman, who looked to be almost on the verge of tears. 'Please, come forward and begin your tale again. You said your husband drowned . . . '

But then he stopped. The next word, half-formed in his mouth, seemed to choke his tongue and make his eyes grow wide. Then his face creased in pain and he clutched at his chest, the purple cloth of his tunic slipping beneath desperate fingers.

There was quiet for a moment, as if the room were waiting politely for the king to regain himself. But then he staggered forward, and shouts of panic erupted. Elissa barely heard them. Climbing over the bench before her, she pushed through shoulders and elbows, and stretched out her arms just in time to catch him as he fell.

'Father?' she gasped, as they lay crumpled together. But his eyes were pressed tightly shut, and the shudder of his breath made her shake with terror.

Chapter 4

TYRE

King Mattan had lain in his bed for three days. Elissa spent most of her waking hours beside him, hunched over on a carved cypress stool so that she could be close enough to hold his hand and hear his thin voice. He was lucid when he spoke, though the words came slowly sometimes and seemed to require an effort that made Elissa's chest tight with fear. His breaths were long and rattling, leaving little flecks of saliva about his lips that he either did not feel or could not summon the energy to wipe away. Elissa grew to hate their glistening – an indignity that looked so wrong on his once proud face, that made his mouth look so slack and aged despite the perfect black of his beard.

'I wish I had done more,' he said to her on the third evening. The two of them had been silent for some time, and Elissa had thought that he'd fallen asleep again. But now she leaned in, her body aching from hours sitting on the stool. 'I wish I had had more time. With you, with your brother.'

And there again came the fear she had been fighting for three days, pressing at her throat. She swallowed. 'Don't speak like that,' she said. 'You are not old yet. You have plenty of time. You will beat me at Hounds and Jackals a hundred times, and I will beat you a hundred times more.' She brought his hand to her lips and kissed it. 'You just need to rest. You have been doing too much, Father. Let Urumilki handle things for a few days.'

Urumilki was her father's secretary. A reserved man, his taciturnity made him seem austere at times, but Elissa knew there was no one her father trusted better. Urumilki would make sure that everything was kept in order for when the king was well enough to continue his duties.

'Yes. Urumilki,' her father muttered.

Elissa was pleased by his agreement, thinking that she had succeeded in putting his mind at rest. But then her father began to shift beneath his gold-embroidered covers, face creasing with effort as he tried to push himself upright.

'Would you send for him, Elissa? Yes, I must have Urumilki here. Ask the guard to bring him.'

Elissa did not want her father to overexert himself, but it was a relief to see his eyes looking less dim. She did as she was asked.

When Urumilki arrived, he had his usual leather bag slung over one shoulder – so much a part of his silhouette that Elissa could not picture him without it.

'Good,' her father said as he saw the short-statured man. 'I need a fresh tablet. You have one?'

It was more a statement than a question. Urumilki opened the flap of his bag and drew out a neat wooden frame. Elissa could see the soft red clay pressed flat against the wood, and turned to tell her father that he shouldn't be bothering himself with decrees and missives. But before she could speak, a long-fingered hand was waved in her direction.

'Come, sit close,' her father rasped to his secretary.

Elissa stood without needing to be asked, and shuffled backwards, away from the bed, so that Urumilki could take her place on the stool. The king had closed his eyes and seemed to swallow with great concentration. When he was finished, his eyes snapped open again, and were as sharp as Elissa had ever seen them.

'Urumilki,' he began, 'you have been my secretary for two decades. You have been the hand that fixes my words in clay, the mind that remembers what I have forgotten. You have been my servant and my friend for all these years, and when I tell you that what I say here in this room now must be recorded with perfect fidelity and exactitude, I know that I am speaking needlessly.'

Urumilki only nodded, his wedged stylus already gripped and hovering above the clay.

Her father took a deep breath and closed his eyes once more, as if to focus on gathering his words.

'I, King Mattan of Tyre, servant of the gods and of his people, by the authority of earth-nourishing Melqart and of bow-breaking Ashtart, hereby give my final and binding testament.'

The pressure that had been building in Elissa's throat became an icy hand, its squeeze so sudden that she choked.

Her father paused as though he had heard it, but he did not open his eyes.

'First and foremost,' he went on, 'my will is that, upon my death, rule of Tyre is to pass to my son, Pygmalion, and to my daughter, Elissa. They shall be called King and Queen respectively, and will share in equal dignity and power. However, until such time as my son reaches his maturity, rule of the city is to be conducted by my daughter, who shall be recognised in the words and in the hearts of every citizen as Queen Elissa.'

Her father opened his eyes now, but Elissa could not imagine the tangle of emotions he found on her face. Surprise. Disbelief. And, wrestling them both, pushing tears into her eyes, an overwhelming love.

'You would trust me with this?' she asked him.

'Like no other.'

She sucked in a breath and briskly wiped away the tears that were hanging from her eyelashes. *Queen Elissa*. His words resounded in her mind, giving life to a future she had never considered. Visions of it rushed at her like a river breaking its dam. She saw herself sitting upon her father's throne, rapt faces awaiting the solutions and solace that her words could bring. She imagined Pygmalion at her side, growing under her care, becoming a king worthy of his father, someone with whom she could one day share the burdens of power. But to let that image live within her, to let it run away and fill her up, was to push her father out. She was not ready to accept the truth he seemed so sure was coming.

'But this is only a precaution,' she said. 'This testament. You are only saying this because you feel tired and afraid. We will not need it. You will have more time. Pygmalion will be strong and grown before you leave us.'

She came towards the bed, brushing against Urumilki on his stool so that she could clasp her father's hands.

'You are right,' he said, and Elissa felt herself loosen a little in relief. 'I do speak from fear. I fear for the future of Tyre, for the hands that it will fall into once I am gone. Your brother is young – only a child. And his mother cannot be given power as his regent. She would not know what to do with it, would pass it off to the noble with the most charming smile or the hungriest hands.' He looked weary and bitter, the sides of his mouth dragged down. 'But do not mistake me,' he continued, raising his eyes to meet hers, and clutching her hands with sudden vigour. 'I have not made this decision because Pygmalion is weak. I have made it because you are strong, Elissa. You are clever. You are wise. You have a heart that beats for this city. You are my daughter, the daughter I have raised. And you will succeed me not as your brother's regent, but as a true ruler. Do you understand?'

She nodded, but his grip remained desperate.

'I understand,' she said.

And she did. All the years of her youth, all the hours playing games in his chamber, all the long days he had insisted she
spend in the petition hall. The way he would watch her, guide
her, ask her strange and challenging questions. All these memories began to take on new meaning. It was as if he had known
all along that he would need her to take his place. That Tyre
would need her. He had shaped her like a tool, tempered her
to withstand the task, sharpened her edges until they gleamed.
But she did not feel used by him. She felt valuable. Worthy. All
her life, he had told her how clever she was, how she would
do great things. And here was the proof of his faith in her.
She had lived up to all he'd hoped she would be – for why else
would he entrust the city to her? Elissa's chest was full with
that thought.

'I will not disappoint you,' she said, fighting to keep her voice
solid. 'When the time comes. When you need me to rule, I will
do it. I will remember all that you have taught me.' She forced
a smile and reached out to stroke her father's cheek. 'But that
time is far away.'

He said nothing, though he looked relieved. The deep creases
of his mouth and brow seemed to smooth as he pressed her
hand. 'You must allow me to finish my testament now,' he said,
speaking to her as if she were a child again, bursting in on one
of his meetings with Urumilki.

'Of course, Father.' Elissa drew herself away, letting her hand
linger on the embroidered coverlet as if it were an extension of
the man who lay beneath it. Once she was standing at the edge
of the room, her father resumed his formal manner, rattling off
instructions about the palace, the temples, about trade shipments and foreign affairs. And all the while, Urumilki's stylus
pressed its little shapes, and her father's words became everlast-
ing. The permanent potential of the clay, its ability to turn mere
mortal breath to stone, made her feel cold.

When his words were finished, her father took up the small onyx cylinder that hung at all times around his neck and rolled it along the bottom of the clay tablet. Elissa could not see its printed design from where she stood, but she knew it well from memory: a string of lions processing among delicate lotus flowers.

'See that it is fired immediately,' he said as Urumilki took the tablet frame from him.

'Of course, my lord,' the secretary said, before he stowed the tablet carefully in his bag, bowed deeply, and left the chamber.

'And will you get some sleep, Elissa?' her father asked gently. A little warmth seemed to return to his cheeks as he smiled at her. 'I have the guards if I should need anything. Please, child. Rest yourself, for my sake. I will be here when you return.'

As ever, she could not deny her father. She kissed his head before she left, and smelled his hair, and squeezed his hand.

She did not see him alive again.

Chapter 5

CARTHAGE

It was a grey day, good for walking. The night's rain had left a freshness in the air and Dido breathed deeply as she made her way along the wooded cliff. There was a secret path she took sometimes, out here toward the north of the promontory, that she tracked by certain rocks and forks. She knew she would never get lost here, but also that she was unlikely to be found. It was necessary to extricate herself from the city every now and then, to allow herself the space to remember who she was without it. She never walked too far, though, always felt its distant energy behind her. She strode away with the comfort that Carthage would always be there when she turned back.

The wind was high but the trees sheltered her, and she enjoyed the rippling rush of their leaves. Dido had only just begun to wear her heavy shawl again, as the autumn twisted towards winter. She wondered whether Iarbas and his flocks had reached Lake Triton yet, and whether his journey had been easy or difficult. She thought of their last conversation and told herself that all frictions were worn smooth in friendships as long as theirs. They would talk as easily as ever when he returned.

Dido's mind was far ahead in spring when her eyes came upon a shape they did not expect. She stopped and stood still, but the man had already noticed her. He had a bow across his back, but his hands were busy with hauling a whole stag by its hind legs. The creature still had one of his arrows sticking from its neck.

The man let go of his quarry, but did not reach for his weapon. His hands were out in front of him, open and peaceful. He was not one of her people – she knew that immediately. But since she did not feel threatened enough to run, she decided the best thing would be to step confidently toward him.

'What is your name?' she asked in Akkadian, the language of diplomacy. It was a good choice, for the man's face broke with relief.

'Aeneas,' he panted.

His hair and beard were dark, tangled black by water and speckled with sand. His tanned brow was beaded with sweat and his tunic stuck to his chest. The overall effect was of a man who might have just stepped out of a heavy mist. He did not seem old – no older than she was, at least, perhaps in his mid-thirties – but his face had a worn quality, and his eyes looked out from beneath his fringe with a fearfulness that put her own worry to rest.

'How did you come here?'

'By ship. Through a storm.' He was still out of breath from hauling the stag, and by the way he spoke, she knew that Akkadian was no more his true tongue than it was hers.

'It is late in the year to be sailing,' she said with a frown.

'We had . . . no choice.' The man paused to gather his voice. 'We were forced from our home by war. We have spent many months upon the sea, and found hospitality on Sicily for a time. But we could not expect our host to keep us through winter. We meant to sail north to Italy, to the fertile lands they say are found there, but the storms tore us from our bearing and now . . . Now I do not even know what land we are in.' He spoke with bitter exhaustion, and when he wiped his brow, his hand left behind a streak of blood and dirt.

'How many of you?' Dido asked. 'Where are the others?'

'A boat full when we left Troy. Overfull. But we have lost some since then.' His lips were tight. 'Those who are left wait on the beach. I said that I would go ahead and look at the land from higher ground. And the stag . . . That would be something, would it not? Something I could do for them. If I could take away their hunger, at least?'

He looked at her as if he were truly asking for assurance. But at the same time he seemed distracted, perhaps pulled away by his fatigue, or by his evident grief, or by something else she did not understand.

She spoke gently. 'Troy. Is that your city?'

'It was. No doubt there is little left of it.'

She thought of the woes that had beset her own homeland, the cities attacked or burned, the fate of once-rich Ugarit. She could not remember if she had ever heard the name of Troy, but she let the stranger's loss affect her as if she had.

'Your countrymen are fortunate to have a scout like you to serve them. They will appreciate the meat, I am sure.' She nodded at the great limp body at his feet and hazarded a smile.

The man seemed to come out of himself. 'I am not their scout. Today, perhaps.' He shook his head. 'Today, I am whatever they most need me to be.'

'Then what are you, to your people?'

'Their prince.'

Dido had a rare feeling of embarrassment, but the man – Aeneas, he had called himself – did not look offended.

'And what are you, to your people?' he asked, looking over her finely embroidered shawl as if seeing it for the first time.

'Their queen.'

He nodded as if he had no energy for surprise. 'Then it is you I must beseech. Do not drive us from this place. We could not leave if we wanted to. Our ship is wrecked. My men are tired and injured. Please, tell your husband that we will be no threat to him. We only wish to recover ourselves, and then we will be away as soon as we are able.'

Dido smiled with a mixture of irritation and satisfaction that she had tasted before. 'I have no husband. There is no king at Carthage. Nor has there ever been.'

This time, Aeneas's surprise was strong enough to overcome him, and she saw his eyebrows rise. 'Indeed? Well, it is good fortune that we have met.' He bowed, and she could see his strong body tense at the effort. He straightened stiffly.

'Come back with me to the city,' she offered. 'You can rest there, and I will send men to escort your people after you. You are all welcome for as long as you need to stay. We have food enough harvested for winter, and timber to repair your ship. Come, you have dragged that stag far enough. My men will collect it for your welcome feast.'

Aeneas's face quivered. 'Thank you.' His head dropped as if it had been hanging on a thread. 'Thank you, sincerely. We will make our way to your city if you only show me the direction. I cannot come with you now. I must return to the beach and speak with my men. They are waiting for me.'

'You are already exhausted.' She recognised his sense of duty, and admired it – just as she admired a prince whose hands were soiled and shaking from a determination to provide for his people – but she also felt a need to protect him from it. If anyone knew the weight of duty upon a grieving soul, she did. 'Your men will be well cared for – you have my word. They will join you in the city.'

'No.' Aeneas shook his head. 'You don't understand. My son waits for me at the beach. He is only young, and will be afraid if I do not return.'

It was Dido's turn to be surprised, though she didn't know why she should be. He was old enough to have a host of sons.

But the stranger's identity was being made with every word they passed, and she understood now that his duty and hers were not entirely the same.

'Of course. Yes, you must go to him. I understand. When you are ready, my city is only a few miles to the south. Follow the coast, and you will not miss it.' She pointed back toward Carthage and smiled warmly. 'We will have food and beds waiting for you.'

Chapter 6

CARTHAGE

It was early evening by the time the Trojans arrived. They brought with them the stag that Aeneas had hunted, strung over a broken ship beam. They brought other things, too, the objects of their former lives carried with them across the sea, strapped across their backs or tucked away in boxes. This must have been what her own people had looked like, Dido realised, a decade ago when they had spilled on to this shore. She looked around at her fellow Carthaginians, who were at their doors to watch the stream of new faces. Did it feel as strange to them as it did to her? As if they were watching their own history played out again?

Thinking back to that time did not make her sad, only resolved. She and her people had been met with friendship then, and she would give out the same now.

'Set your things down in the palace porch,' she called as the line of men and women approached. 'They will be safe there. Rest, now, for you are guests of Carthage.'

Some of the Trojans smiled gratefully, or thanked her as they passed. Others were mute with exhaustion, and looked about them with dull eyes. They were in need of refreshment, and Dido was well prepared to offer it. Meat had been roasted and stewed, bread baked, and wine jars unsealed.

She spotted Aeneas among the file of refugees. He looked less storm-washed than he had earlier, but his face was still lined with cares as he took in the buildings of the city and carried his young son upon his shoulders. The boy was squirming to get down and his father obliged, leading him by the hand for the last steps towards the palace. Dido smiled at them, but Aeneas did not see it.

There was no woman walking beside the prince, she noticed. Perhaps the boy's mother was one of those lost on the journey. It was a cruel pity, Dido thought. And yet the boy was fortunate, too, to have survived all that he had and to have a father who so clearly loved him. The boy jumped over the palace threshold with all the lightness of one so young in years, for whom each moment is new and separate, unweighted by the past.

Dido made a show of having the stag taken away to be cooked. The Trojans had carried it with great effort, and she knew that they had brought it as a gift of sorts, a contribution to the feast of friendship.

What she did not anticipate were the further gifts that Aeneas brought to her table. When all were seated and the food was about to be served to the hall, the prince approached with his son trailing behind him. In his own arms he carried a sumptuously woven dress, with a border of yellow acanthus flowers. Resting atop it were a string of perfect pearls, and a fine-bladed dagger with an ivory handle and case of silver. Dido gasped at the beauty of the gifts, but before she could speak, Aeneas ushered his young son forward.

'This is Ascanius,' he said proudly. 'My son and heir. He has his own gift to present.'

He nodded at the boy, who raised up his doughy arms. In his hands was a gold diadem, delicately wrought and gleaming with polished amethysts. It was the first time the boy's shy eyes had met hers, and she felt a tender part of her unlock.

'It's for your head,' he said simply, and she beamed.

'Oh, it's wonderful. These are all marvellous gifts.' She found her hand absentmindedly touching the ruby-studded fillet that already sat across her black hair. 'But your generosity is too great. I cannot take these treasures of your homeland. You have carried them so far. They are too precious.'

To her dismay, Aeneas's expression darkened. 'It is right that a guest should give gifts, and a host receive them.' He looked at her pointedly. 'We are not without wealth, though we are without a home. It is my honour for you to have these things, which are as fine as can be found in any land.'

She knew then that she had hurt his pride, and hurried to amend her mistake. 'Of course. I only wished to express my appreciation of their value. As precious as they have been to you, they will now be to me.' She smiled smoothly and laid her hand across the bundle to indicate her acceptance. 'Now come, sit at my table. The food is being brought. Let us feast together as friends and allies.'

The dark cloud cleared from Aeneas's face as he took a seat along from Dido. He put his son Ascanius between them, but she did not feel affronted. She was pleased to have the child's lively energy beside her, novel as it was, and laughed as he began to take enthusiastic fistfuls of food from the plates within his reach.

Between watching Ascanius and seeing to her own appetite, Dido let a few of her glances go sideways to the prince of Troy. She noted how he half-filled his plate, how he picked at what he had taken, how his own gaze seemed to cast restlessly about the hall. The men and women who had come with him from the beach seemed well contented with her hospitality. They ate heartily, laughed and sang with one another as their cups were refilled. She was pleased to see their aching bodies relaxing, their eyes brightening gradually under the torchlight. But Aeneas watched them as if he were a shepherd far from home with clouds closing in above him. His noble face was alert, his mouth chewing distractedly.

Dido wanted to say something that might ease him, but she didn't trust herself to find the right words. She did not know him well enough, and had already pricked him once. Before long, he rose from his seat and took a position in the corner of the room, leaning against a pillar and half-obscured in shadow. His eyes continued to trace over the convivial benches, but Dido could not tell whether what he saw brought him any solace. She could tell little at all from that face, in truth. The cares she imagined were woven from what he had said, and embroidered by her own experience.

Her preoccupation with the half-shadowed prince was disturbed by an unusual sensation – the warmth of a small hand clasping her arm. She looked down in surprise as Ascanius leaned himself against her. His eyes were battling to stay open, and his little body sighed contentedly. No wonder he was sleepy, she thought, now that his belly was full of bread and baked quince.

She smiled and tried to keep still in her seat, to avoid unsettling him. Perhaps he had forgotten that he sat in an unknown hall, that the woman beside him was a stranger. Or perhaps, in the little time that had passed since their meeting, he had decided that she was no longer a stranger, that the gentleness of her voice and the soft cloth of her dress were all he needed to know about her. It was enviable, she thought, to trust so easily, to take comfort simply because it was desired and because it was there to be taken. She found herself relaxing into this new intimacy that Ascanius had granted, accepting it as freely as she was accepted. The two of them sat in joint comfort as the child fell asleep against her.

When all the platters had been cleared and the wine jars were empty, Dido sat alone in the hall. The Trojans had been shown to their beds, and her own people had sloped away to theirs. Dido was sitting with a cup of dregs, trying to summon a will to follow them, but her chair was comfortable and she was savouring the success of the feast.

'Still here?' Anna appeared around the doorpost, wearing the grin that always made Dido want to smile too.

She sank more deeply into her seat and spread her arms. 'May a queen not enjoy her hall?'

'She may,' said Anna. 'Though perhaps a humble subject such as myself will be permitted to join her?' She gave an exaggerated bow, which made Dido laugh.

'I do permit it. Indeed, I insist upon it.' She pulled out the empty chair beside her, the same one on which Ascanius had lately fallen asleep.

Before Anna took her seat, she peered into the cups that scattered the table. 'No wine left?'

'Afraid not. It seems the Trojans are as fond of it as any sensible people. Did you have some earlier? And some food?'

'Yes, I came in for a while. I was as curious as anyone to get a look at our guests. There were some handsome ones among them, I'd say.'

Dido rolled her eyes.

'Don't pretend you're above noticing such things.' Anna pushed her arm playfully.

'We are too old to act like gawking maids.'

'Tch. You talk as if we ought to be stepping into our graves. And besides, one should never outgrow the appreciation of beauty.'

'You may appreciate all you like. My care is for the well-being of my guests.' Dido assumed her formal voice. Her queen's voice. But if there were anyone at Carthage who was impervious to it, it was Anna. They had been friends for as long as Dido had had her city, for as long as she had been Queen Dido. Ten long years, in which so much had changed, and in which Anna's tongue had grown no less irreverent. Dido was glad of that.

'You had the prince at your table, I noticed.' Anna's look was casual in design, but curious in intention.

'Is it not right that I should?'

'I caught your eyes on him more than once.'

Dido scoffed. 'Would you have me stare at my plate?'

'No.' Anna's voice softened. 'I would have you look at that which pleases you.'

'You're speaking nonsense.'

'Admiring a man is no shameful thing.'

'I did not say that it was.'

'It is not a betrayal, Elissa.'

Dido stiffened on her chair, the carved wood suddenly pressing uncomfortably against her thighs. She picked up her empty cup. 'Don't, Anna. I don't want to talk about this.'

'I never knew your husband,' Anna persisted. 'But I know that he loved you. He would not chain you as you chain yourself.'

'Stop. Please. I am too tired. This wine has made my head spin.'

Anna fell thankfully quiet, readjusting her dress in the corner of Dido's vision. Dido leaned her head against her palms, pressing them into the ruby studs of her fillet.

'You told me you and your husband had no children,' Anna said eventually. 'Not even ones that didn't survive?'

Dido was confused by the new path of the conversation, and shook her head without looking up. 'None. Not even the stirring of one. I would have told you if I had lost a child.' She heard the sharpened edge that had entered her voice.

But Anna, as always, was unperturbed. 'It's just you seemed so natural with that little boy. The way he warmed to you. I thought . . . Well, it was a silly thing to ask. I know you would have told me something like that.'

'The boy has lost his mother, I think.' That was how she had explained it to herself. It allowed her to put all her pity upon the child, and not to think about the feeling he had stirred in her own heart. She had never been a mother, though she had often helped to care for children – Pygmalion included, when he was young. For many years, she had thought this would be practice for her own, but many more years had passed since she had given up that imagining. Her people were her children, in a way. She liked that thought, and it had fed her well. But she was pleased, too, by Anna's observation, and by the memory of Ascanius resting against her. 'He is a sweet child,' she said simply, and kept her other thoughts to herself.

Chapter 7

TYRE

Elissa had never seen the hall so full. Every merchant in the city seemed to be there. Every priest, every diplomat. All the great personages of Tyre had come to witness the announcement of the royal succession. And that really meant all the great men. Elissa could not pick out a woman's face among the crowd. There was only herself, Barce and Queen Meret.

People still called her that, Elissa noticed. And why should they think to do otherwise? Meret was widow to the late king, mother to the prince. By all rights of tradition, it was the proper title. And yet Elissa knew that by the end of the day, it would become hers instead. *Queen Elissa*, her father had said. Even to hear the echo of his voice in her head sent a stab of grief, and she had to dig her nails into her palms to bring herself back to the present.

She would need her whole self today. She could not be split by loss, half-leaking into her memories, half-lingering in the world she had shared with her father. The people of Tyre needed her now, even if they did not know it yet. They would need her for the rest of her life.

Elissa sat silently, appreciating how odd it was that among all these masses of great and privileged men, only she knew what was about to happen. Had Urumilki revealed the details of her father's testament to anyone else? She did not think so. No one had treated her any differently since her father's death. A part of her had expected them to – after all, nothing stayed secret for long on their little island. She had prepared herself for a flurry of flattery and ingratiation, but none had materialised. It would begin soon, she had no doubt – as soon as the testament was read. And she would be ready for it, with the same subtle, enigmatic smile her father had given when he wished neither to promise nor to offend.

She was pleased, really, that Urumilki's discretion had bought her the time to mourn in relative peace. Time as well to appreciate the final days of her present life before she was thrust into a new one. She must remember to thank him, Elissa thought. Though, as she scanned the crowded hall, she could not find his face.

Between her and Meret sat Pygmalion, not bored and fidgeting as he usually was at such formal occasions, but filled with excited energy. He was old enough to know what today meant, and what it would mean for him. Though the reality might not meet his expectation exactly, Elissa was pleased to see him smiling. Father's death had been a loss for both of them, and she had never felt closer to her brother than when she had held his shaking body just days ago, and felt their grief pour out together. Elissa even smiled herself, to see all the looks that shot straight past her to fix on her brother. It was an amusement only she could enjoy. She thought of how all those faces would change when the testament was read, how their eyes would swivel, their mouths drop open. Better to imagine their surprise than any other reaction that might come instead – anger, objection or, perhaps worst of all, laughter.

Elissa forced those possibilities from her head. Tyre's people had loved her father and trusted his judgement. They would follow his word, even in death.

The chatter in the hall grew louder and louder, as each man raised his voice to be heard above the next. It was not until Ahiram, the ivory merchant, raised a hand toward the ceiling that the din began to recede.

'Esteemed friends.' He looked around the hall, with hands now clasped together. His beard was immaculately trimmed, his hair slick with perfumed oil. The yellow tunic he wore was edged with purple, and sewn with little pearls around the collar. Elissa though it looked garish, but his outfit left no doubt as to his wealth.

'I do not need to tell you why we are gathered. We have all mourned the death of King Mattan, taken cruelly from us before old age had crowned his head with silver.'

Ahiram allowed his solemnity to breathe a moment, but Elissa wished he would continue. The longer he lingered on her father's death, the more she felt her composure erode.

'I speak now not for myself,' he went on finally, 'but on behalf of the Council of Elders and, by our authority, for all Tyre's people. The city suffered a great loss when King Mattan passed, but today she will be blessed with a new ruler.'

Elissa saw a few faces turn towards her brother, but tried to let nothing show on her own. She could feel herself vibrating, her heart racing, her limbs trembling. Every word from Ahiram brought the destined moment closer.

There was some shuffling among the crowd as one of the palace scribes, whom Elissa recognised from the archive room, brought forward the clay tablet. Elissa saw that it had been enclosed within a sealed clay casing. Urumilki's idea, she presumed. It explained how the contents had remained so secret, and she again found herself thanking the secretary for his diligence.

Ahiram took the clay package from the scribe, held it up for the inspection of the crowd, and then broke the fragile case with his hands. Once the tablet was free, he held it ceremoniously before him and began to read.

'I, King Mattan of Tyre . . . '

Elissa edged forward on her seat, sweating palms pressed against her skirt as Ahiram's voice rang out.

' . . . hereby give my final and binding testament. My will is that, upon my death, rule of Tyre is to pass to my son, Pygmalion.'

There was barely a murmur from the hall. Heads nodded, and Pygmalion began to rock in his seat as hands gestured to him in respect.

Elissa sat stunned. At first she thought that Ahiram had simply not finished reading, but as he lowered the tablet, her consternation was like a fist gripping her chest. It dragged her to her feet.

'That is not right,' she said, forcing her voice to reach across the hall. 'That is not what my father willed. Come, read the rest of the tablet. That is not all that was written.'

She had Ahiram's attention, but he shrugged his richly dressed shoulders. 'There is nothing more, Princess.' He displayed the tablet for those eyes that were closest to him, and they seemed to murmur their agreement.

'Let me see it,' Elissa said, more boldly.

The tablet was passed around the edge of the hall, with each man glancing over it as it came to his hands. When it reached Elissa, she took it desperately, feeling the eyes of the crowd upon her as she scanned the small block of triangular markings.

All was as Ahiram had read it. As her father had spoken it, too, except that the clay only recorded the beginning of his words. Her own name did not appear.

'This is not the proper testament,' she announced, turning the tablet in her hands as if the missing words might reveal themselves. 'I bore witness to King Mattan's testament. Where is the true record? This is not it.'

Her words had brought a hum to the hall, as men muttered to their neighbours, but Ahiram's hand dampened it.

'I can assure you that this is the document. The final decree of King Mattan, signed with his personal seal, and kept secure since his death.'

Elissa looked down at the tablet again, traced her finger over the relief left by the seal. It was her father's – there was no doubt. But she had seen him press the same pattern on to the true tablet. This one was either a mistake or a forgery. She could not think about what that meant, not in this moment. Instead, she found herself scanning the crowd once more for Urumilki's face.

'Are you satisfied, Princess?' Ahiram perhaps meant his tone to sound sympathetic, as he addressed the poor young girl whose mind was addled by her grief, but to Elissa it only sounded patronising.

'I know that this is not the true tablet,' she said, straightening herself. 'Because I spoke with my father before his death, and he told me that he wished for me to succeed him, as Queen of Tyre, alongside my brother. That was his final testament, which was recorded by his secretary, Urumilki. If you will only summon Urumilki, he will confirm what I say . . . '

But her words were drowned out by the din of the crowd. She heard jeers of disbelief, and felt eyes fixing her with an outraged intensity. Elissa kept her chin high, her body still, despite the pounding in her chest.

Again, it was Ahiram's hand that regained control of the room, though it waited in the air for some time.

'King Mattan said many things before his passing. Some with clarity and some with the cloud of death upon them. I have no doubt that he wished you to assist the young king in his new position. There are many who shall share the duty of advising King Pygmalion, so that he may lead the city with strength and wisdom. Your contribution will be valuable, of course, and always welcome, as would be the contribution of any member of the royal house.'

'No.' Elissa's voice was taut like a bowstring. 'That is not what my father intended. He wanted me to rule until Pygmalion comes of age, and then for the two of us to rule together. A king and a queen. As equals in power. He explained it clearly in his testament.'

'And where is this testament?' Ahiram looked about the hall with a frown. 'We have only one here, which you have seen with your own eyes. And we must honour it.'

'Urumilki has it.'

'And where is he?'

Elissa had no answer. Where was Urumilki? Not in the hall. She tried to think of the last time she had seen him. The days since her father's passing had been a tangle of grief and anticipation. She could not find Urumilki's face within them.

Ahiram took her silence as an answer. 'Then I think we must move on with proceedings. Tyre must have its king, and we the people are ready to honour him.'

'But this is not right. This is not what my father wanted.' She knew it was a feeble protest. Without the tablet, there was no proof. And why else should they believe that her father had meant for her to rule, that he had planned for it before Pygmalion had even taken his first steps? Because they had played a thousand games of Hounds and Jackals together? Even in her head it sounded ridiculous. She could not bear for these men to laugh at her. She could already see their faces twisting, their sideways looks, their embarrassment on her behalf.

'I fear the noble Princess has been overcome by her grief,' Ahiram said sadly, and waved for a pair of guards who were stationed at the doorway. 'May she feel better once she has rested.'

Elissa resisted as the guards took her arms, but their grip was gently persistent and she found her feet moving as they led her away. She could not find any more words to speak, could no longer look at Ahiram's serene expression. Instead, her eyes roved over the faces in the crowd as her mind burned hot with one question.

Where is Urumilki?

Chapter 8

TYRE

There was no time for bitterness. When Elissa thought back to that crowded hall and her useless feet leading her away, she felt her anger bubble. Perhaps there was something more she could have done, but even now, in the cool quiet of her chamber, she could not think of it. And even if she could, it would be no use. She could not undo the moves that had already been taken; she could only plan the next to come.

Elissa sat on the edge of her bed, fingernails scratching the weave of the cloth. It was frustrating to be so still, but she was where she needed to be. She had sent her maid, Piddaya, to find the answers she needed. A maid drew no whispers, could shuffle through the palace halls with barely a glance in her direction. A maid could speak with the other invisible creatures that kept the city alive, and elicit a candour that a royal face could never hope for. So, as much as Elissa longed to be on her feet, she rooted herself to the bed and waited.

The day's light was mostly spent, and Elissa had just lit the first oil lamp in her chamber, when the door creaked inwards.

'Piddaya.' She found herself whispering, and closed the door firmly behind her maid. 'I was beginning to worry.' This was true, but biting behind it was the question she was desperate to ask. 'Did you find him? Did you find Urumilki?'

Piddaya shook her head. 'No, Mistress.'

But just as Elissa's shoulders began to sink, her maid went on.

'I found his nephew instead. He works with the dyers.' She wrinkled her nose as if the pungency of the murex vats had followed her back to the palace. 'His fingers were full purple, you know! He had a charm to him, though. Not much like his uncle at all, I thought. But Gilben told me I'd find him there, and there he was.' The girl smiled, pleased with herself or with the memory of her encounter with the purple-fingered young man.

'And did he tell you anything? About where his uncle might be?'

Piddaya seemed not to notice the impatience creeping into her mistress's voice, for she went on cheerfully. 'Oh, yes! Well, no. He wouldn't tell me where his uncle was. But I told him that you needed to speak with him. I told him my mistress is the noble Princess Elissa, and that he has a duty to help us if he can.'

Elissa cringed a little, wondering how many ears might have heard Piddaya mentioning her by name. 'And what did he say?'

'He went off for a while. Told me to wait, so I sat watching the dyers. Started to think he'd taken me for a fool, but then he comes back again. Tells me his uncle won't go near the palace, but he'll be at the Great Betyl at dawn tomorrow. He said if you want to speak with Urumilki, that'll be your chance.'

Elissa was nodding, already trying to work out how she would get to the Betyl without drawing too much notice. If Urumilki was so reluctant to come to the palace, she couldn't risk bringing the palace to him. A royal escort might be enough to make him flee, and then she would gain none of the answers she so desperately needed.

'Thank you, Piddaya,' she said distractedly, as the girl's expectant face hovered before her. 'You've done well. But that will be all for today. I need to think.'

The girl took her cue with a neat bow, before retreating to the doorway.

'Wait.'

Piddaya stopped just as obediently, though her hands fidgeted with the sash around her waist. 'Something else, Mistress?'

'Could I borrow something from you?'

Piddaya's dress scratched at Elissa's skin. It had always looked comfortable enough on her maid, but now that she was wearing it, the coarse weave felt a world away from the fine linens she was used to. Her discomfort was made worse by the fact that her young maid had the body of a girl, slight and straight, and a dress to match it. Elissa's more womanly curves pressed against the cloth in all the wrong places, her thighs straining the seams as she strode purposefully through the city streets.

It was best to walk with purpose, as the working women did. Though the sky was still grey with the vestiges of night, some were already about their business, carrying baskets of fish from the harbour, or on their way to the granaries for the day's flour. They nodded to one another, and Elissa dipped her head, too, so as not to stand out. Even those that got a full look at her face showed not a blink of recognition. Without her fine clothes, her make-up, her cloud of perfume, she was no different from any other woman of Tyre.

The island on which the city nestled was small, like a bead fallen from the fabric of the mainland. Every day, ships threaded back and forth across the narrow sound, as if they were trying to stitch the island back into place. Their shallow hulls brought water, grain, oil and wine – the stuff of life that the city herself could not provide. There was no space here among her winding streets, no fields, no rivers. Only buildings of wood and stone, floors upon floors, reaching upwards into the sky when there was no more ground to occupy. Elissa loved the closeness of it, the thrumming energy of lives pushed so tightly together. The palace lay at the heart of it all, and there was no place in the city she could not reach by her own feet.

She entered the precinct of the Great Betyl just as the sun began to break from the horizon. As she approached the sacred stone, she realised how much smaller it seemed now that she was grown. Elissa still remembered the first time her father had brought her here, when his hand could still envelop hers, and she'd had to trot to keep up with his strides. He had told her the story of how the goddess Ashtart had seen a star fall from the sky and travelled across the wide world to find it. When she did, she took it up in her hands and brought it here, to Tyre's blessed isle, and laid it on the ground so that her people might have a piece of the heavens for themselves.

The stone was black as charcoal, smooth as if it had been polished, and yet so irregular in shape that it could not be the work of a craftsman. It had an aura of the divine, which Elissa felt now just as she had when she had stood before it as a child.

A sound came from behind her, so gentle that the breeze almost carried it away. A subtle clearing of the throat.

'Urumilki,' she said as she saw him. There was a relief in the word. A part of her had thought he would not come.

Urumilki did not greet her, but drew his scarf close about his face. What was left for her to see was grey and haggard. The man's black eyes, usually glinting with intelligence, were sharp with something else. It looked like fear.

'Were you followed?'

'No,' she said, trying to sound confident of the fact.

'Does anyone know of our meeting?'

'Only Piddaya. My maid.' Elissa was beginning to feel a little affronted. She had expected that she would be the one to do the interrogating.

Urumilki regarded her for a moment, his brow deep over his eyes. 'Ask what you must ask. I do not wish to linger in this place.'

Elissa faltered slightly. She had arranged the questions in her head on her walk across the city, but now they jostled against one another. 'What happened to the tablet? My father's testament. He trusted it to your keeping.' Her anger, so well contained since the events of the hall, began to leak into her voice. 'He ordered you to have it fired.'

'And it was fired. As soon as I left your father's chamber. I saw it done with my own eyes. And I sealed it and kept it in my room, hidden away. But then, after the first day of the funeral, I returned to find my door broken, my things torn apart, and the tablet gone.'

'Why did you not put it into the archive?' she asked incredulously.

'Do you think it would have been safer there?' he snapped. 'I kept it myself because I knew there were those at the palace who would object to it. And the false tablet – yes, I have heard what came about at the announcement of succession – who do you think made it? One of the scribes you seem so willing to trust, no doubt. There are webs that stretch across the palace, invisible like gossamer, and deadly to those caught in them.' Urumilki's expression was dark, his lips twisted in bitterness.

'You were not at the announcement,' Elissa said, though some of the force had left her voice. 'I tried to tell them the truth. I needed you, and you were not there.'

Urumilki shook his heavy head. 'After the tablet was taken, I knew what would come, and I knew that I would be in danger. So, I fled.' He met her hard gaze from between the folds of his scarf. 'You think me a coward. But what difference would it have made if I had stayed? I am not a powerful man, Princess. I was useful to your father while he was alive, but now that he is gone, I am only a scribe with too many secrets. Sooner or later, the things I know will get me killed. And despite what you may think, my voice would be no aid to you. I have no followers or armies to support it. If I speak, they will blow my words to the wind, and yours with them. They will say you have seduced me, or some such scandal. You may scrunch your face all you like, Princess, but this is the way these things usually go. You are a woman, and I am a common man. They will keep us in our places or stamp us out entirely.'

Elissa was taken aback by this profusion of words from Urumilki. In all the years she had known him, she was not sure he had spoken as much as just now. As she sifted through what he had said, she struggled to find anything she could argue against. But she could not just let her questions dissolve on her tongue, and her hope with them.

'Do you know where the original tablet could be now?'

'Ground to brick dust, most likely.' He sighed. 'And perhaps that is best. Once I am gone from this rotten island I will think no more of it, and neither should you.'

'How can you say that?' Elissa's voice rose high. Urumilki put out a warning hand, but she ignored it. 'How can you betray my father like this? Why did you agree to meet me if you refuse to help?'

'It was for your father that I agreed to meet you. For his memory and the respect he showed me. I knew him as long as you did. Do you think I have no feeling?' His low voice quavered uncharacteristically. 'I loved your father, as my king and as my friend. And I know why he named you in his testament. I do not doubt the wisdom of his choice, but in the real world, we cannot always pursue what is good and just. Not if we want to survive. And for his sake, I hope that you will listen to what I have said. I hope that you will survive.'

48

Urumilki looked at her with a sincerity that chastened her. She felt her anger soften, its edges curling into guilt. The dark shadows under Urumilki's eyes told of sleepless nights, of the fear she had sensed throughout their meeting. He had risked much to come here. The nervous angles of his body screamed of a man desperate to leave, and yet he stayed.

'Where will you go?' she asked quietly.

'I have been waiting for a ship to Egypt. I have a brother there.' He smiled faintly as if to reassure her, though Elissa could see his sadness. He might call Tyre rotten, but it was his home as much as it was hers.

'May Ashtart protect you,' she said, and reached out a hand to touch the Betyl.

Urumilki did the same, and for a moment they stood silent, so that the goddess might hear them.

'Thank you,' she said eventually. 'For speaking with me. And for all you did for my father. I will keep you here no longer.'

As Elissa walked back towards the palace, with the morning sun now blinding her eyes, she thought that she ought to have asked Urumilki more about the intrigues of the court, about whom she might trust, and who might have conspired against her. But perhaps he did not know. Or perhaps she could already guess. The nobles who had so enthusiastically welcomed the news of Pygmalion's accession came to her mind and, before them all, the condescending smile of Ahiram. She felt as if she had been living in a box before, sheltered there by her father. But Urumilki had opened the lid, and now the 'real world', as he had called it, awaited.

Chapter 9

CARTHAGE

Dido had not had time to walk to the grove today. With the city full of guests, there was much to be done. She had sent her best shipwrights to assess the Trojan wreck, and had made sure that the palace ovens were fired at all hours to bake the extra loaves that were needed. She knew they had grain enough, but she'd checked in with the storemaster nonetheless, double-counted the jars herself. Perhaps they were a little low on oil, she noted, but they would make it stretch. She would put limits on perfume, reduce the number of lamps in the palace. She could ask the priests to make their libations with milk instead, but no – that was a measure too far. Light and scent were luxuries to be trimmed, but the favour of the gods was not. Her father had known that, and her husband too. She imagined what each of them would say to the mere suggestion of curtailing holy rites, and smiled to herself. It was a comfort to know that even now, with so many years passed, she could summon their voices.

So no, an escape to the peace of the grove was not possible today. But a visit to the temple was almost as good. She felt grounded there. The gods who heard her prayers in that place were the same she had spoken to across the sea in Tyre, across the span of her life and the lives of those she had loved. They watched over Carthage as they watched her homeland. They watched over the darkness below just as they rejoiced in the light. It was humbling to put herself before them, to know that against theirs, her power was so small. A queen needed to feel that way sometimes.

Dido crossed the sacred threshold just as the sun was streaming its last light over the rooftops. The colours of the temple walls were muted at this time of day, and yet the details of their carvings were thrown into greater relief, almost coming alive as the light moved across them. Dido, as ever, was pleased to look upon those walls, raised and shaped by her own people, where a decade ago there had been only flat earth. They honoured the gods, of course, gave shelter to their most sacred rites, but they were also a testament to Carthage, telling the history of the city and her people in painted stone.

Dido paced around the temple, taking in the scenes she had looked upon a thousand times. Scenes she had lived. There was still pain in some of them, and in others pride. She followed them in their course, around one corner and then another. As she came around the third, she almost collided with Prince Aeneas.

'Oh, excuse me,' she said, stopping her foot just in time to avoid stepping on his. 'I did not expect . . . I did not see you. Forgive me.'

He looked at her, though his expression was oddly distant. She thought his eyes might have a glaze of tears, but it was difficult to tell in the low light.

'Nothing to forgive,' he muttered, then turned his attention back to the section of wall before him. He did not seem in a mood for conversation, and Dido could not allow herself to be offended by that. She understood the need for solitude, especially for those who carried such responsibilities as they did. She nodded her head and made a wide arc around him.

'It's so strange.' His voice was soft, and for a moment she thought he might be speaking only to himself. But when she turned, he was facing her. Then his eyes were pulled back to the temple walls, and his hand reached up towards the carved relief. 'I feel as if I could be looking at the walls of Troy.' His fingers hovered over the image of Tyre, standing proudly over the sea. 'But I know I am not.' He shook his head ruefully, before turning to face her once more. 'Will there be any to remember my city so beautifully as this, I wonder? Where does her memory live, other than with me and my men? She is ash and ruin, and we the only ones to survive her.'

To Dido's surprise, he smiled then, though she could see his mouth dragging at the edges.

'It is a fine temple,' he said hoarsely. 'The style is different to those at Troy. Those that were at Troy,' he corrected himself. 'Though not greatly different. I am pleased to discover a pious people upon this foreign shore. A value we share.' He forced the corners of his mouth upwards again, and Dido had the distinct sense of speaking now with Aeneas the prince, as if Aeneas the man had taken shelter behind him, withdrawing to somewhere private. 'Tell me, what god do you honour here?'

She wanted to chase the injured man she had seen so briefly, and speak with him again. But Dido slipped into her diplomatic role as naturally as Aeneas had.

'The temple is dedicated to two gods, in thanks for the aid that was given to us when we crossed the sea and built our new home, and for the continued protection they each grant us. Their altars burn with equal reverence. The first, Melqart, was our patron at Tyre.' She swept her hand towards the relief beside which Aeneas stood, the stone walls of her home etched in grandeur. 'Lord of the City. That is his holy title. He defends us now as he did then, and gives life to this new land. We know his favour by the bounty of our harvest – which is great.' She allowed her pride to swell, but while Aeneas listened with attention, he did not react. 'The other god,' she went on, 'we call Baal Zaphon. Lord of the North. Lord of Storms. In his wisdom, he brought us to this land, and he allows our trade ships to sail across wide seas.'

'Perhaps we offended this Baal, if he controls the skies as you say. It was a storm that broke our ship upon your shore.'

'Even with proper rites, the sea is treacherous. Baal allowed your people to live, so perhaps you have his favour after all. Your arrival here may be a blessing, as it has been for us.' Dido smiled, but Aeneas looked unconvinced.

'You give sacrifices here to both gods?' he asked, perhaps only to redirect the conversation. 'And they share one house?'

'Yes,' she said simply. 'This temple was the first building we erected, before even one hall of the palace was built.'

Aeneas nodded at that, and Dido was pleased to feel his approval. She did not explain that there had, in fact, been much disagreement about which god should be honoured by Carthage's first temple. Dido had wanted to found a cult of Melqart, while her Head Priest favoured Baal Zaphon. And so, the resulting construction was as much a monument to compromise as it was to piety.

The conversation had fallen into a lull, but Dido didn't want to lose an opportunity to learn more about her guest.

'And which gods do you worship?' she asked.

'We had many temples at Troy. But the gods I have brought with me are the Penates. Our home gods.'

'Brought with you?'

'I snatched their holy statues from my own shrine, before the flames could devour them.' His tone was one of satisfaction, churned with sadness. It reminded Dido of her feelings when setting up Melqart's new altar here in Carthage. 'The Penates protect our home; they connect us with our ancestors. They hold us to what has been left behind, and preserve some piece of it. I could not save my home, nor bring it across the sea. But I could bring them. And my heart is thankful for it. Forgive me; my words are unclear, perhaps, Do you understand?'

Dido wanted to tell him that she understood more deeply than he knew, but her throat was tight and she hesitated. She adjusted the ruby fillet that crowned her long black hair.

'You know what it is to leave a home behind,' Aeneas said in sympathy. 'I have learned that much about you – about your people, I mean.' His eyes glanced away, to the carvings of the temple wall. 'I can read some part of your history here. But I think there are some parts you will have to explain to me.' Suddenly, he stepped around to the back of the temple, and she followed. 'Such as this, here.' He pointed at a section of the wall before him. 'Is this an oxhide? What meaning does it have?'

His eyes were sharp with curiosity, and she smiled to see it. Since his arrival, Dido had felt a desire to understand the prince from Troy, to know him beyond titles and the gestures of guest-friendship. She told herself that it was more than a personal fancy. It was the duty of a queen to understand a stranger she had welcomed into her city. A necessary caution, even. And now, for the first time, she felt her interest reciprocated.

'There is much to tell of how we came to leave Tyre and build our new city here.'

'And how you came to be its queen? That is a story worth hearing, I am sure.'

She felt her cheeks warm. 'I will not spoil it with a hasty telling. Come, share a drink in my hall this evening and I will give you the beginning, at least. And the rest . . . Well, you shall have to be satisfied by these painted walls for now.'

Dido flashed a smile and was relieved to see it returned. Somehow, she felt that if she gave her story over all at once, the prince may lose his interest in speaking with her. And, at the same time, she knew she was protecting herself. Just as Aeneas kept one foot in shadow, so would she. Even wounds long closed were painful to expose.

Chapter 10

TYRE

Over the following days, Elissa thought about what Urumilki had said. The memory of his fearful eyes was not easily forgotten. He had spoken as if assassins were waiting around every corner, as if mere whispers would be enough to draw their blades. But as Elissa returned to the daily hum of the palace, she had trouble believing it. Aside from her father's absence, and the ache it had left in her heart, things felt unchanged. The women still baked their bread in the courtyards, and the yeast of the beer troughs still pinched her nose. The men still spoke of the price of silver, the delays their ships had suffered in this storm or that port. Incense still burned on the altars, and the people prayed for the same things as always. A good harvest. A healthy child. The safe return of a loved one. Tyre had lost her king, but as long as the throne was filled, she did not seem to mind much who filled it.

Elissa's own name, which had peppered the palace whispers for a good week after her spectacle in the hall, seemed barely to be spoken now. She no longer drew furtive looks as she passed through the rooms of her home, only the genial smiles she had known before. They made her angry, somehow.

Urumilki had been right about one thing. The truth was no more than words without power to support it. She had seen that in the hall. And she had no more power now than she'd had then. But what she would not do was sink into the hole of irrelevance that was opening up for her. She would not be a ghost in her own home. It would be an insult to her father, and the path he had so deliberately laid for her. So, when the noble men smiled at her, she smiled back, as one might to a worthy opponent. She would find her power yet.

It was the first day of petitions since the king's death, and though it galled Elissa to step into that hall again without the authority that should rightfully be hers, she knew she must attend. There was a flutter from the nobles as she entered, a nervous shuffling that gave her some satisfaction. She walked past them and took a seat close to Pygmalion.

'Princess Elissa.' Ahiram, who was seated beside her brother, acknowledged her with a stiff smile. 'We did not expect to see you. Your mourning has not ended, after all.'

'It is a daughter's duty to mourn her father,' she said calmly. 'And a sister's duty to aid her brother. Did you not say that my advice would be valuable? The young king must have our support.'

'Of course,' he said, with an incline of his well-oiled head. 'Your commitment to duty is an inspiration to us all.'

Elissa sensed that he was mocking her, but she would not let herself be barbed. Even a flicker of emotion would be something he could use.

As the petitioners entered and made their cases, Elissa noticed that they seemed unsure where to look. Should they address the king? This nine-year-old boy whose royal mantle slipped from his shoulders each time he shifted impatiently in his seat? Many looked instead to the Council of Elders, their eyes darting from one bearded noble to another, not knowing where to settle. Others, to Elissa's own surprise, addressed their pleas to Elissa, at which she adopted what she hoped was an engaged, concerned demeanour, such as the one her father had mastered. And all the while, she resisted the temptation to look at Ahiram's expression.

Around midday, just as Elissa's stomach was beginning to complain at the long hours since breakfast, a grey-haired woman entered the hall. Her shoulders were hunched, the colours of her clothes faded, but when she stopped before Pygmalion, she spoke with a straightforward dignity.

'I have come from the mainland, from Usha,' she began. 'My husband has a vineyard there – had a vineyard.' Her mouth wrinkled at her mistake, but she went on. 'He died last month.'

'Our condolences,' Elissa said softly, then turned to her brother with an expectant look.

Pygmalion, who had been fiddling with a string of leather, put his hands in his lap and bowed his head. ' . . . condolences,' he echoed.

'Thank you, my king. The reason I have come is that my brother-in-law is claiming now that the land – my husband's land, my land – should pass to him. It is my right as a widow to inherit. We were married most of our lives – but now my brother-in-law claims that since we had no children, it was not a true marriage.' The woman's voice began to crack. 'I have worked that land, my king. My fingers are rough from those vines.' She held them up as if they might see the calluses. 'If it is taken from me, what will I do? I have no husband, no children. Who will support me if I cannot support myself?'

Elissa, moved by the woman's plea, leaned forward. She summoned words of reassurance, but Ahiram's voice overtook hers.

'Surely, you must have your dowry set aside? A woman can always rely on that.'

The petitioner shook her head. 'No. It was spent some years ago, to pay my husband's debts.'

'You should not need it,' Elissa interjected. 'The land is yours by right. We will have this dispute resolved.'

She turned towards her brother, but Ahiram was speaking again.

'What is the name of your brother-in-law?'

'Barekbaal.'

'Ah, yes. Then I'm afraid the matter is settled. Barekbaal has already made his petition for the land, and it has been granted.'

Elissa stumbled for a second. 'What petition? I have attended every audience and have never heard such a claim come before my father.'

'It was a private petition. Brought some days ago, after King Mattan's passing.' He did not even turn his head to face her.

Elissa felt her skin prickle in anger. 'And what was the price of this private audience?' She could imagine well enough. A share of the land, a cut of its profits. Ahiram was not a man to grant favours when there was a deal to be made instead. Her father had known it. He had managed all the merchants to ensure that their grasping fattened the city as much as their own coffers. But what would Pygmalion do?

'The matter has been settled.' Ahiram ignored her question, turning instead to her brother. 'Do you not agree, my king? Let us end the morning session and take some refreshment.'

Pygmalion's eyes brightened at that, and he nodded. 'It is settled.'

'Brother, this is not right. Father always said that it is our duty to protect widows and orphans. Do you remember?' Her voice was soft but urgent, her attention drawn by the grey-haired woman's hanging head, her shoulders slumped in dejection. Elissa pulled her eyes back to her brother. 'The land is hers. We must follow the law.'

'My stomach is growling!' Pygmalion pushed himself up from his throne. 'Do you think we can have honey almonds?'

The Council members were leaving their seats too, drifting towards the open door. The petitioner remained rooted, hands clenched together, until a guard came to move her away. Elissa wanted to call after her, but what could she say? An apology would not give the woman a roof or a hearth. And it was pride, too, that stopped her tongue. To speak would be an admission of her failure. Ahiram had outmanoeuvred her, with a false move taken before she even knew the game had begun. But next time, she would be ready for him.

'You must not let the Council of Elders make all your decisions for you.'

Elissa had been unable to speak privately with her brother at midday, among the throng of people and the distraction of his appetite. Now, the palace was quiet again – as quiet as it ever was – and she had caught up with Pygmalion on his way to his bath. Thankfully, the afternoon's petitions had concerned no stakes so high as a woman's home and livelihood, but still Elissa had bristled each time one of the noble merchants swept through a ruling that suited his own interests. And, as the day had gone on, another feeling had grown beside her frustration. An unfurling awareness that this was exactly what the nobles had planned when they had schemed for her brother's accession. She cursed herself that she had not realised it before now, that she had only assumed there were a set of men who would always favour a king over a queen. No, these men were shrewder than that. They favoured a boy who would flow like water around whatever plans they constructed, over a woman who might block their way like a stone.

'This is not what father intended. He said that a city must be ruled by justice, and above all by a care for its people. He protected those who could not protect themselves, and he would tell you to do the same. So I am telling you. Do you hear me, Pygmalion?' She touched his arm, and he turned his young face up to hers. 'You must have your own mind, and speak it.'

Pygmalion's mouth puckered as if he had eaten something sour. 'You cannot tell me what to do just because Father is dead. I am the king now.' He narrowed his eyes, as if daring her to disagree. 'And I hate listening to all those people. I don't care what the merchants decide. That's their job, isn't it?'

'They are supposed to counsel you, not rule in your stead. You must take your duty seriously, Brother. Else why should you be king at all?'

'Stop talking,' he commanded, pulling his arm away. 'You're not my father and you're not my mother. You're not anyone, really. You're as bad as Barce, telling me what I must wear and when I must go to my bed.' He looked scornfully at his nurse, who lingered nearby. 'I don't need either of you.'

He marched off, leaving Elissa with her wounds. Had she not always loved him? As if he were her own mother's child? Had she not sworn to care for him, to always defend him? Pygmalion was still a boy, she forced herself to remember. He spoke words in haste, not thinking how his sharpness might cut her. And he needed her, no matter what he might say. She would have to be more subtle, perhaps, but she would guide him just as Father had guided her. If she could not be queen, let her at least do this. She would help Pygmalion to be the king that Tyre deserved.

'Excuse me, Princess.'

The voice pulled Elissa out of her thoughts.

'Yes?' She took no care to hide her annoyance.

The man who stood before her was dressed in long, plain robes, with head and chin shaven clean – a priest. His bare head was misleading at first, but when she examined his face, she judged he was only a few years older than she was.

'I am sorry to interrupt you,' he said. His confidence seemed tempered by her shortness, but he went on. 'I only wanted to say that I admired your contribution in the petition hall today.'

'You were there?' she asked, but it was a witless question. Many of the city priests were members of the Council of Elders, though they stood somewhat apart from the more numerous merchants.

'I have lately become Head Priest at the temple of Melqart.' He dropped his chin humbly, yet it was no small thing that he had said. Melqart was the patron god of the city, and of the king. His priest was the most esteemed of Tyre's religious servants.

'You do not seem old enough.' It was an honest response, though Elissa realised too late that it might offend.

'I am young, yes,' he replied genially. 'But you can be sure the Rising God's offices are safe in my care. I have been prepared for the role since my infancy.'

Something they shared, Elissa thought.

'Well, I thank you for your kind words.' She smiled tightly. 'I only wish that I could – ah, what am I saying? Forgive me. It has been a long day, and I must be on my way.' Her mind was returning to her earlier thoughts, already forming new plans to deal with her brother, with Ahiram, with the nobles. This priest and his gentle smile had become a cloud she must shoo away.

'Would you come to the temple?' he asked.

'The temple?'

'I would be pleased to show you the work that we do there. If you would honour us.'

Elissa hardly had time for chants and incense, but more than anything she needed this man to go away and leave her to her thoughts.

'Yes, yes. I'll come. But now I really must go.'

He swept gracefully aside to clear her path, and with a polite nod she hurried on towards her chamber.

Chapter 11

TYRE

The temple of Melqart stood not far from the palace – an appropriate setting, given its vital role in the preservation of Tyre's monarchs. Melqart, Lord of the City, was not only patron of the king, though. Through his living, dying and yearly awakening, he ensured the prosperity of every citizen, and made the land and the sea plentiful.

Elissa had celebrated the festivals of the Rising God all her life, had anointed his statues and spoken prayers to Melqart for her father's health. But this was the first time she had visited the temple alone, without the ceremony of a feast day, or the overshadowing attention given to her father and his entourage. Those memories floated about her, pulling at her with bitter sweetness as she entered the sacred precinct.

It was full of life, more so than she had expected. Away in the corner the ovens were burning, with a large table nearby for the loaves already baked. A queue of people – ordinary people, with tanned faces and empty baskets – ran along the walled edge of the precinct, up to the table of loaves. In another corner, great pots of steaming broth were being ladled out. The faces that waited there had a more desperate look. One or two were bare-chested, and another had no sandals on his feet.

Elissa shifted her gaze away, suddenly aware that she might be staring, and looked instead to the temple itself. It was not a large building, but the strong cedar beams and fine details of the frontage gave it a robust majesty. As she stepped nearer, she saw the doorway was carved with fruit and berries, ears of grain nestled between figs and pomegranates, vines heavy with grapes weaving between lotus flowers in full bloom. It was a work of beauty, and she wondered that she had never studied it before.

'Princess Elissa.' The priest emerged from the dim interior of the temple, and as he walked towards her, she thought he was taller than she remembered – though perhaps it was only the conical cap that now sat atop his head. The red felt suited him somehow, not only as a distinction of his honoured role, but as a blot of warmth amid his otherwise insipid attire. It brought out the youthful flush of his cheeks and drew Elissa's attention to the bright eyes that greeted her.

'You have come.' Though he smiled widely, he sounded a little surprised to see her. It had been over a month since his invitation, so perhaps he had thought she would not honour her word. Elissa was pleased to prove him wrong.

'Of course.' She nodded graciously. 'Though I must beg your pardon, for I did not ask your name on our first meeting.'

'It is Zakarbaal.'

'Zakarbaal, the priest. I shall not forget it. But tell me, Zakar-baal, have I disturbed you on a feast day? I did not expect the temple to be so well attended.'

'No, not at all.' He looked about him with a hint of pride in his expression. 'You find us at our daily activities. In fact, this is what I wanted to show you.' Suddenly, his gaze seemed drawn by something beyond her. 'One moment, please.' He stepped away towards the corner where broth was being served, and Elissa followed awkwardly behind him. 'Aqhat,' he called to one of the attendants. When the young man was close, the priest lowered his voice. 'These men are in need of clothes. We have a few items in the storehouse. Will you bring what you can find?' The attendant trotted away, and Zakarbaal returned his attention to Elissa. 'Many are the garments gifted for the sartorial pleasure of our Lord Melqart, but his holy statue may only wear one outfit at a time.' He grinned and seemed to watch for her understanding. Or was it her approval?

Elissa nodded. 'The gods begrudge no man his dignity.'

The priest seemed pleased at that, and Elissa felt her own face relax. But even as it did, Zakarbaal's brow became serious.

'There are many here in the city who rely on the temple, as you see. And we are pleased to aid them. But lately their numbers grow. The temple gives what it can, from the tithes we collect, from the donations given by those whom Melqart has blessed. But we can only do so much.' He paused and cast his eyes across the precinct before settling on her again. 'I had hoped, Princess, that you would see our situation, and that I might persuade you to act as our patron. I have heard you during the petitions. I know you have a care for the needs of the city, and all who look to it for protection.'

His last words were pointed, and though she was flattered by his observation of her, Elissa felt a familiar gripe in her stomach. The priest seemed to overestimate her power.

'I am aware,' she began cautiously, 'that care of Tyre's citizens may have been . . . neglected of late. Though I did not expect to see such circumstances as these, so soon after my father's death.' She gestured widely at the queues of people. 'Matters have become worse than I had realised.'

'Forgive me, Princess.' Zakarbaal lowered his head, and his words seemed to stick on his lips. 'The citizens have been in need of our aid for some time now. Since before King Mattan's passing. For over a year, the raids on the mainland have been increasing. These people from across the sea . . . Who can say where they have come from, or how long we must suffer them? Our shores are not the first to be harried by them, so perhaps – Ashtart defend us – they will move on in time. But as things are . . . ' The priest pinched the bridge between his tired eyes. 'Every month, more people are driven from their farms, seeking safety here on the island. But they have no work here. No homes. I find positions where I can for those who are young and healthy, but what is there for the rest? Only their prayers and our charity.'

Elissa was prickled by what Zakarbaal had said. But even as her skin grew hot, she felt an uncomfortable admiration for his honesty. He was brave to speak so plainly of her father's shortcomings.

'Do not mistake me,' he went on. 'I know that King Mattan devoted himself to Tyre. That he had her best interests always in his heart. He did what he could in circumstances which had become challenging. Which continue to test us, and will test the new king also.' Again, he was watching her face, perhaps gauging the level of offence he had caused. 'All I ask is that you see the challenge we face. That you help us to make others see it – the king not least of all. Blindness will only allow these troubles to grow. Then, perhaps, we will be beyond the help of even the gods.'

Elissa was quiet. Her cheeks still burned from Zakarbaal's talk of her father, and the directness of his gaze did nothing to help. She wanted to turn her head, to stare across at the people who queued patiently for their bread or refocus herself on the ornate carvings of the temple. But there was something in the priest's openness that would not allow her to close herself to him. All he spoke was true – she did not doubt that. There was no call for guile here, no need to position herself for battle as she had become so used to doing in her dealings with the Council. His aims and hers were in alignment. The people of Tyre

68

needed voices that would speak for them – even more than she had realised.

'I will aid you, as you ask,' she said levelly. 'I will spread word among the court of what I have seen here, and the reasons for it. And I will lend my support to any action you may propose that would benefit the people of the city. All I ask,' she added, before the priest could give his thanks, 'is that you support me in turn.'

Zakarbaal held his tongue, and a wrinkle appeared between his dark brows.

'You have observed, no doubt, that I am often at odds with certain members of the Council. I wish only to guide my brother in making decisions which will be for Tyre's good, and the good of her people. But for that, I need allies. And your position makes you a valuable one.'

Zakarbaal seemed surprised by her candour, and his lips parted.

'Are we not speaking plainly with one another?' she asked. 'You strike me as a man who values honesty. So I am asking, honestly. Can I count upon you? Will you be a friend to me, when I am in need of one?'

Elissa extended her hand and set her gaze steady. For a moment, she feared that he would reject it, but then the priest put forward his own hand and took hers firmly. She expected his fingers to be soft, smooth like his shaved face, but they were hardened by work.

'Let us be allies, then, as you say.' His mouth twitched as if he wanted to smile, but he was regarding her thoughtfully, and Elissa could not read what he found in her.

She nodded and drew her hand out of his. 'I will see you at the next audience of the Council, then.'

If he'd heard the question in her voice, he did not answer it. 'Thank you for visiting,' he said instead, with a half bow.

'Sincerely.' His eyes caught hers again before she turned away and released herself.

Walking back across the precinct, she could already hear Zakarbaal's voice instructing the temple attendants to order more grain. He sounded buoyant, though maybe it was only the lightness of her own step that made her think so. It gave her hope to feel that there was another who cared for Tyre as she did. There had been no battle to fight here – she was right on that count. But that did not mean there had been nothing to gain.

Chapter 12

CARTHAGE

Dido sat in her hall, as she always did around midday. In the early days of Carthage, she had practised weekly petition hearings, where she would sit from dawn until dusk and hear anyone who wished to speak with her, from farmers and fishermen to merchants and architects. It was what her father had done. She knew no better model. And yet often, when dusk came, there would be those who had not yet gained her ear, who were sent away to sit in their troubles for another week. Or there would be urgent matters that could not wait upon a queen's schedule. People would stop her on her way to the temple, or as she tried to slip away to the grove. Things moved quickly in a new city, and she heard every issue willingly. Better to know the problems her people were facing and resolve them if she could.

It became clear that weekly petitions, as well as they might have served Tyre, were not what Carthage needed. And so now she made herself available for a short period each day. The people knew that if the sun was at its highest point, they could find their queen on her throne. Some days she sat in silence, and others there was a queue into the courtyard. But all who came were heard.

Today was a quiet day, so Dido sat picking individual seeds from a pomegranate, letting them burst on her tongue. Her head felt thick with last night's wine, and she was relieved not to have a stream of citizens before her throne. She even took a moment to close her eyes, but they snapped open as footsteps echoed.

'Prince Aeneas.' She smiled to see him approach, with his son pulling at his arm. 'And little Ascanius.'

The boy seemed suddenly shy on hearing his own name and hung back beside his father's knee.

'Would you like some dried apricots?' she asked, and was pleased to see Ascanius's uncertainty melt into delight. He skipped towards her with hands already outstretched for the golden treats.

When Aeneas eventually came to join the two of them, his look was apologetic.

'He asked if I could take him to see the lady in the purple dress. I think that's you,' he whispered, with more humour in his eyes than she had seen yet. 'I'm sorry if we have disturbed you.'

'Not at all. As you see, I am without company. It seems today is one of those rare days when everything is running smoothly. And so I am quite useless.'

'I'm not sure that could ever be true.'

She smiled at that, and tried to determine whether his expression fell more on the side of earnest or amused. Either way, it sent a warmth through her chest. She looked away to where Ascanius sat happily on the stone floor, chewing on his first sweet apricot.

'You are a masterful storyteller,' Aeneas said, drawing her gaze back to him. 'It was an honour to hear you speak of your beginnings last night. My men all said so,' he added quickly. 'To hear you describe your home in Tyre, I felt I had visited the city myself. And you did much service to the memory of your father. That is something to be admired.'

She felt the sincerity of his words. Perhaps this explained the new regard she sensed from him. Some of the distance between them had closed since yesterday, and she was glad of it.

'It was a pleasure to share these things with my guests.' *With you*, she had almost said. 'Tyre will always be a part of me, as Troy is part of you. And the same is true of our fathers.' She spoke gently, not wanting to sour the pleasant mood between them with unhappy thoughts. Perhaps she had said the wrong thing, for he fell quiet.

'There has been no greater influence upon my life than that of my father,' he said eventually. 'I know that you understand what that means.' He looked at her, and she nodded. 'Until recently, I still had him to guide me. If I had known how it would feel to be without that . . . ' Aeneas closed his eyes as if he were trying to summon his father's memory. 'I know that my men are look-ing to me. That my son needs me more than ever. Yet how can I guide them when I feel so lost?'

She knew it was not a question he expected her to answer. She had felt that same despair more than once, of finding her-self aboard a ship with no rudder, and no map to the stars. She could not navigate those waters for him, but she could remind him that he was not alone.

'I know your grief, and I am sorry for it. Was your father lost in the war at Troy?'

To her surprise, he shook his head. 'No. He boarded the ship with me. I carried him out of the city myself. Gods know where I found the strength. His sight was gone and he was too frail to run, so I took him on my back and kept Ascanius beside me, held his arm so tight he screamed for me to let him go. But I couldn't. I couldn't let either of them go. One my past and the other my future. I would have got them to that ship and let the flames take my own body as payment. But somehow, we made it out together.'

Aeneas's face had a haunted look – not sad so much as bitter. Dido was stiff with shock. This was the first detail the prince had given of his escape, and it burned brightly in her imagination.

A desperate man dragging his kin through deadly flames. She glanced down at Ascanius as if she might still find black ash in his hair, or see the bruise left by his father's grip. The child seemed unscarred, as if neither body nor mind recalled the events that had so clearly left their mark on his father. That was a blessing at least, she told herself.

'My father, Anchises, died on Sicily,' the prince explained. 'Several months after we had left Troy. Perhaps it was his fated time. Or perhaps he could not recover from the destruction of his home. We laid him to rest in that foreign soil. I only wish that we could have buried him at our new settlement, wherever that was to be. Italy, I suppose. It was he who said we must go north. He had dreams of how we would prosper there. He was sure that if we could only carry the Penates to that land, we would found a new Troy, as noble as the one we had seen consumed by flames.' His eyes shone as if that awful sight were still before him. 'My father died before he could see his vision become truth.'

Aeneas was silent for a moment, then seemed to come to himself. He cleared his throat.

'You must scorn my grief,' he said, hardening.

'Not at all,' she began, baffled by the declaration. But she could say no more before he went on.

'You, who lost your father when you were still young. I enjoyed many long years with mine beside me. I should count myself fortunate to have had so much time with him.'

'Fortunate? After all you have suffered, I do not think many would call you that.'

But it was as if he could not hear her. 'Fortunate, too, that I survived the fall of our city. How is it that I came away when so many did not? I saw great men cut down – greater warriors than I. But perhaps that is why. If I had a true warrior's heart, I would have fought until all my blood was spilled. Wouldn't I?'

This time he seemed really to be asking her.

'You had people to protect.' She looked down at Ascanius, as if to remind him. The child had heard the change in his father's tone and was watching him with worried eyes.

'I had a whole city to protect. And yet I could not do it. I put on my armour and charged out to cut down any Greeks in my path, but I could barely tell enemy from friend in the dark chaos of that night. When they swarmed the citadel, I stood upon my roof, firing arrow after arrow, kicking away each fire-brand as it was thrown on to the tiles, knowing that even one might destroy all that I cared for. And then some part of the roof caught alight, and I realised that I could not even protect my own house. And so I took my family and my gods, and I fled.' He stopped to breathe, and Dido saw that he was shaking. 'But if I had known how it would feel, to survive when so many others did not . . . ' His face contorted and he put a hand to his chest as if it were burning with pain. 'I often think I would rather trade my lot with theirs. I should have died with them. I ought to have died. But who can change that now?'

Dido had no answer. Her own chest was tight with sympathy. With horror, too, at what he had described and at the black thoughts that plagued his mind. She knew these were no idle words. He spoke them as if it were a release to do so, as if they had been circling him for some time.

Then he shook his head as though to throw them out. 'I'm sorry. I have never said such things aloud. And to you, whom I hardly know and who has been such a gracious host. You must think me ungrateful. Forgive me. Perhaps it is easier to speak them to you. What would my men say if they knew I harboured such thoughts? They need to trust in me. Who else can they depend on?'

'They depend on you, and they are right to. But who can you depend on?'

'Upon the gods,' he said blankly. 'All that I do is no more than a ripple against their tide. I know that in my heart. If I have survived Troy, it is by their will.'

Dido nodded. She knew the solace of that conviction. When she had suffered her great loss at Tyre, when all the world had seemed ripped out beneath her and she had tortured herself retracing every step of the how and why, the gods had been her island in the storm.

'But who can you speak to? Not by prayers,' she added. 'Who can you really speak to?'

'Well, to you, apparently. Strange as that is.' He looked surprised and even faintly amused, which eased her worry. She could feel that he was about to apologise again, so she stopped him.

'I am glad.'

Chapter 13

TYRE

For once, Elissa found herself looking forward to the next petition hearing. Those since her father's death had been an exercise in enduring defeat, in which she could feel her patience straining beneath each unjust ruling, her pride churning to the point of sickness as she was spoken over again and again. This time would be different. She had an ally now. Already she could imagine Zakarbaal's face amid the benches of nobles, his open smile a succour she might look to when she felt her frustration rising. He would speak for her, as he had promised, and she for him. There was a strength to be drawn from that.

The audience was still some days away, and yet Elissa's mind was already fixed on it. As she sat in her chamber, she imagined exchanges between herself and the noble men of the Council, or the gentle words she might speak to her brother. There was little point to these imaginings. She could not know what cases would be brought until the petitioners were standing before her. But what else was there to think about? Her weaving? Her stitchwork? These idle activities that men seemed to think were enough to occupy a woman's mind? She scoffed to herself as she saw her abandoned loom in the corner.

What she wouldn't give for a game of Hounds and Jackals with her father. That was the best distraction for a wandering mind. But the thought of it stirred her grief, so she pushed it away.

Just as she was considering a walk through the palace, there was a tap at Elissa's door. Opening it, she found one of her brother's servants on the other side.

'King Pygmalion wishes to speak with you.'

Elissa felt a kick of surprise, but kept her face smooth. 'Of course. I am ready as I am. Lead the way.'

She felt a growing sense of promise as she followed in the servant's measured steps. She tried to speak with her brother most days, but he was more often than not kept busy by his duties – or, at least, that was what she had been told. All she needed was some time with him, to remind him of the bond they shared, to guide him as she knew their father would have wanted. That he had called for her was a good sign, and Elissa was pleased to think that he might value her advice on some matter. Who could he trust better, after all, than his own blood?

She was confused when they did not turn towards Pygmalion's royal chambers, but instead towards the petition hall. It seemed a grand room for a private meeting, and as the servant pushed open the door, Elissa's step faltered.

The benches were occupied by members of the Council of Elders. Not all the members – she immediately scanned for Zakarbaal's face, but could not find it. No, the men who sat on either side of her brother's throne were merchants and guild leaders, those who seemed always to be speaking into Pygmalion's ears, and against her own counsel.

'Brother,' she said, trying to conceal her disquiet. 'You wished to speak with me. Though . . . I did not know the Council would be meeting today.'

'This is not a public matter.' Ahiram's voice set her nerves on edge, and she avoided turning her eyes to him. 'These men are here only as friends and supporters to the king. And to share in the happy news.'

'And what news is that?' Elissa asked, still looking deter-minedly at her brother.

Pygmalion hesitated. He glanced aside at one of the noble men, who nodded. 'It has been decided that you shall marry, Sister.' The words were slow and deliberate, as if rehearsed. But then the expression on his young face softened into something more natural. 'Is it not glad news? Mother says weddings are the most splendid parties.'

His excitement was so genuine that Elissa almost wished she could return his smile. But her lips felt numb.

'Marry?' The word was still floating in her ears. She shook her head.

'It is a happy thing, is it not?' Her consternation seemed to give Pygmalion some doubt.

'It is, my king.' Ahiram rose to his feet, and this time Elissa could not avoid looking at him. 'And the princess is past old enough. Near twenty, are you not? You must surely be craving the joy of motherhood.'

His smile made her stomach turn, and in it she saw the truth of this scheme. Wed her off, give her a husband and babe to occupy her. What threat could she be with a child at her hip, another at her breast? They would weigh her down with womanhood. Or better yet, send her to some foreign prince. Remove her from her brother, from Tyre, so that they might be free to do all that they liked without the irritation of her opposition.

'I do not wish to marry, Brother.' There was an intensity in her voice, but perhaps that was needed for Pygmalion to hear her, for him to know that this was not a game being played. That there was more at stake than a splendid party.

'Come, now. It is natural for a bride to be nervous.' Ahiram's light tone was pitched to blow away all her seriousness. 'But rest assured, we shall find you a kindly husband. The search has already begun. Do not fret yourself, my dear.'

Her stomach rolled again.

'The decision has already been made.' Ahiram turned to Pygmalion with an expectant smile.

'The decision has been made,' her brother repeated.

'I cannot marry while you still have need of me, Brother,' she said, trying another approach. 'I promised Father that I would always care for you. If I marry, I shall be forced to go away. Is that what you want?' She watched him, desperately hoping that it was not. 'Allow me to continue in my duty to you. At least for some years more.'

'Is it not the duty of a royal woman to strengthen her house?' Ahiram turned again to Pygmalion. 'An advantageous marriage would do much good for Tyre's future and for your own security, my king. As I have already advised. As we here have all advised.' He opened his arms to the room, and roused sounds of agreement from the assembled men.

'This is the best course,' called Gereshmun, from the guild of silversmiths.

'Assuredly so, my king,' chimed Iliya, a red-cheeked merchant with fingers ringed in gold.

Pygmalion looked between the men, and finally back to Elissa.

'The decision has been made,' he said once more. Then, after a pause, 'You may leave now, Sister.'

Elissa was not one for weeping. When she had cried as a child, as all children cry, her father would put a finger to her cheek and brush away the tears.

'What's this now?' he would say, in his softest voice. 'Is there not enough water in the world already?'

Elissa wished she could cry now, though. Was it not more dignified than screaming? As she sat in her chamber, she felt herself burning, her body shaking with an energy she was desperate to release.

'My lady?' Piddaya's voice was fearful, her skinny arms wrapped around one another as she observed Elissa from the corner of the chamber. The girl had come across her on the way back from the petition hall, and had fallen into her usual trot beside her mistress. Now, the silence of the chamber had become so thick that her little voice could not help but break it.

'I am to be married,' Elissa said without looking up.

'Oh.'

She could feel the girl grasping for something more to say, but Piddaya knew well enough not to sprinkle cheery words on her mistress's fire. Elissa was grateful, until the girl finally did speak again.

'I'm sorry.'

Those words, kindly meant, seemed to chime with her own despair. They were a permission, somehow, and Elissa felt her body's response. When she finally met the girl's eye, her own were stinging.

'What will we do?' Piddaya asked.

It was a surprising question. Piddaya was looking at her with total trust – a look she usually took for granted. Trust that her mistress had a plan, that she would know what to do or where to go or whom to speak with. For a moment Elissa felt warm, to be under that gaze, to have this girl ready to aid her without knowing what game she might play. Then that warmth began to cool into something more solid: a will to be as Piddaya saw her.

What would she do? Refuse marriage? She had tried that. She could try again, but she had no new arguments to help her. The influence of the merchants seemed to grow by the day, and even with her new ally, their voices would always outnumber hers.

She could flee. But even as the thought appeared, she knew it was ridiculous. Flee from the very city she was trying to serve? Flee from her father's legacy, from her brother, who needed her guidance? Ahiram and the councillors would like nothing better. She would do as well to let them marry her to a foreign prince.

No, the one thing she would not do was leave Tyre. She could not. But nor could she stay still. The longer she delayed and deliberated, the more opportunity she allowed her enemies to trap her in the very worst outcome.

Beneath Piddaya's patient gaze, a plan began to grow in Elissa's mind.

'We will go to the temple of Melqart.'

'Princess Elissa, to see Head Priest Zakarbaal,' she announced to the startled attendant who was hurrying across the precinct with an armful of kindling.

'The priest is within, I believe.' He pointed towards the temple. But as Elissa took a step towards it, he moved to block her path. 'Ah. I'm sure I need not tell you that Great Melqart admits no women across his threshold.' He smiled placidly, but there was a firmness to his warning that she did not expect from so timid a frame.

'Of course. I will wait.' She smothered her impatience and nodded to send the attendant on his way. 'Women and swine,' she muttered to Piddaya, who hovered at her elbow. 'Let neither befoul the sacred house of Melqart. Do they think we hide trotters beneath our skirts?' She turned with a grin, and the girl hid her laughter behind a pious hand.

It was strange, perhaps, that she should be making light when her chest still felt so heavy. But that weight sat differently now that she had a plan. It propelled her towards her next move. *There is no standing still. Don't let yourself be trapped, Little Jackal.* She summoned her father's words, breathing the incense of the precinct altars as if it were the spiced scent of his chamber.

When Zakarbaal finally emerged from the temple, Elissa strode to meet him.

'Princess. I did not expect to see you again so soon. Is all well?' Behind his smile there was a shadow of concern.

'May we speak? Privately.'

The shadow reached his eyes. 'Of course.'

He led her behind the sacred chamber of the temple, to a storeroom with thick stone walls. There, between the sacks of grain, the jars of oil and wine, the disused tripods and shining metal bowls, Elissa found the words she needed to speak.

'My brother has ordered me to marry,' she began. 'Or rather, his advisors have ordered it. I have tried to speak against them, but Pygmalion will not listen. He is only a boy and he does not understand what this will mean. He doesn't understand any-thing – or he doesn't care.'

That was the more painful thought. That she should be owed no care from the brother for whom she cared so much. Elissa felt her anguish rising, her words running out of her control. And Zakarbaal must have felt it too, for he put a steadying hand upon her sleeve.

'You want me to speak on your behalf,' he said.

'No,' she said. 'I am grateful. But no, I fear it would do no good. That is not why I have come.' She paused, tried to swal-low the dryness in her mouth.

Now that she was here, it seemed a madness. He would laugh at her. She was suddenly sure of it, could feel herself retreat-ing. Why should she care so much what this man thought of her? And yet she did, with a deep instinct – the same that had brought her here, that told her to go on speaking.

'I need you to marry me.'

The words hung for a moment, and Elissa watched Zakarbaal's face. He did not laugh, but the deep crease in his brow was little better.

'I must marry someone. That seems unavoidable. If I wait for a husband to be chosen for me, they will send me as far from Tyre as they can manage. But if we marry, I can remain in the city and continue to serve her. And you are young and . . . unmarried?' She took his silence for an answer. 'And my brother could not object to such a match. Often is royal blood bonded with that of the priest class. My own great-grandfather was priest of Ashtart. The Council would have to accept our union.'

'I am flattered that you consider me a worthy prospect,' Zakarbaal said dryly.

'I have offended you,' she muttered, unable to tell whether the curl of his lip was from ridicule or disdain. 'I only wanted to explain why I had come. I hoped that you would be persuaded. That you would help me, if you knew my position. Did you not promise to help me?' She felt her confidence crumbling under his gaze, and resented the warmth that flooded her cheeks. She dropped her head. 'Please know that I would not have asked this if I did not hold some trust in you. I admire the work I have seen here at the temple, and I admire you, as little as I have been able to know you. I expected too much, though. I understand that now. Please, forgive my presumption.'

Elissa turned towards the storeroom door, desperate to leave this cramped space and stride away before her embarrassment could fully catch her. She took a step forwards, but a hand caught her arm.

'Do you speak so much that you would speak for me, also?' Zakarbaal's gentle grasp turned her away from the door, and she forced herself to look up at him. 'I admit I was surprised. This is the last thing that I imagined.' His face seemed smoother now, his eyes brightened by the light from the doorway. 'But the gods fill our lives with surprises. And this, I think, is not a bad one.'

He smiled, but it took Elissa a moment to realise his meaning. She took the hand that still touched her arm and pressed it firmly.

'Do you swear it? You will do this thing? You will be my husband?'

'If you are sure you want me, then I will take you gladly.'

Chapter 14

TYRE

If the wedding party was splendid, it did not seem so to Elissa. It was a feast like a hundred others she had attended. Yet she barely swallowed two mouthfuls of food and refused to touch her wine. She kept herself alert, to the sounds of the hall and the glances of the men who surrounded her. All had been arranged swiftly once Zakarbaal had brought his marriage suit to the king. Ahiram and the merchants had made no opposition strong enough to reach her ears, but that fact had not settled her. Perhaps her act of resistance was not that at all, but only a different flavour of what they had schemed for her. Still a trap, but now one of her own design.

Or perhaps there was a silent scheme still at play to prevent the marriage after all. That was why she watched the room, waiting for some signal that she would not in fact be allowed to walk from the palace along the path she had chosen.

But instead, there came a disturbance of a different kind, as the music suddenly rose to a livelier pitch and she was jostled by inches through the crowded hall and out to the front gate. She felt almost as if that great building, that had been her home for nearly two decades, were spitting her out. And though her brother stood beside her, smiling up at her with his fresh face, she wished beyond all else that her father could be standing there instead. She would have known from one flash of his dark eyes whether her decision was the right one, just as she had when she was a child, touching her fingers upon one of her ivory jackals. She imagined that she did see him now, held him before her like a mirror so that she could remember her own reasons, stir again the determination that had sent her to Zakarbaal's temple.

Zakarbaal had not been at the feast. He waited for her at his own house, with another meal laid out that she would not have the stomach for eating. She made herself recall the priest's open smile, his steadiness that made her feel steady, and told herself that these things were enough until she had more.

The streets outside the palace were full, and the king's attendants had to cut ahead to clear a way through. Elissa should not have been surprised to see so many people. Who does not like to look upon a bride in her finery? And a royal bride could only draw more curiosity. The crowd sang the wedding song as she made her slow progress. Her arms were heavy with gold and her embellished skirt dragged at her thighs, but the smiles of the Tyrians emboldened her. Elissa held her chin high, inviting them all to look upon Mattan's daughter and to celebrate her.

Pygmalion walked beside her, like a bejewelled shadow. She felt his hand brush hers as if he wanted to take it, so without looking down, she wove her fingers into his.

'I shall miss you.' His small voice was difficult to hear above the wedding song.

'I am not leaving you,' she said. 'I will still be here in the city, whenever you need me. Just send for me and I will come. Always, Pygmalion. I will be at your side as often as you need me.'

If he replied, she didn't hear it. The sound of the crowd swelled around them, and all Elissa could do then was squeeze her brother's hand with as much feeling as her words had carried.

She guessed that they were nearing their destination. She scanned ahead for the face of her betrothed, and discovered it in the doorway of a house she scarcely had the chance to examine.

Once Zakarbaal had caught her gaze, he held it, and she found herself smiling with relief, even as she knew how strange that was. She smiled at him as if he were a well-worn friend, though in truth they barely knew one another. It was trust that kept her moving towards him – trust in her own instincts, and in what little she had observed of his.

As the procession slowed, she let her brother's clammy fingers fall from hers, and gripped the tightly embroidered cloth of her skirt instead. She looked across at Pygmalion and hoped that he would remember what she had said to him, that he would remember the love knitted between them for nine years. *Let it stretch this small distance*, she willed. The final steps to the doorway were longer than the entire rest of the journey, so it seemed, and when she stopped in front of the house that would now become her home, her legs were shaking.

'Princess Elissa.' Zakarbaal's voice was stately, but she saw his nerves in the hand he put forward. She had touched that hand only once before, yet she remembered its warmth. It ought to be an easy thing, to slip hers into it. And a part of her was eager to. So that she would not feel alone in that pressing crowd. So that she could stop fearing that her legs would fold beneath her. She hesitated, though. Once she crossed this threshold, she could not go back through it. Once she chose to live with this man and share his house, his meals, his bed, she would be bound to him, and he to her, as husband and wife. Even here, with his patient eyes on her, with the city singing for their union, she asked herself whether this was the best move that she could make. In walking into this marriage, was she preserving more of her freedom than she was giving up? Was she protecting the power that her father had grown in her, that her brother and her city would need from her? As she searched the priest's eyes, and wrestled her own gut, she told herself that she was. Zakarbaal did not seem like a man who would force her to shrink.

Elissa pressed her hand on to that of her husband, felt the reassuring grip of his fingers, and stepped into his house.

Once the door was closed, the world fell quiet, and Elissa's ears felt oddly empty now that they were not filled with the clamour of the crowd. Her heavy dowry chest had been carried in behind her, filled years ago by her father, and now her maid Piddaya stood awkwardly beside it.

'Your room is past the kitchen, Piddaya,' Zakarbaal said warmly. 'You may rearrange things as you like them.' The girl took her cue gratefully and headed off through the door that Zakarbaal had pointed to. It occurred to Elissa that she had not introduced them to one another; the priest must have enquired as to the name of her maid. She smiled faintly at that.

'We ought to eat something,' Zakarbaal said, as he stood beside the neatly laid table. 'It is traditional, though I've not much appetite.'

Elissa watched his face crease with uncertainty and thought, not for the first time, that it had a quiet handsomeness.

'Neither have I,' she said, relieved. 'I could barely eat at the palace.' For a moment, she wondered whether that might offend him in some way, to confess the depth of her apprehension, but he only smiled.

'Just a little fruit, then.' He picked up two quarters of fig from the table, and bit into one as he stepped toward her. He held the other out and, misunderstanding his intention, Elissa bit into it while it was still in his fingers. There was an intimacy to the moment that surprised them both, and Elissa felt her cheeks flush with something more pleasant than embarrassment. There was a stirring in her stomach, nervous and hopeful. And when Zakarbaal leaned down to kiss her, there was still the sweetness of fig on his lips.

Chapter 15

CARTHAGE

Dido walked with Aeneas and his son by the shore. She had happened to meet them as she was leaving the palace, and it was the prince who had suggested they go out of the city together – an offer that delighted the restless Ascanius. Now her sandals slipped over fine sand while the rhythmic breaking of the waves sighed in her ears.

How long had it been since she had walked along this beach? Or passed an afternoon in light company? Her time away from the city – from the duties of her audience hall, of the temple, of monitoring the stores and workshops, of meeting with her scribes and advisors – was in such short supply that she usually spent it alone. She carved out silence so that she could hear her thoughts, untangled them as she strode to the grove or along her private path on the cliff. Such outings were never frivolous, never without purpose. Her visits to the grove least of all. They were a duty to her husband and his memory, as pious in her mind as pouring libations at the altars of the gods.

Today's walk had a different pace and weight. So much that, even as Dido found herself enjoying the sounds of the shore, the salt smell on the breeze, the rare aimlessness of her own body and mind, she felt guilty. She blew away that feeling by reminding herself that proper attendance of guests was a duty in itself. And there was no law to say that a duty could not also be a pleasure.

Ascanius was entertaining himself by running into the surf as it receded, and squealing as a fresh wave came to splash over his knees. The sea had lost its summer warmth, but he did not seem to mind – the cold likely added to his thrill. Dido found herself laughing as she watched him, and made her eyes wide every time the child turned around to share his excitement.

'It is a shame that a woman such as you should have no children,' Aeneas mused as they walked in parallel. 'Ascanius has known you barely a week and he adores you.'

His words warmed her, but there was a scratch to them too.

'I know you said that Carthage has never had a king, but you did have a husband once, yes?'

'Yes.'

'And he died?'

'Yes.'

'In Tyre?'

'Yes.' Dido knew that the prince was searching for answers longer than she was willing to give. And she knew, too, that it was unfair of her to withhold them when he had revealed so much of his own pain. He did not sound frustrated, but she was afraid to make him so and spoil their pleasant outing.

'That was one of the reasons for our leaving Tyre,' she offered. 'It is a long and . . . unpleasant story. Best told when there is wine to hand.' She turned and gave a crooked smile, which he seemed to understand.

'And you never had children?'

'Not one.' She spoke without bitterness, but it was another topic she preferred not to linger on. 'And you and your wife . . . Was Ascanius your only child?'

'Yes. I was late to marry. Creusa and I were only wed a few years.'

Creusa. Dido noted the name. This was the first time he had spoken of his wife.

'She was young still, and I had hoped we would have many more children. That would have made things easier, I think. If Ascanius had siblings beside him. As it is, I feel I must be all things to him. He has no one else, since even his grandfather has left him now.' Aeneas stopped on the sand, and Dido turned to face him. 'I wonder sometimes how it will affect him, to be without his mother's love. It seems so cruel that he has been robbed of it.'

'He has a father who loves him. Who protects him and does all he can for him.' She smiled warmly but resisted reaching out her hand. 'I was little older than Ascanius is when I lost my own mother. But my father filled that space with as much of himself as he could spare. And I have survived well enough, have I not?' She threw up her arms and posed playfully, inviting him to verify her claim. She began to turn on the spot, and his laughter made her beam with satisfaction.

'Yes, you are right. There are many who endure without mothers. I never truly knew my own. Only what my father told me of her. I do not think she died – my father never confirmed it – but she left me, in any case. The way my father spoke of her, you would think she had been a goddess, but when I was a child all I wanted was a real woman, to hold me in her arms and wrap me in her love. Like the mothers other children took for granted. Ordinary and irreplaceable.' His face was soft as he spoke, and he seemed suddenly much younger than his years. Dido listened in fascination. 'I suppose I just hoped that my son would have what I did not. Do we not all wish such things for our children?' He caught himself then, and looked apologetic. But Dido smiled.

'We all wish that things will be better than they have been. Such hopes are never foolish. Though they may come to pass in ways we do not expect.'

She had wanted to give comforting words, but Aeneas's expression shifted in a way that confused her. She felt as if he were looking into her. The intimacy of it was so close to intrusion that she turned away to watch Ascanius kicking the waves instead.

'How was it that Creusa died? Was it the war that claimed her?'

'She was lost in the fall of the city. She . . . ' Aeneas's throat made a sound as if it were closing up, and Dido felt sorry that she had asked the question.

'She was killed in the fighting.' She thought to save him the pain of speaking, but Aeneas found his voice again.

'No. Or perhaps. She . . . In truth, I do not know how she died. She was with me when we left our house. I told you that I had to carry my father, that Ascanius was beside me. And Creusa walked behind. I thought that she was following. But when we were near the ships, I turned around and I could not see her. I was afraid to call for her and draw the attention of the Greeks. So I left my son and my father at the shore, told them to keep silent in the darkness with the others who had made it that far. Then I went back into the city to look for Creusa. By then, everything was aflame. I could not hear my own voice above the screams. I made it back as far as our house, but I could not find her. And what could I do then? Stay and burn and leave my kin without protection? So I went again to the shore, and she had not found her way there either. So . . . so we set sail without her. But I knew in my heart that she was dead then. Whether by sword or smoke or terror. She could not have survived.'

Dido stood without words. There was the shock of sympathy for a man forced to make such desperate decisions. Of course there was that. But behind it, she felt something closer to disappointment. That the prince who cared so greatly for his own blood had let his wife slip away from him. Could he not have kept her in his sight, as close to him as the son she had borne him? Did that bond have so little value? He had given his whole body to his aged father, and to his wife not even a hand or an eye. Dido could not help picturing the poor woman, stumbling behind unnoticed, calling out when she was already too far to be heard. It made her heart twist uncomfortably. She told herself – knew, without hesitation – that her own husband would not have left her. That she would never have left him. The bond between them had been more precious than any other in her life. And while she knew it was unfair to assume that Aeneas should feel the same towards his own wife, she could not dismiss the cold feeling that came over her.

'I loved my wife,' Aeneas said, and she knew then that he could sense her judgement. Perhaps he expected it.

Her silence had stretched too long, but the only words ready on Dido's tongue felt spiked and dangerous. Aeneas's taut body was turned towards her, his gaze uncomfortably direct. But she could not return it.

'You think that I should have done more? That I could have?' His voice was rising. 'What do you know about it? You cannot understand all that I have suffered.'

'I know more than many,' she murmured.

'Because you have lost a home? But your city still stands, does it not? It was not torn down. You simply left.'

Now Dido's own blood was rising. She felt it in her cheeks, pulsing in her neck. Did the prince truly think he owned all the world's pain? That he understood loss better than she did?

'There was nothing simple about it.' Dido's hands gripped her skirt, shaking with anger and something else besides. A vulnerability. A feeling that his words had stabbed at something sacred. Aeneas had learned nothing of her at all, if he did not know how deeply her heart ached for Tyre, for all that she had been forced to leave behind there. Even if the city still stood, it was burned for her.

Before she could rally her thoughts to say more, she realised that Ascanius had stopped his playing. He stared at her with a quivering frown that was like a bowl of water over her fire. This was the first time he had heard her voice so sharpened.

She felt the breath go out of her and half-turned towards Aeneas without meeting his eye. 'I should return to the palace.'

Dido granted the prince a curt nod before hurrying away over the sand, wishing that it would stay firm beneath her feet for a more dignified escape. She was still angry, still gripped her skirts as if they were the reins of a chariot, but the further she walked, the more sadness rose in her throat. The day had been so pleasant. She wished that she could go back and make it so again. But things had passed that could not be retrieved. Aeneas had disappointed her, and she had shamed him. They had wounded one another, in the clash of loss against loss.

She should not have been surprised. Pleasantness was hard to hold in hands such as theirs. The roughened hands of queens and princes, refugees, ocean-crossers, bearers of more than their own grief. Both she and Aeneas carried their pasts like heavy cargo. And while Dido had enjoyed learning about the prince from Troy, as he'd unloaded each box and pried off the lid for her to look inside, she should have known that one of those boxes might contain a snake.

Perhaps that was it for them now. It would be for the best, she told herself, if he were on his way across the sea as soon as his ship was repaired. She had more than performed her duty towards him. Let him dare to say that Queen Dido of Carthage was not a generous host. He could carry the rest of his history away with him, and she would keep hers sealed. What good could there be in sharing it? Only more hurt for both of them.

As soon as she was back in the city, she would call a meeting with the shipwrights, and make sure that all was progressing as swiftly as it could be. Yes. She could feel herself calming with each stride. Dido always felt better once her next move was decided.

Chapter 16

TYRE

Elissa held the faience scarab in the palm of her hand. The little beetle, long out of the kiln, felt cool to the touch, and its blue glaze gleamed like polished turquoise.

'Perfect, as always. You are a master of your craft, Shapashuru.'

The white-haired man smiled, but shook his head. 'You will rarely find me at a kiln these days. This is the work of my apprentices.' He gestured to the tray of identical scarabs he had laid out for her. 'My time is too far stretched managing the matters of the guild. Between my own workshop and the business of the glassworkers, I barely find a moment of peace.' He did not seem to rue the fact, but beamed with a humble pride.

'In any case, your contribution to the temple of Melqart is appreciated. May the Rising God bring you all that you need.' Elissa nodded solemnly and rose to leave, as Piddaya took up the rattling tray of scarabs.

'I hope that you will come again yourself next month, Princess.' Shapashuru held open the door of his office. 'It gives me pleasure to see Mattan's daughter. You have so much of his bearing.' The guildmaster's eyes were glossed with nostalgia, and though Elissa smiled, she felt a pinch in her chest. So rarely was her father's name spoken now.

'I am proud to serve Tyre, as he did,' she said quietly. 'You will see me again. Do not doubt it.'

As she and Piddaya made their slow progress through Tyre's streets, Elissa still felt a little unbalanced by Shapashuru's mention of her father. It had called her back to a different time, to a different version of herself.

This was the sixth winter since her father's passing. Six years was not so very long, and yet how changed the world felt – or perhaps it was only she that was changed. She had been so angry then, striding around like warlike Ashtart, as if she were meeting the entire world in battle. She had been no more than a child, really. A child desperate to find her place. Well, she had found it now.

The temple of Melqart came into view, and Elissa could already see Zakarbaal waiting by the precinct wall.

'You've returned.'

As soon as she was within reach, he took her into his arms. She might have been embarrassed by such affection, but the temple had already emptied of its daily visitors, and there was only Piddaya to witness it. She let herself soften into his embrace, before pulling away.

'Did you think I would not?' she teased him with a smile.

It was strange, she often thought, how she could miss her husband after only a few hours apart, how she could be so pleased to see his face again and hear his loving voice. They worked together each day and lay beside one another each night, and yet she never tired of being close to him. Elissa wrapped her hand around his and led his gaze towards the tray Piddaya was still holding.

'Beautiful, are they not? I think the guildmaster added a few more than last time.'

'That is well. We are in need of generosity. Come, Piddaya, let me take those to the storehouse.'

The maid looked relieved to have the tray taken from her, and let her aching arms drop to her sides. She was past twenty now, but still only a slight woman. She stood a little taller than her mistress, but in that she was no different to much of Tyre.

As Elissa watched her husband carry away the tray, she felt satisfied by her day's work. The collecting of tithes was only one of the ways in which she served the temple, but it was an important one. Each of those gleaming scarabs would be bought by a worshipper wealthy enough to afford it – a small piece of comfort that they might press to their palm and know that Melqart was watching over their affairs. Those who could not afford such beautiful charms would benefit from whatever wealth they generated, meted out in grain and oil.

That evening, Elissa lay in bed with her husband. Their house was not as grand as the halls she had grown up in, but neither was it meagre. Three storeys, with a small, shaded courtyard, and a generous room for Piddaya. It was too much space, really, for only the three of them. But it was the priest's house, granted to Zakarbaal when he'd gained his position, and convenient for its closeness to the temple.

In the days after she had wed her husband, as she had walked through the vacant rooms of her new home for the first time, Elissa had felt a kind of threat from them. They had seemed so expectant. Waiting to be filled with children, with their crying and their laughter, with their incessant calls for comfort that only a mother could answer. She had feared that, she remembered. And though the memory seemed almost amusing now, it tasted bitter, too. For a moment, she wished she could go back and tell that girl she need not fear the cage of motherhood. No children would come. Perhaps that knowledge would have brought her comfort then. But, not for the first time today, she realised with a pang how far she had changed from the girl she once was.

'Are you here with me, my love? Or away in your mind?' Zakarbaal's face was tired from a long day, but it lacked none of the warmth that seemed always so abundant in him. He drew her close and kissed the top of her head.

'I am here. Mostly.' She smiled and let her head rest on his chest, breathing in the smell of him. Smoke, incense, the sweat of labour and the faded notes of his resin perfume. This was one of the many things she had come to love about her husband. Some things had made their impression quickly – his open smile, his generous heart, his confidence that was not arrogance, his touch that could be gentle and strong at once. Other things had taken months or even years to fully unfold themselves. The depths of his moral spirit, his shrewdness, his particular wit. The way he could read her so thoroughly, but never judged her. There was not one singular moment in which she had realised that she loved him, but a thousand moments, piling upon one another. Elissa's love for Zakarbaal had come, not like a rush, but like a steady drip that becomes a trickle, a river, a whole ocean.

'Would you like me to attend the petition hearing tomorrow?' he asked her softly. 'I have not been for more than a month, since there is always so much to be done at the temple. But I will go if you wish me to. It may serve us to know the dealings of the palace, if nothing else.'

'It may,' she conceded. 'Or it may serve only to tell us things we have no use for. Things we have no hope of changing.' She felt her old frustration spike. 'At the temple, we do real work. We help those who need it. We serve the gods and the city. Is that not a more worthy use of your time? Of our attention?'

'Yes, my love. You know you do not need to convince me. I only thought to ask.' Zakarbaal was not a man lacking in passion, but he did not let his passions burn him as Elissa's did. It was another thing she had grown to appreciate in him, the way his coolness could soothe her.

'I'm sorry,' she said, pushing herself up so that she could look at his face. 'Go to the hearing, if you think you should.' She kissed him and settled back down against his bare chest. 'You may do whatever you think is best.'

'Oh, may I?' He laughed lightly and stroked her long black hair away from her face, but she did not look up again. She was back in her thoughts, pulled there by his talk of the palace.

She felt so distanced from that place now, despite having the ability to walk there in a matter of minutes. She was distanced from the people, from the lives that carried on there without her, from their thoughts and their decisions. Distanced from the court, from the Council. From her brother.

She saw Pygmalion on feast days. She smiled and nodded to him – acknowledgements he usually returned – but she had long abandoned her hope of closeness or influence with the king. She had pursued it for a time, even after her marriage. She had tried to attend the court. But she found she no longer knew her place there. Should it be beside her brother as a member of the royal house, even though she was no longer of his household? Was it on the benches with her husband? She was not a member of the Council of Elders, and could at best hope to be admitted as his accessory. Or was she supposed to find her place among the wives of the court, in Queen Meret's band of gossips, where information was shared but rarely used?

Her meetings with her brother – the only times she might actually be of help to him – had become rarer and rarer, until, within the first year of her marriage, she had realised that her desire to serve the city was more fulfilled by her work for the temple than it ever could be at court.

And so this was her life now. Not the one her father had planned for her, but one she hoped he would admire. It gave her an odd feeling to think how far it had strayed from her own imagination. The very cause of her marriage to Zakarbaal – her will to remain at her brother's side – had fallen into dust now. And the very thing she had feared from their forced union – the burden of motherhood, as she had seen it then – had not come to be. It was a cruel joke of fate, perhaps, that fear should turn to longing. But Zakarbaal did not fret as she did. He said that the gods granted all that should be, in time. And he was so often right about things, even if she did not share his patience.

As she lay against him, pressing as much of her skin against his as she could manage, she thought of what Zakarbaal had said so many years ago, on the day he had agreed to be her husband. He had told her that life was full of surprises. And of all the surprises Elissa had met with since that day, the joy and comfort she had found in their marriage was surely the greatest.

Chapter 17

TYRE

Elissa stood at the entrance to the precinct, like a stone that forks a stream.

'Those who have come for bread, join the queue on this side. Have patience. We have enough for everyone. You have an offering for the temple? This way, please. May Melqart hear your words.'

Many faces she recognised. They were the same who came each day, though not always for the same purpose. One month a man might come in desperation, and stand in the long queue for bread with hands wringing. The next month, when his fortune was brighter, he would come again with a gift in his hands – a basket of fish, a jar of wine, a pot of salt – a repayment of his debt, though none was asked for. And his gift would keep another man – a whole family, perhaps – from falling to a place from which they could not recover themselves. And so it went on.

'Melqart bless you,' murmured some of the men and women that passed her. Sometimes a hand would grasp hers and squeeze tightly, expressing what words could not. Elissa squeezed back, uncertain whether to smile. Would it be heartening, or patronising? After six years at the temple, she had grown used to gratitude, but a part of her wondered how much of it was deserved. It was Zakarbaal who had begun these endeavours, who had seen the city crumbling and done something to prevent it. The needs of the people had only grown since they were married, and yet somehow he always rose to meet them. And the people did, too. They helped one another with what they could afford to give.

Elissa played her part. And whether or not it was enough to earn the beaming smiles and desperate thanks she received, she could not deny that she enjoyed the feeling of it. The feeling of being needed, being seen. Of being someone who meant something to all these people – her father's people, her people.

Zakarbaal had gone to the petition hearing, but she did not mind. She could manage the precinct well enough without him, and the lower priests would take care of the altars. After a long morning, though, her throat was beginning to feel ragged. She longed to get a cup of beer from where they were being passed out with the bread. But as she took a step in that direction, there was a tug at her skirt.

'Princess?'

The voice was small, and she turned to find a young girl looking up at her. Her eyes were wide and wondering, her fingers still stuck in the soft folds of fabric.

Elissa crouched down. 'What is it?' she asked softly. 'Are you hungry? Where are your parents?'

'My papa needs to speak to you,' she said, with a confidence so surprising it made Elissa smile.

'And where is he?'

The girl pointed to a thick-bearded man in a goat-skin cap, waiting anxiously at the precinct wall.

'Come, then. Let's go to him.'

The girl took Elissa's hand without her offering it. The press of those little fingers made her chest warm and tight at once.

'Why do you not come into the precinct?' she asked as she reached the man. 'The temple of Melqart is open to all.' She tried to smile, but the man's expression was dour.

'I have not come for the temple. I came . . . Forgive me, Princess. I can see that you are busy. No doubt there are people in there with greater woes than mine. But I didn't know where else I could go. And my daughter – Ashtart defend her – she's in a bad situation.'

Elissa looked down at the girl, bitten by concern.

'No, my lady. Not this daughter.' He brought the girl close to him and she let go of Elissa's hand. 'No, my eldest. Donatiya. Her husband has been beating her. He doesn't even hide it, the shameless coward. Beats her right on her face. Cut her cheek with his ring. I'd have fought him myself, but I can't risk that. Not with my other children relying on me.' He put a hand on the girl's head and messed her curls. 'Donatiya has no children to be concerned with, so she has asked for a divorce, as is her right. And I have supported it. But the coward her husband will not return her dowry. Without it, she cannot remarry. So what is she to do?'

Elissa listened carefully, her brow heavy with sympathy. 'I am sorry for what your daughter has suffered. And the dowry must be returned, of course.' She paused. 'But why have you come to me? You must go to the palace and speak for your daughter there. The king is hearing petitions this very day. It is only noon. There is still time if you—'

'I have been to the palace,' he said. 'I was turned away this morning. And now I have been trying to think where else I could go.'

'You were turned away? For what reason?'

'We were all turned away.' The man's mouth became hard. 'The king will no longer be hearing petitions from any citizen except those of the noble classes. That's what they said. Some waiting there had come all the way from the mainland. And who is to hear us now? I thought of the temple, and how you and the priest, your husband, help so many people. Perhaps I was wrong to come to you, my lady. But what else can I do for my daughter?'

Elissa was quiet, trying to absorb what the man had told her, while feeling the great weight of his gaze. He looked so lost, and she could not send him away without some hope.

'I will speak with my husband, and we will see what can be done concerning the dowry. What is the name of your daughter's husband?'

'Danel. He is a fisherman.'

'Very well. Leave this matter with me.'

The man's body seemed to fold, and he breathed deeply with relief. 'Thank you, Princess. Tyre is blessed to have you.'

As the man led his young daughter away, Elissa was washed with the familiar feeling of gratitude not wholly earned, mingled with pride that people such as this man trusted her, that they might look to her for help when her brother had disappointed them. It was a feeling brewed in the knowledge that, though she had been denied the power she was meant to inherit, she had found herself power of another sort – one that was more satisfying for being built rather than bequeathed.

She walked back into the precinct, feeling a flame at her heel. There were people in need of clothing, she saw, and she let her momentum carry her to the storehouse where the spare garments were kept. She piled them into her arms without really seeing what she picked up, and stumbled back out into the muted winter sunshine. All she could think of was Zakarbaal's return from the palace, and what she would tell him when he arrived.

'They are not hearing petitions from ordinary citizens.' Her husband's indignation was exactly as she had predicted, and she loved him for it.

'I know.'

'You do? How?' He deflated a little.

'A man came to the temple. One of those who had been turned away. He brought his petition to me instead, and I said that we would help him, but . . . How can they do this?'

'I don't know.' Zakarbaal sighed and they sat together on a bench in the empty precinct. 'I spent the day listening to merchants asking for better trade levies, and courtiers complaining about the shortage of good wine from the mainland. How can these be the matters most in need of the king's attention?' He looked so dejected. Elissa put an arm around him, but his body remained tense. 'Every day we are battling against Tyre's problems. The raids continue, and people are hungry, without work. We give them all we can, but it will not be enough while the king insists on remaining ignorant.'

'What did the other nobles say?' she asked. 'Were there any on the Council who objected to the change?'

'A few.' He nodded slowly, and his face lost some of its hardness. 'Yes, I was not the only one who spoke against it. But what could we do? Even if half the Council were in dissent, we know which half holds Pygmalion's ear. And a king may do as he decides.'

He rubbed his face with one hand and fell quiet. The two of them sat looking at the peach sky.

'But what of this man who came to you?' he asked eventually. 'What was his petition?'

She explained all that the man had told her.

'You were right to say you would help him. We will speak with this fisherman and make sure the dowry is recovered.' For a moment, he seemed brighter, as his spirit found a solid purpose. 'But I fear there will be many more requests like this one, brought to the temple if they cannot be brought to the palace. If the king intends to keep to his new course, this will be the first of many. And will our work allow us to answer them, I wonder?'

'We will do what we can, as always.' She tried to sound encouraging, but she felt as much doubt as his face showed. 'I wonder,' she began, with her throat faltering, 'if we may have made a mistake in distancing ourselves so much from the court.'

'Well, that is something I never thought I would hear.'

It had been Elissa who had convinced him that their work at the temple was more valuable, that nothing at court could be influenced by them. And she hated to admit that she may have been wrong.

'I never thought that things would go as far as they have. Pygmalion is changing the very fabric of the city, degrading his responsibilities as its king. Perhaps if we had been at court more often, we might have prevented this. Or at least been more prepared for it. I . . . I don't know.' She looked up at him. 'I thought I had found a way to serve Tyre, but maybe I only abandoned her.'

'That is not true.' The firmness of Zakarbaal's voice was something she could hold on to. It always had been.

'Then how shall we save her? What can we do now? Take on every task for which my brother has no appetite?'

'No. You know we cannot.' He took her hand and laced his fingers through hers. 'I think you are right. We cannot always be reacting. We need to know how the palace moves. Both of us. There will be a meeting at the end of the month, between the king and the Council of Elders. It concerns the Great Awakening festival, so of course I must go. But you, also, would have every right to attend.'

The thought of returning to the court, after so many years away, made Elissa's stomach twist. It meant returning to her memories of that place, her disempowerment, her injured pride, her anger mixed with grief. But the press of Zakarbaal's hand reminded her that he would be there with her, that she could never feel small or unimportant when his eyes were on her.

'We will go.'

Chapter 18

TYRE

Elissa was annoyed by how uncomfortable she felt. Had she not lived in the palace for most of her life? Had she not been born here? Had she not grown here, sat on her father's knee in this hall, and sat beside him as he did his duty? It felt like the home of a stranger now.

Or perhaps she was the stranger. That was how she was made to feel, under the suspicious attention of the nobles. They looked at her as if a wild goat had wandered into the court, to begin chewing the bench cushions and making its mess on the floor.

Why did their wrinkled brows sting her? Why should she care what these obnoxious, soft-bellied, stain-toothed merchants thought of her? She had the love of the people. She felt it every day as she stood on aching feet and let their thanks fill her to the brim. She did not need these men to love her, nor even to like her. But she wished – far more than she would admit – that they would respect her.

'I should not have come,' she whispered to Zakarbaal. 'There is no gain in me being here.' She shifted in her seat, trying to summon the courage to stand up and walk out of the hall. But just as she began to rise, a voice called to her.

'Princess Elissa.'

Shapashuru had just entered, and he cut across the floor to where she and Zakarbaal were sitting. He beamed at them, his head hardly higher than theirs due to his aged stoop.

'What a pleasure it is to see you again. And your noble husband, of course.' The guildmaster dipped his head even lower.

'How are the affairs of the guild?' Elissa asked eagerly, relieved that she had an opportunity to speak rather than endure silent stares.

'Oh, we do well enough,' Shapashuru replied with thin cheerfulness. 'Though, with things being as they are, there are few who can spare the indulgence of our pretty baubles.' His smile was crooked. 'Still, we have our foreign trade. I had a ship return from the north just yesterday, but it came with troubling news. Ugarit fares badly. Fires and sieges, so they say. Praise to Melqart that he keeps Tyre safe from such calamities.' He turned his face to Zakarbaal and bowed reverently. 'I sometimes feel your prayers at the temple might be the only thing keeping us from disaster.' The guildmaster's voice fell to a hush, and he looked aside as if to see whether anyone had heard him. 'Melqart preserve you both,' he added, as he clasped their hands with hurried sincerity, before shuffling away to take his seat.

As Elissa sat on the bench, her thoughts of leaving the hall forgotten, she began to see other faces that smiled as she looked at them, or nodded with polite acknowledgement. Had they not been there before, or had she not seen them? Shapashuru's warmth stayed with her, and she smiled tentatively at those nobles who seemed to reflect a little of it.

The hall filled slowly, and the last to enter was the king. He came flanked by two guards and swathed in purple. Beads of carnelian hung from around his neck; bands of gold encircled his arms. Black kohl lined his eyes, and a bejewelled fillet sparkled in his black hair. But beneath all his splendour, Elissa could see the boy who had been her brother. Still a boy, really, even now. A suggestion of fine hair grew about his lip and chin, but his cheek and jaw were smooth and doughy. He sat upon her father's throne with an acquired confidence, and looked about with a leisureliness that came with knowing that nothing would begin until he began it. Elissa sat anxiously, waiting for him to notice her presence, but his gaze passed over her with barely a pause.

'What is the purpose of this meeting?' Pygmalion asked eventually, addressing the bench of nobles sitting closest to him.

'To make preparations for the Great Awakening festival, my king.'

The men's faces remained undisturbed, but Elissa wondered how. Were they not embarrassed to sit before a king who knew not why he was there?

'Head Priest Zakarbaal,' her brother called, and the attention of the hall shifted in their direction. 'Should you not be the one to speak first?'

Elissa's husband put a hand on her knee before rising to his feet. 'Of course, my king.'

She hoped that he would stay beside her, but he moved to the floor of the hall so that all could hear him.

'As you know, every springtime we must perform the Awakening of our patron Melqart, to rouse him back from the land of sleep and darkness and ensure his bounty returns to the land. With winter being at its end, the time to observe this duty is nearly upon us.'

There were nods around the hall, some solemn, others impatient.

'But further to that, the nature of Melqart's divine cycle is such that every seven years, he requires a more vigorous rousing, to bring him back to us from greater depths of oblivion and, consequently, to stir from him an even greater flourishing of the land. This festival we call the Great Awakening.'

As Elissa watched her brother, she saw that he nodded casually but listened carefully. He would have been a child when their father led the last Great Awakening, only months before his death. Elissa remembered it well, but perhaps for Pygmalion it had blurred together with every other city festival. She realised then that Zakarbaal was speaking above all for the king's benefit, so that he would not expose his ignorance, or perhaps more so that he would understand how vital the festival was for the city's prosperity.

'Every man in Tyre,' Zakarbaal went on, 'knows he must contribute to the Awakening. By his voice, by the stamping of his feet, and by the pleasing things we offer to stir Melqart's appetite for the living world. I hope that the guilds, too, understand that to receive the Rising God's bounty, they must first provide. Therefore, I ask each merchant guild represented here – ivory carvers, silversmiths, winemakers, dyers, lumber traders, glass and faience workers' – he looked at each guild-master sat along the benches – 'to provide sacrifices equivalent to seven rams.'

There was some turning of heads, a few muttered words that Elissa could not hear, but no one objected. Most men of the Council were old enough to have contributed to several Great Awakenings, so her husband's request could be no surprise. Elissa felt herself relax on his behalf. But just as Zakarbaal opened his mouth to continue, a man rose from his bench. Ahiram. Of course it was Ahiram. Elissa's chest grew tight at the sight of his face rising above the rest.

'The guilds will always provide for Tyre's need,' he said in his usual unctuous tone, while he flashed his teeth at Zakarbaal and bowed towards the king. 'But tell me, Priest, what will the temple be contributing to this great festival?'

'We will prepare the sacrifices, and—'

'Our sacrifices.' Ahiram's voice cut across him like a knife.

'Yes. We will prepare the sacrifices, of course, and we will tend the altars, and build the sacred pyre, and lead the people in their devotions. All this I'm sure you know, for this is not your first Awakening.' Zakarbaal smiled, but Elissa saw how her husband's dark eyes glinted.

'Is it not curious, though,' Ahiram went on, 'that you should ask so much from us, and yet sacrifice nothing yourself?'

'The temple is not a guild,' Zakarbaal said levelly. 'We do not profit and prosper as merchants do. We serve Melqart, and benefit nothing, ask nothing, but safety and bounty for the city.'

'And yet,' Ahiram said, spreading his long fingers before him, and turning his gaze around the room, 'do we not see much wealth entering the temple of Melqart? Tithes and gifts, flowing in your direction every day. Surely you prosper more than any from the Rising God's bounty.'

'As I have told the Council many times,' Zakarbaal replied with admirable patience, 'the wealth gathered by the temple allows us to sustain the people of the city. And we have less of it than we need. No doubt our worshippers will give what they can for the festival, but we can pledge no more than that.'

Ahiram watched Zakarbaal for a prolonged moment, then seemed to accept his response. 'As you say.' But the look he sent to Pygmalion as he sat down gave Elissa a prickle in the gut.

'Are we concluded, then?' the king asked as he slouched beneath his purple cloak. 'The sacrifices will be given as you ask.'

'There is another matter we must discuss, my king.' Elissa heard her husband's hesitancy, saw it in the way he twisted the ring on his finger. 'That of the sacred dance.'

Even the word summoned memories in Elissa, of the last Great Awakening and those of her childhood, of her father dressed in his finest robe, his powerful body leaping and turning, her eyes stuck on him, her heart full with pride. Did her brother share such memories? The blankness of his expression made her doubt it.

'An Awakening always requires dancing, of course,' Zakarbaal explained, 'but the dance of the Great Awakening is a most holy rite, essential for the festival's success. It is performed on the third night and will involve men and women of the city. But these men and women must be led, my king.'

'And who leads them?' Pygmalion asked.

'Usually, they would be led by the king and his consort, as your father and mother led the dance at the last Great Awakening.'

'I will lead them, then, as I am their king.'

'I'm afraid that would not be suitable.' Zakarbaal's eyes glanced down for a moment, and Elissa saw him swallow. 'You are not yet married, my king. There must be two leaders of the dance, one for the men and one for the women.'

'Then my mother will lead with me. She has performed this rite before, as you say.'

'No. No, it cannot be the Queen Mother.'

A curious expression passed across Pygmalion's face, and Elissa wondered how long it had been since someone had last said no to him.

'No, the leaders of the dance must be bonded by marriage. It is a rite of fertility, of unity, that brings forth fruitfulness. I'm sure you see that your mother would not be suitable, and as you have no wife . . . '

'But who is better to lead the people than their king? If this is the most important rite, then I shall be the one to perform it.' Pygmalion spoke decisively, and yet he must have felt the cloud of doubt that hovered over the hall. 'What other option can there be?'

Zakarbaal did not answer. It was rare for Elissa to see her husband without words, but she knew as well as he that he stepped upon treacherous ground. A colour had come into Pygmalion's cheeks, and his soft jaw seemed to tremble with tension.

Her husband was saved from his paralysis by Shapashuru.

'My king,' the guildmaster began, rising from his seat. 'If I might propose a solution, I believe the priest Zakarbaal and his wife, your sister, would be fitting candidates for this duty. I am old enough to have seen many Great Awakenings, and it has been known for a priest of Melqart to lead the dance, when the king himself was prevented by youth or infirmity. How fortunate we are that our priest has a wife, and that she is of your own royal house. In what better hands could we place the well-being of the city?'

Elissa felt a surge of appreciation towards the guildmaster, and her surprise at his proposal only grew as she heard other men among the rows murmuring in agreement. She saw none of her own feeling on Zakarbaal's face, though. He must have known of this precedent, and yet he had said nothing to her.

'And this would please the gods more?' Pygmalion scoffed, pushing himself forwards on his throne. 'To have the dance led by an unroyal husband and his childless wife? Will this be our symbol of fruitfulness? Surely a king and the woman who bore him would be more fitting.'

He looked around the hall, as if seeking the approving nods he felt his wisdom deserved. Elissa saw a few heads submit, but her own mind was burning. Pygmalion had thrown out the insult as if it were nothing. And though it was true that she had no children, she felt horribly exposed by his words. Of all the things she knew her brother to be – indolent, careless, spoilt – she had never thought that he was cruel.

'What does our priest think, I wonder? Should we not be guided by him in such matters?' Shapashuru turned to Zakarbaal, and the whole hall sat silent, waiting for his reply.

'I think that we cannot know which course the gods would prefer. Not without investigation.' Zakarbaal put his hands together and spread his feet as if trying to anchor himself. 'I propose that we seek to divine their opinion on this matter, by means of belomancy.'

There was favourable muttering across the benches, but Zakarbaal's attention was upon the king. Pygmalion's eyes roved over the members of the Council, but when it was clear that no one had anything further to offer, he gave a resistant nod of assent.

'Did you know?' Elissa asked as she and her husband left the palace gate and headed back towards the temple. She was a little breathless, though from excitement rather than the pace of their walking.

'Know what?' Zakarbaal's voice was clipped, as if his mind was elsewhere.

'That we might be called upon to lead the dance?'

'I knew it was a possibility,' he said. 'I should have prepared for it. I might have handled it better.' His frown confused her.

'Better than what? Is this not a good outcome? If the gods favour us in the belomancy, we will lead the city in its most vital moment. I will stand where my father stood, and you beside me. The people already look to us. We will show them we are worthy of their confidence, give them hope for the new year and Melqart's bounty. Is that not important? Especially now. Come,' she soothed, linking her arm through his. 'This feels like a victory, I think. There were many who agreed with Shapashuru. I saw it in their faces. We have more favour with the Council than we thought.'

'Pygmalion was not pleased.'

'My brother does not like to be challenged. Perhaps this will be good for him.'

'I am not so sure.' His voice was so low she had to lean in to hear him against the sounds of the city. 'We must be careful, Elissa. The people look to us because they must, but we should not be seen to court their favour. Nor that of the Council. Not if it goes against the king.' He looked aside at her, and shortened his steps so much that they almost came to a stop. 'You know your family's history, and Pygmalion must know it too. Your own great-grandfather was priest of Ashtart before he killed his king and usurped his throne.'

Elissa knew the meaning of her husband's warning, but she did not share his worry. 'You are not that kind of man. My brother knows it. Everyone in Tyre knows it.' She looked at him with all seriousness, in the hope that he would be reassured. 'This is why you have proposed the belomancy, yes? You do not wish to put yourself before the king. But if the gods choose us, how can you be blamed? It was a clever move, my love.' She smiled up at him, but his face was still drawn with thoughts he did not share.

As they fell into silence, Elissa was determined not to let her husband's heavy brow sink her mood. She felt as if she had won something today, without even having to speak. Already, she imagined herself leading the dancers, standing at the head of the line as a thousand faces stared back at her. It was a feeling she could not let go, that worked itself deeper and deeper into her heart even as she walked the short journey home. By the time she lay in bed that night, she had forgotten that it was only a hope and not a promise.

Chapter 19

CARTHAGE

Dido had spent several days feeling uncomfortable in her own palace. Every time she entered a room or crossed a courtyard, she worried that she would find Aeneas there, and have to bow her head awkwardly or change her direction. Each time she caught the silhouette of a Trojan entering the main hall, her eyes darted up to see only some other man. And she would breathe silently with relief.

But as the days passed, her anxiety at the possibility of seeing Aeneas turned to concern that she had not. She knew then that he was avoiding her. What else could explain it? For all that Carthage had grown in her ten years, the city was not that large.

Dido revisited their conversation on the beach again and again. So few words spoken in anger, and yet they had unravelled much. The story of his first wife, of Creusa left to Troy's flames, had shocked her. Frightened her, even. But she had shamed the prince for something he had not intended, a memory that pained him, that he would go back and reverse if he could. Didn't she know something of that?

She had told herself then and since that there was nothing lost in her friendship with the prince, that Aeneas would soon leave on his ship and that anything that had passed between them, whether harsh or pleasant, would fall into the dividing sea. But even so, she felt a regret about how she had walked away from him on the shore and left him in his hurt. It was not right that he should now have to hide himself, when she had promised welcome and friendship for as long as he needed it.

This was what she told herself, how she explained the gnawing need she felt to speak with him. It became the anchoring thought Dido repeated as she made her way to Aeneas's chamber on that fourth morning after their sharp words. She had set aside a generous room for him and Ascanius here in the palace, on the first night when they had arrived smelling of sea salt.

Dido realised how tightly her hands were gripping the gift she carried, and forced them to loosen. A queen should not be nervous, not when she walked over foundations she had helped to lay, past walls she had ordered to be built. This was her home, her domain. She drew in one slow breath and let it seep all the way out before she knocked on the door.

'Queen Dido.' Despite his formality, Aeneas did not bow but stood with a hand still on the door as if he wanted to close it.

Dido chose not to be offended. 'Prince Aeneas.' She inclined her head even if he would not, hoping this small sacrifice of her pride would warm the air. Perhaps it worked, for she saw his hand relax a little on the wood. 'I have come to apologise for what passed between us the other day. I judged you when I had no right. Forgive me. I did not wish to cause you more pain.' Another sacrifice, to admit her part while ignoring his. But her words were mostly true. She did regret hurting him.

Aeneas was looking down, his fingers tapping silently on the door. 'I do forgive you,' he said eventually. 'And I am sorry for my own sharpness. I should not have spoken to you as I did.' He looked up then, and his dark eyes were sincere. They asked for forgiveness in turn, even if his lips did not.

'You have been missed in the hall,' she said lightly. 'I hope that we will be able to pass more evenings together before your ship is repaired. Not too many, I mean . . . I know that you will be eager to leave when you are able. But until then, please know that you have my friendship. That is all I came to say.' She moved to turn away.

'Are you sure that is all?'

For a moment, Dido was thrown. Her heart began to patter nervously, until she saw that Aeneas was looking at her hands. She laughed. 'Oh, of course. Yes, I brought this for Ascanius.'

Aeneas smiled and she felt all tension leave her, brushing her neck like a feather as it fled.

'Well, I didn't think it was for me.'

As if summoned by mention of his name, Ascanius appeared behind his father, half hiding and half desperately leaning to see what Dido held in her hands. She set the wooden toy down on the floor – a carved and painted goat, with bright eyes of quartz, and little wheels beneath it. There was a leather string tied around its neck that Dido held out for the boy to take.

Ascanius looked up at his father for permission, then stepped out from the doorway and took the string. As he leaned down to stroke the wooden creature, Dido felt her chest warm. 'You must take good care of him,' she said. 'And give him a name, perhaps.' The boy was already leading the goat towards the light of the courtyard, and Aeneas had to step past Dido to follow him.

'Thank you,' he breathed. 'I do not deserve a friend so good as you.'

But before she could disagree, he was away after his son, as the wooden wheels of the goat bounced over the flagstones. Dido was left with his brief, soft words, spoken so close to her ear. And the smell of his foreign perfume.

'You have made up with him, then.' Anna strode across the hall to where Dido sat on her throne.

'With whom?'

'The handsome prince of Troy.' Anna grinned, but Dido kept her face flat. 'You've been so miserable the last few days. Hide it all you want, but I can see you're happier now. You were beaming this morning outside the temple.'

'So you've been spying on me.'

'Not spying, no. Just looking out for an old friend.' Anna's smile softened, and she drew up a cushioned chair. 'And speaking of old friends, I saw Piddaya on my way to the palace. She looked very well, if rushed off her feet, the poor dear. I told her she must come and have a drink with us, leave those children with their father for a change.'

'You mean now? I can't, Anna. I'm here for the petitioners.'

'I don't see any waiting, do you?' Anna twisted herself around in an exaggerated motion, throwing a hand across the empty hall. 'Any that wanted to see you have been and gone. Now, you won't turn Piddaya away, will you? She already said she'd come.'

Anna had a look of satisfaction on her face, since she rightly knew that Dido would not turn away Piddaya, of all people. She leaned over and tipped the wine jug to check its contents – well watered and likely not what she was hoping for – then poured out three generous cups. 'To friends old and new.'

Dido could not help smiling as she raised her cup and took a sip. She had not seen Piddaya for more than a greeting in months. Though she knew she could call at her house, or summon her to the palace, it felt like an intrusion somehow to demand time from the woman who had given her so many years of it, who had her own family to be concerned with now. She could not bid her as she had done when Piddaya was her maid, and she was afraid to cross back into that habit. But there was no one with whom she had shared so much of her life – no one still living, in any case. They had grown to be almost like sisters, Dido had often thought, through all that they had experienced together. And if Piddaya had been her first sister, then Anna had become her second. Siblings to replace the one she had lost.

When Piddaya entered and pulled up her own chair, Dido could see shadows under her eyes, but her friend beamed as she took up her cup.

'It has been so long,' Piddaya said, 'since we were all together.' Her voice was breathless, parched. She took a long drink and relaxed into her seat. 'I hardly have time to stop at the moment, now that our youngest has found her feet. She makes good use of them, may Ashtart bless her.'

'And you are well, all of you? I have told you before and I will say it again, that if you need anything from the palace, you have only to ask.'

'Oh, we are quite well. We have all we need, thank you.' Piddaya stretched out a hand to Dido's and squeezed. 'You must not worry for my sake. I am contented, truly. I would rather hear about your lives.' She glanced between her two companions. 'With so many new guests at the palace, you must have things to tell.'

Dido could feel Anna's look without turning her head. She kept her neck stiff.

'Anna, I know that smile.' Piddaya's voice was pitched with intrigue. 'You have taken one as your lover. What is his name?'

Anna paused while her lips twisted playfully. 'I have thought that I might. There are many handsome men among our guests from Troy. Would you not agree, Elissa?'

Dido chose that moment to take a sip of her wine and swallowed it awkwardly.

'There is some meaning here between you,' Piddaya murmured. 'Do not be cruel and leave me out of it. What is there to tell? You have not . . . I cannot think that *you* have taken a lover.' Piddaya's expression was markedly less entertained as she beheld Dido. Her voice fell to a whisper. 'Have you?'

'How can you ask me that? Of course I have not.' Dido pressed her shoulders against the back of her chair. 'Anna has amused herself with a foolish notion. And a false one. You both know the vow that I made. All of Carthage knows it.' She heard her own voice rising and dragged it down. 'I have sworn that I will never love another man. Zakarbaal was and is my husband.'

'You swore not to marry again,' Anna said, with surprising softness. 'But you are still free to love.'

'To me, they are the same thing. If I loved a man, he would be as my husband. It is a bond that cannot be broken, except by death.'

'Not all love is like that. It does not have to be.' Anna leaned over her cup and held the base with restless fingers. 'I have loved many, and married none.'

'That is well for you,' Dido said. 'But we cannot all love so freely.' There was dismissal in her tone, and Anna heard it.

'Do you think that my love is worth less because it is more easily given? That yours is so precious because you lock it away like gold?' This sharpness was rare from Anna, and Dido regretted stirring it.

'No, I'm sorry. That was not my meaning. But I cannot make myself the same as you. Our lives are not the same. Our pasts are not the same. I love you, Anna. You know that I do. But I do not always understand you. Nor you me.'

The three of them sat silently for a moment. Once Anna had taken a long drink from her cup, she spoke again.

'When I left my family, it was to escape a marriage. To end it before it could begin. I could see my life stretching out before me, with a man I hardly knew or cared to know. It was a safe life, perhaps, but terrifying in its certainty. A home and children – both cages I would not be able to leave. That was how they felt to me,' she added deliberately, with a half glance at Piddaya. 'Since then, I have loved men, yes. But I love them lightly. There is a power in that, in knowing that when they leave, you will still be the same person you were before you met, that they cannot rip anything from you. And they do leave, eventually. Because I have never desired to be a mother, and in the end they all want to be fathers. And I'm almost relieved when they go, because I do not have to wait for it anymore. If they stayed, I would end it myself to be rid of that waiting.'

'But you have loved women, too,' Piddaya said quietly. 'There was no dread of children then.'

'You are right.' Anna nodded slowly. 'But still I found myself binding to this other person, my own cloth woven into their threads. And I did not like that feeling. To lose my independent self, who has been the best and most sure companion I have ever known. I could not lose her for loving too tightly. So I keep a loose hold.'

'You are afraid to love deeply because you fear being hurt,' Dido said, trying to keep her voice gentle. 'Your lightness makes it impossible. You can admit the true reason.'

'Can you admit it?' Anna's gaze was piercing without being spiteful. 'Your vow began from faithfulness. From love for your husband, and your grief for him. I do not doubt that. But it has become something else, Elissa. A way to barricade yourself, to keep people at a distance and silence your own feelings. Because you cannot bear to lose someone like you lost Zakarbaal. I understand that – and perhaps the way that I love is not so different. But I at least allow myself a little joy. I wish that you would.'

Dido resisted her instinct to argue back, to win this game of words and draw comfort from that victory. She knew that Anna was not trying to best her, but to help her to see herself. And that was an uncomfortable thing. Dido felt herself resisting, retreating to the absoluteness of her vow and the stability it had given her for a decade, the sureness she had felt when she had made it. She had returned to that feeling many times over the years, in soft moments she had shared with her friend Iarbas, when she felt her identity as the widow queen beginning to blur. She would recall her husband's face, and the love and grief she felt for him, and she would wash herself with guilt and wrap herself in noble fidelity. It was the habit of a decade, one that had won her both praise and preservation. And she was terrified to give it up.

'The Trojan ship is almost repaired.' Dido met Anna's eye steadily. 'Aeneas will be gone before the month is done.' She did not hide her sadness at that fact, nor her relief that the turmoil she felt would soon come to a natural end. She glanced between her sisters and knew that they understood. Piddaya looked sympathetic, even worried for her former mistress. Anna's eyes were bright, but her mouth was set seriously.

'Then I suggest you enjoy his company while you have it.'

Chapter 20

TYRE

When they left the island, there was still a mist over the water, and Elissa's arms were pricked by the coolness of morning. She sat close to Zakarbaal, leaning into his warmth, pulling her star-patterned shawl tight around her shoulders as they swayed together with the bob of the waves. The boat was small, only large enough for herself and the priests. Another, grander boat would carry her brother across the strait, along with the guards who seemed never to leave his side.

Through the mist, Elissa began to see the edges of the coast emerge. On a clear day, you could see farms and vineyards, orchards of apple and quince and pomegranate trees, and behind them the cedar-covered hills that became mountains. Those mountains were the boundary of Tyre's claim on the land. Of what lay beyond, Elissa had only vague notions. But why should she care to know? Everything she had ever loved had lived within this crowded cradle of earth. Island and mainland. City, field and forest. That was all she knew or needed.

There was a bump as the boat came aground. Elissa rose on stiff legs and followed Zakarbaal on to the shore.

'I hope this mist lifts,' he said as he looked out to the water for a sign of the king's barge.

'There is a humour in it, almost.' Elissa grinned and took his hand. 'Just when we are trying to see the gods' minds, they make it so that we cannot even see one another.'

She was pleased to coax a smile from her husband. He had been quiet all morning, as she chattered to herself about the belomancy and its outcome, as she began to make plans for the dance. 'Just in case,' she had said more than once, each time she found his eyebrow rising. But in truth, she knew the gods would choose them. Hadn't they proven their devotion? And wouldn't they lead the dance better than anyone else could?

They waited for some time before Pygmalion stepped ashore, on high shoes that teetered on the stones of the beach. He was forced to take the arms of his guards, who near enough carried him to the more level ground of the road.

The air was clearer now, at least, and they made the rest of the journey to the precinct as one group. They walked in solemnity, but Elissa also took opportunity to look about at the fields and trees dormant from winter, and to imagine the life that would soon bloom here once Melqart had awakened. All Tyre relied upon it. Upon the beans and barley and wonderful, sweet fruits that this land would provide. That Melqart would bring up from beneath the earth.

Suddenly, she felt something stir in her chest, a cold anxiety. They were walking now to decide the course of the Great Awakening. And for the past days, she had thought about her part in it, the part she might enjoy and be proud of. But here, between the empty fields, she realised that there were greater weights hanging upon today. If the festival should fail, so would the city. Tyre would starve. As she watched her brother walking ahead, still stumbling occasionally as he held the hems of his fine robe out of the dust, she knew she could not put the city into his hands. The gods would know it too, she told herself.

The rural precinct was very different to the one in which Elissa spent all her days. There was no temple, only a wide plateau beside a grove, where birds sang their shrill tunes. There was a peace to the place. Even the air smelled less busy, without the markets and the dyers and the smoke of ovens.

It was the priest of Ashtart who carried the bow, and a quiver over his shoulder with only two arrows. He unslung the quiver and laid it down carefully upon the stony ground of the precinct, with the bow resting on top.

'Let us pour out the libations,' he announced, and gestured to the lower priests, who had carried the necessary jars all the way from the city. Nearby there was a receptacle for the offerings – three bowls close together, half sunk into the ground. One for wine, another for oil, and the last for honey.

'I must purify the perimeter,' Zakarbaal said quietly, brushing her arm. 'You'll be alright here?'

'Of course.'

Elissa watched as the priests began to speak their prayers and unstop their jars. It was nothing she had not seen a thousand times before, though perhaps today she had added cause to wish the gods pleasure from it. Even so, she found her eyes wandering from the priests, pulled toward the bow and the arrows that had been left on the ground beside her. Through these, they would know the gods' will. Around each of the two arrows, a delicate ribbon of cloth had been tied. She crouched to examine the first.

KING PYGMALION AND QUEEN MERET was stitched in neat script. She took up the second ribbon and found a shorter text embroidered there: *ZAKARBAAL, PRIEST OF MELQART.*

She stared at the ribbons for a moment, passing each between her fingers, turning them over in case she had missed something. She might have been back in the palace hall, turning over the tablet of her father's will that refused to reveal what she knew to have been written there. She felt the same spike in her chest that she had then.

Then she rose, calmly, and approached the priests at the libations, where Pygmalion also stood.

'Why is my name not recorded on the ribbon?' she asked, trying desperately to make her voice sound light.

The priests acted as if she had not spoken, or perhaps they were simply focused on their task.

'Need it be?' Pygmalion asked. 'The priest's name is there.'

'Your mother's name is written.'

'The gods will know who is intended,' he said impatiently. 'Or do you doubt that?'

Perhaps he meant to silence her by a suggestion of impiety, but Elissa's blood was running too hot for that.

'You omitted it on purpose,' she murmured. And suddenly she could hear herself, sounding like a petulant child. Was she not the one who was grown? Who had spent so long moving beyond the pains of her past? It was only a name on a piece of cloth. She collected herself, drew in a breath of the crisp, rural air. What was the purpose of her complaining? The gods would know, as he said. And was that not all she needed?

But then Pygmalion laughed. 'Do you imagine I have so much care for you? That I have sat with needle and thread and embroidered these ribbons myself? Sister, you over-esteem your role. You are only here because of your husband, after all.'

It was as if a splinter had gone in under her nail. But she did not react. Elissa only stepped away, for fear of throwing out words she could not take back. Treasonous words.

She had hoped, in all these years of distance from her brother, that he might still hold some affection for their childhood together. Some memory of the love she had given him. But he seemed now as if he were not her brother at all. No child of her father. Only a mocking shade of him, which sat upon his throne.

And yet he enjoyed all that her father had built. Enjoyed and wasted and depleted. He had been handed that privilege for no reason other than his own weakness, and the advantages it might provide for those sharp enough to take them. Meanwhile, she had strived for all she had. Hadn't she? She would not let him tell her that she was, after all her work, only a wife.

As she burned with hurt and with anger, Elissa's mind went again to her latest preoccupation: the dance. She would prove herself then, with the eyes of the city upon her, with their feet stamping to her step. They would know and she would know that she was as capable and as worthy as her father had always told her she was. Pygmalion could not disdain or dismiss her then. No one could.

But as bold and as compelling as that image was, it was not decided yet. The arrows still lay in their quiver.

She moved towards them again and knelt on the hard ground. There did not seem to be anything of the divine about them. If it were not for the holy symbols scratched on the heads, they would seem utterly ordinary. And yet these shafts of wood held such power over her – even over the fate of the city.

She ran her finger over the closer arrow and saw her brother's name curl along the ribbon. No god could favour him. She was sure of that. And yet surely no god would favour his kingship – no god that cared for Tyre. But they had not stopped it. Perhaps they could not. Perhaps the course of human action had run too strongly against them. All the more reason for them to make their will known now, to show their disfavour.

But what if they were silent again? What if their ears were too full with the desperate prayers of the people, for them to give heed to the flight of two arrows? Divination was a tricky art. Zakarbaal always said so. It could not always be depended upon.

Her fingers had moved from her brother's ribbon to the stiff feathers fixed with resin. She touched them gently, as if waiting for a response. A warning. But the priests were still busy with the libations, and her own heart felt still.

If the gods objected, they would stop me, she told herself, as she carefully, forcefully, bent the feathers of her brother's arrow.

Chapter 21

TYRE

'Everything alright?' Zakarbaal cupped her cheek and smiled over his concern. Her husband knew her too well. He could always tell when she was agitated.

'Yes,' she muttered. 'Just something Pygmalion said. Got me in a temper. But I'm alright now.' She met his hand with hers and squeezed his fingers. 'Have you finished the purification?'

She barely listened to his reply. Her mind was still on the arrows. It took a desperate will not to look down at the quiver. Her heart, which had been so still for the act, was hammering now.

The priests were putting the stoppers back in their jars, which meant the libations were done. The belomancy would come next. The priest of Ashtart would pick up the quiver and inspect the arrows and discover what she had done. Elissa only realised how tightly she was holding her husband's hand when he pulled it away.

'What did Pygmalion say to you?' he murmured. 'Ah, it doesn't matter. You will tell me later.' He pulled her to him then, as if his arm would guard against all the world's upsets. 'We must be quiet now.'

The priest of Ashtart approached. He bent to pick up the bow and quiver, and Elissa felt suddenly dizzy.

But then the quiver was on his shoulder, and he was striding away with bow in hand. She felt her heart calm a little and allowed her limbs to untighten. He had not noticed. And why should he? It was not such a great thing that she had done. Only a few twists of her fingers. Barely anything at all. And yet, as the priest took his stance, she found herself eager to see the result that her innocent fingers had wrought.

He reached a hand over his shoulder and drew the first arrow from the quiver.

'Zakarbaal, the priest,' he announced, with a glance at the ribbon, then settled the shaft against the bow, drew back the string, and let go.

The arrow arced across the precinct, cutting through the air almost faster than Elissa's eyes could follow. It landed somewhere beyond the perimeter.

There was a general nodding among the assembled men, but their attention was soon back on the priest of Ashtart, who drew the second arrow from the quiver.

'King Pygmalion,' he called, without reading the ribbon.

Elissa's brother stood ahead of her, and she could see he was as rapt as anyone. He held his posture unusually upright, as if he were posing under the scrutiny of the gods.

The priest raised his bow and let the arrow fly. At first, it followed the same smooth course, but at the height of its arc, the shaft began to wobble and it came down less gracefully than it had gone up. They heard the faint clatter as it hit the earth, and without delay, two priests were dispatched to observe the distances.

Though they went with unhurried dignity, Elissa wished they would run. Or that she could go herself and confirm what her instinct and the evidence of her eyes already promised. She felt Zakarbaal's tension by his stillness, by the stiffness of his arm around her.

The priests returned, each with an arrow held high, the ribbons trailing in the light breeze. As soon as they were close enough to be heard, the elder shouted:

'The arrow of Zakarbaal flew further. By our witness, he has the gods' favour.'

Elissa had known better than to celebrate her victory before her brother and the priests. She had forced her lips to remain stiff, imagined two weights in her cheeks. But all the while, she felt her heart brimming with satisfaction.

Now, in the privacy of her home, she allowed herself to smile. Sitting in the courtyard, she cradled a cup of sweetened wine as if it were her own libation.

'You are pleased with the result, I see,' said Zakarbaal as he stepped outside.

'As you should be,' she replied. 'Piddaya has prepared some wine. Come, drink with me.'

Her husband shook his head and sank on to the bench beside her.

'There is nothing to worry about now,' she said softly, leaning against him. 'I know you feared that Pygmalion would dislike our leading the dance, but he cannot complain if the gods have ordered it.'

'He can still dislike it.'

'Oh, let him.' She said it with a little more vim than she intended.

'You have not told me what he said earlier, that made you so angry.'

'It seems almost silly now,' she said, shrinking from where she knew this conversation might lead.

'If it has hurt your feelings, then it is not silly to me.'

She felt a rush of love for her husband, followed by a strong pang of guilt, that she could hide things from this man who was so good and honest. Who would never cheat at anything or do some impulsive thing behind her back.

'He spoke as if I were no one. As if I did not deserve to be there. As if all that I do is only a reflection of you and not of myself. As if he has forgotten that I have my father's blood in me, as much as he has.' Elissa felt her hands shaking, and put down her cup for fear of dropping it.

'Then he is a fool,' her husband said, taking her hand and pressing it to his lips. 'You should not let him disturb you so.'

'How can I not? When he has so much that he does not deserve? Perhaps he is only a fool, but he holds power over all that I love. Power that should rightfully have been mine.'

Zakarbaal turned towards her fully and took her other hand. 'Why do you hold on to that, after all these years? Your envy only upsets you. What do you gain from it? You have built something for yourself, whatever your brother may say. You have influence of a different kind. You do good for the people of this city.' He paused and pulled her hands towards him, as if tethering her to him, to the truth of what he was saying. 'I saw how eager you were today. How much you wanted us to be chosen above the king. Why should it mean so much to you?'

Elissa could feel her eyes stinging, and blinked angrily. 'You do not understand,' she snapped.

'Then help me to.'

The directness of Zakarbaal's gaze had always been her weakness. She knew he would not look away until she answered him. But there were things she could not say aloud, even to him. How could she tell him what she had done today? She imagined the way he would look at her – disbelieving, even outraged.

'I have told you of how my father raised me. What he always intended for me. To win. To lead. To rule. To make the decisions that others cannot. He wanted me to be someone in this city. He wanted me to have power. He trusted me to have it.' She sighed with frustration. 'In failing to fulfil that, I fail him, and all he envisioned for me.'

'I know that is what you have told me.' He nodded. 'I know you believed it once, and let it drive you. But I think that it has gone beyond that now. This need is within you. It hasn't been about your father for a long time.'

She sat astonished. Her lips stuttered, reaching for denial.

'You know it yourself, I think,' he went on in his soft voice. Though she pulled away, he still held her hands. 'This is something more. This fire in you. If you do not face it, perhaps it will consume you. Come, tell me truly. Why do you need so desperately to win?'

'Because . . . ' She searched for the words to give form to the feeling that crouched within her, that had leapt up so strongly at the precinct. 'Because they are incompetent. My brother and the merchants. They bring everything to ruin. They do not know how to rule for Tyre, only for themselves.'

'That is them,' Zakarbaal said calmly. 'Why do you need to overcome them?'

'Because I am better than they are,' she said fiercely. 'Because they say I cannot. Because . . . ' She delved within herself, to the tender place she avoided, filled with memories of her father's death, of a hall full of pitying faces, of a tablet that betrayed her eyes and sent her stomach sinking, sinking. 'Because I do not want to lose.'

Elissa's cheeks were burning, her breaths ragged. Zakarbaal was watching her, his dark eyes reflecting her pain. Then he blinked and rubbed her trembling fingers gently between his.

'And this life we have,' he said quietly. 'The one we have made together, you and I. Does this make you feel like you are losing?'

There was a fear in his question, as if he thought she might say yes. But she let herself fold into him and pressed her head against his chest.

'No, my love,' she whispered. 'No, don't ever think that. Please.' His arms closed around her, and she breathed deeply into the simple cloth of his robes, let his scent fill her and felt the thud of his heart. 'You are more precious than anything. You know that. I hope you know that.'

She could not see his face, locked as she was in his embrace. But she felt his reassurance as he rocked her. He did not doubt her love, did not need her to swear it. He only meant to remind her of the happiness she had. And he was right. There were greater things to strive for, greater things already within her grasp, than some petty triumph over her brother. The most important victory of her life had already been won years ago, when she had found the man to see her and love her for all she was. She would hold on to that, she told herself.

Chapter 22

TYRE

The Day of Mourning was at an end. It was Elissa's least favourite of the three festival days. Yesterday, they had performed the Rites of Death and burned Melqart's effigy on the great pyre. Perhaps that was supposed to be the darkest phase of the Awakening, as they watched their god succumb to the destruction that all life must meet with. Perhaps it felt sorrowful to some, but not to her. No, there was a spectacle in the flames reaching towards the black sky, and a nostalgia in the smell of woodsmoke, from festivals she had witnessed as a child. And there was a power, too, in the fierceness of the heat, in the waves of warmth that flushed the watching faces, in the mesmerising light that held the attention of all present, and bound them together in this one event.

There was no such magic on the Day of Mourning. Only sombre songs and aching laments. Slow processions of weeping faces. Did they weep for the god, Elissa wondered? For him alone? Or, like her, were their hearts stirred by the memory of other losses?

She was glad to wash the ash from her hands. She raised the cloth from the basin and washed her face, too, washed off the sorrow of the day so that she could begin looking forward to tomorrow. The Day of Life. The dance.

As she rinsed the cloth and the water became grey, Elissa heard her husband enter their chamber. She knew him without turning, by his step and by his breath. And when his steps drew closer, and he put his hands on her waist and began to press his thumbs into the sore part of her back, she put her hands on the edge of the basin and let herself relax into his touch. There was no comfort like the warmth of her husband's hands, the feel of his touch on her skin. If all the world were to dissolve, she thought, let her keep only this.

'You did well today,' he murmured over her shoulder. His breath sent a delicious tickle down her neck, and she felt her depressive mood melt away, like ash in water. 'There were many looking to you to lead their song. I know it was not easy.'

She turned around to face him, and smiled as he pulled her close.

'There will be many more looking to us tomorrow,' she said.

The flutter in her chest was not fear but anticipation, and as Zakarbaal kissed her it grew stronger, filled her limbs, down to the tips of her fingers. She kissed him back and held on to him wherever her hands could reach, moved her mouth to his neck, felt his body press against hers. She could not say why she wanted him so urgently, but his desire seemed to match hers.

When Elissa had married, there were women who had told her what would be expected of her. That she must let her husband take her. They had made sex sound like a capitulation. But no. She had soon discovered that it was a game for equals, where nothing was lost, and all victories were enjoyed together. At least, that was how it was with Zakarbaal. But sometimes she would think of those women and pity any who gave over to her husband what should have been theirs to share.

They lay on top of the covers afterwards, their skin hot despite the cool air. He stroked her neck while her fingers traced invisible lines through the hair on his chest.

'I'm glad you must not shave all of yourself to please the gods,' she said softly.

'Melqart has my devotion,' he whispered. 'But there are some things which I save only for you, my love.'

'Is that something a holy man ought to say?' she asked with mock sternness.

'Why should it not be?' He smiled, and his dark eyes shone in the light from their lamp. 'We owe our happiness to the gods, and they rejoice in it. They would not begrudge the love of a man for his wife.'

'Nor that of a wife for her husband, I hope.' She kissed him slowly, lingering on the softness of his lips now that her urgency was spent.

'I have something for you,' he said when she drew away. Elissa was surprised, and watched with curiosity as he rose from the bed and crouched down to open a chest in the corner. They were not in the habit of giving gifts.

'For the dance,' he said simply, holding a strip of fabric across his hands. As he came back into the light of the lamp, Elissa sat up for a better look. It was a fillet of red cloth, dyed to a deep colour. And along its length there glistened a row of rubies set in gold.

'Where did you get it?' she gasped.

'I ordered it from the palace jeweller. To match the red dress you wear when you want to look fearsome.' He grinned, and she knew exactly the one he meant.

'It is too much,' she said, even as she ran her finger over the line of jewels. 'Have you not said we should be cautious? That we should not be seen to promote ourselves? What will this say, if I wear it before the entire city?'

'Only what is true. That you are a Princess of Tyre.' He took the fillet and laid it over her hair, leaned closer as he tied the strings at the back of her head. 'There,' he said with satisfaction.

She felt as if she were glowing under his gaze, as if the polished rubies were emitting their own light and not only reflecting that of the lamp. Was this how her brother felt, beneath his regalia? Was this how she might have felt, if she had been queen? Wrapped in that feeling, it was easy to forget that she was still naked.

'I'm sorry,' Zakarbaal said suddenly. 'For my caution. For my worrying.' He held her cheek and kissed her. 'You deserve to enjoy this victory. The gods themselves have granted it to you.'

Her stomach clenched at that, but she held his gaze.

'Tomorrow we will lead the people, and you will show them just how worthy you are.'

His words filled her with a feeling she could not define. A relief of sorts, a permission to let go of the parts she had been holding back. She felt herself expanding, spreading towards the potential he saw for her and which she had so long seen for herself. If it was only for a day, let it be for a day. She would nourish herself with the memory of it.

Elissa's hands shook a little as she opened the ivory case. An elegant duck, with wings that swept aside to reveal the black kohl kept within. It had been her mother's, apparently. A wedding gift from Elissa's father. The charming little thing was older than she was, and its carved eyes had an uncanny sharpness.

She was glad she had Piddaya to apply the kohl for her. She needed everything to be perfect, and a trembling hand would not achieve that. Her outfit was already chosen – the red dress to match her new fillet – and she would wear a string of lapis lazuli and golden glass around her neck.

When her make-up was finished and she was fully dressed, she went down to the courtyard where Zakarbaal was waiting. He had been at the temple since before dawn, making all the preparations for the sacrifices, but he had promised to meet her at the house so that they could enter the precinct together.

Elissa stepped into the sun, and there he was. Somehow, her husband managed to look refined even in his plain linens. His bare head was covered by his priest's cap – red like her own attire.

As she swept over the flagstones, his mouth fell open and she beamed.

'A Princess of Tyre, indeed,' he said. He moved towards her but she put out a hand.

'You cannot kiss me, or Piddaya's work will be ruined.'

He took the outstretched hand and kissed that instead. 'Are you ready?' he asked.

The nerves in her stomach leapt higher, but she ignored them. 'Let's go.'

Elissa could not remember seeing the temple precinct so full. Wherever she looked there were men, women and children jostling against one another, packed into every corner, sitting on walls, or pressing up to them in the hope of a view of the rites to come. There was an excitement running through the crowd, but Elissa thought she sensed something else too. A desperation. With so much depending on this day, she could hardly be surprised. And yet the tension of all those pressing bodies put her on edge.

As she and Zakarbaal cut a path through the crowd, faces turned and recognised them. Many smiled, others cried out blessings. Some hands reached out, and Elissa thought that they might be overwhelmed, but the crowd seemed to push them onwards. Word of the belomancy had spread quickly, as all things did on their small island, and it seemed everyone knew the role she and her husband were to play.

When they made their way to the centre of the precinct, Elissa found, to her relief, that a wide area had been kept clear, spanning from the temple itself to a large altar near the south wall. Beside the temple entrance hovered a bundle of priests and attendants, and a little apart from them there waited two other groups – one of young women, and one of young men. All fresh-faced and beautiful. The prime representatives of the city. Some were of noble families, but not all. They came from across Tyre, and from the mainland too.

Elissa found herself assessing the men and women. Did they seem athletic? Were their limbs toned with practice? Would their feet hold to a rhythm? She shook the useless thoughts from her head. She must trust the judgement of those who had nominated them. And, in any case, there were the offerings to see to first.

The aromas were already drifting from the temple door, as if the building itself were a great oven. It was not long before the first tray was brought out – a dozen roasted quails. This was the offering that Zakarbaal himself was to carry, for it was known that Melqart was especially partial to the delicious smell of those birds. As her husband took them gracefully from the attendant, another man stood close behind with a tray for her. Silver-scaled bream, baked whole with salt and citron. They made her mouth water, and she muttered a prayer that the Rising God would find them as tempting.

More offerings followed – a tray piled high to be carried by each of the men and women who had been chosen. The men's trays were laden with legs of lamb and goat, trussed game birds, fat geese and lean rabbits, all roasted with the most aromatic herbs. The women, meanwhile, held platters of shellfish, of nuts and preserved fruits, of delicate cakes sweet with honey or spiced with cardamom. The whole array seemed enough to feed a city. And later, once the god's portion had been burned and it was time for the feast, the city would be fed. But first, they must wake their god.

Elissa and Zakarbaal took their places at the head of each line – she leading the women, and he the men. Then the procession began.

They took slow, rhythmic steps towards the altar, and with each step the crowd stamped their feet, so that Elissa felt as if her own paces were causing the earth to shake. When she reached the altar, parallel to her husband, she raised her tray up towards the sky, then settled it carefully on the table of stone. As soon as it was down, she moved aside for the woman behind her, whose own feet were urged forwards by the stamp of the crowd. Elissa threaded her line of women back upon itself, as each left her offering for the god, and Zakarbaal's line of men were their mirror, until all trays had found a place at the altar and their carriers were unburdened for their next duty.

The stamping of the crowd did not stop, but rather became the beat behind new sounds. The clash of tambourines. The trill of pipes. The plucking of lyres. Each gave their part to the swell, and all came together to call with one voice: *Rise, Melqart.*

Elissa felt the vibration in her head, in her limbs. She took the hand of the woman beside her, and she the next hand, down the line until they were a great chain. And again the men were their mirror. Elissa met her husband's eye, let his steady smile fill her just as the music did, let her feet begin to step in time to the music, and raised her hands to begin.

A jump on to one foot, echoed along the line. A switch to the other. Back and forth as the tambourines held the beat. She leapt into the air, down to the ground, sprang up again, back into the stamping rhythm of the crowd. She whirled around, turned the watching faces into a blur, while the clamour of their voices rushed in her ears.

The dancing women watched her too, following her lead, matching their steps to hers. And the men followed Zakarbaal.

They were two lines alive with energy, sometimes drawn together, sometimes springing apart. One would leap as the other went low, but they were all bound by the same beat.

Elissa's heart pounded like an extra drum. Her fingers slipped against those of her neighbour. Her thighs quivered as they thrust her upward. But she did not tire. She could not stop or slow, not with all those eyes willing her on. The music began to rise. The stamping quickened. And still she stepped and whirled and leapt. She could feel the end coming, in the great crescendo that filled her ears. She looked across and saw that Zakarbaal felt it too. With no signal between them, they each made their final jump, and the lines came down with them.

Crouched on the ground with her lungs burning, Elissa heard the music stop, the stamping too. And in its place, a great roar of cheers, of whistles, of prayers that could not be made out by mortal ears. But what did that matter, if they were meant for a newly roused god?

Chapter 23

TYRE

Pygmalion had not attended the dance. Perhaps he resented the fact that the gods had not chosen him to lead it. Or perhaps he did not want to attend and allow his royal eminence to be overshadowed by a priest, or by his own sister. Whatever his reason, it had been a mistake, Elissa thought. For the king to be absent at that moment of great community not only increased the distance between himself and his city, but it also prevented him from taking any share of the credit for a successful festival. Already, the earth was stirring; green shoots scattered the fields, while delicate sprays of blossom crowned the orchards. Elissa felt the mood of the people lift at these hopeful signs, but she heard no thanks or prayers offered for the king.

The services of the temple – both spiritual and vital – were as much in demand as they ever had been. The promise of spring was not enough to sweep away Tyre's heavy troubles, though at least the weather that blew in with it would be kinder to the growing number of citizens who found themselves without a home.

The raids on the mainland continued, forcing people to the relative shelter of the island, but as more and more supply ships were intercepted or kept away by fear, there was not enough of anything to sustain a city so thronged with people. Even water was becoming a scarcity, for there was no fresh source on the island. The temple, as always, distributed what it could, and when there was no more left, they nourished the people with the solace of prayer.

Elissa had noticed one curious change since the Great Awakening. Each day, a number of well-dressed, gold-trimmed men would cross the threshold of the precinct. They came not only to give conspicuous offerings at the temple – which they did – but also to speak with her husband or with Elissa herself, to discuss the affairs of the city, and in particular those that concerned their dwindling coffers.

Elissa found some gratification in this. These men were not like the common citizens who came to her because they had nowhere else to go. These men, draped in purple and smelling of myrrh, could have the ear of the king if they wanted it. And yet they preferred to have hers.

Zakarbaal did not like this change.

'The nobles should not be consulting with us,' he said one evening, as he ran an anxious hand over his head. 'How does that look? We cannot be something apart.'

She knew what he meant. They could not allow themselves to be seen as something apart from the palace, apart from the king. To be set apart was to allow the possibility that one might be set above.

Zakarbaal had convinced her that they must continue to attend the court, not least to show that temple and palace were united. So when the next meeting of the Council was called, they took their seats on the cushioned bench and waited for the king to appear. Pygmalion was late, of course, and his eventual entrance was flustered – a change from the bored nonchalance that seemed to carry him through life. The mood of the room changed as he crossed it, as lips were suddenly tightened and grave expressions were assumed. The eyes of the nobles watched her brother with an intensity that surprised Elissa, and almost as soon as Pygmalion had reached his throne, the first merchant was on his feet.

'We must discuss the ships, my king.'

Her brother blinked. 'Which ships?'

'Our ships. And the foreign ships that prevent them from sailing. Do we even know where these raiders come from? They appear on the horizon and stop our trade, stop even our own water and food from reaching our harbour. And what is being done?'

Pygmalion was silent and raised his steepled fingers before his face in the way their father used to do. But his eyes were not sharp as King Mattan's had been. They were glassy, uncertain. He turned towards Ahiram, who seemed never to be far from the king's elbow. 'What is being done?' he muttered.

'We have written to the pharaoh in Egypt, as the king wisely instructed.' Ahiram's voice was overly loud, as if he were addressing a much larger room. 'Egypt has long been our ally and patron. They will send ships and soldiers to deter these raiders. We must only be patient.'

'And how far is our patience to stretch?' asked another merchant, rising from the bench. Elissa had spoken with him at the temple the previous week, though she had forgotten his name. He was a wine trader, she recalled. 'This is not the first time we have asked Egypt for aid. Nor the second. Our missives go unanswered. How many more will you send, Ahiram, before you admit that we must seek another solution?'

There were noises of agreement from the benches, and Pygmalion had turned again to his advisor. The young king looked expectant, even irritated, but Elissa was more interested in watching Ahiram, whose usually immovable features seemed perturbed. He had the look of a man who was fighting a scowl, and had decided his best defence was a plastered smile.

'I am sure that you do not mean to criticise the decision of the king,' he said smoothly. Perhaps Ahiram was losing his touch, for none of the displeased faces along the benches seemed to alter at all. They saw well enough, as Elissa did, that although he invoked the king, he was truly only defending his own wisdom. To admit that their hope in Egypt had been misplaced, that their failed appeal had delayed and continued to delay proper action, was to admit that he had provided Pygmalion with bad advice. And as dangerous as it was for his standing to admit this before the Council, it was more dangerous by far to admit it before the king.

Elissa should not have been surprised that such a man as Ahiram would put his own position above the needs of the city, and yet the blatancy of his display, only a few feet from her in this crowded hall, set a fire in her gut. When she and Zakarbaal had agreed to attend the meeting, she had understood that they were going to be seen and not to be heard. They were heard too often, as Zakarbaal saw it. People came to the temple every day to seek their judgement or advice. And that was the danger, the very reason that they were sitting here. They had come to blend themselves into the fabric of the court, not to start pulling at threads. And yet Elissa felt her knees bobbing restlessly, and she gripped the bench as if to hold herself down. Zakarbaal put a steadying hand on her thigh, but it was like spider silk tethering a bull.

'If Egypt will not answer, we must take action for ourselves.' She was on her feet, with the eyes of the hall upon her. She tried not to let herself be unbalanced by the weight of their attention and turned directly to the king. 'We must do something, Brother. Tyre is being squeezed and her people are in great need. I see their troubles every day. Something must be done.'

'*Something*, you say. *Something*, as if it were so simple.' Ahiram's voice dripped with derision. 'You give the people some bread and think yourself their saviour. But real politics requires more than a bleeding heart. There is a reason the other members of the Council do not bring their wives to the hall.' He looked around and was gratified by some scattered jeers from the benches.

Elissa's cheeks burned hot, and her tongue faltered. Ahiram's words cut with added sharpness. Was it because there was some truth in what he said, or because he was the one to say it? This meeting was more important than her long-held loathing for the ivory merchant. Her city was in peril, and here she was, unable to find the words to save it. How foolish she must look, like a fish gulping air.

She felt a hand grasp hers, and realised Zakarbaal was on his feet beside her.

'Perhaps you have forgotten whom you address,' he said coldly. There was a vibration in his voice that Elissa was not used to hearing. 'My wife is the daughter of King Mattan, and sister to King Pygmalion. She serves this city every day. She understands its needs as well as any of you.' He looked around, as if daring one of the men along the benches to dispute it. Some averted their eyes, while others nodded or murmured in quiet agreement. From among them, a familiar face caught Elissa's eye, and Shapashuru rose to his feet.

'If I may speak for myself and for others, we should like to hear what the noble princess would propose. How are we to stop these raiders, if the pharaoh will not stop them for us?'

The old man looked at her with such expectation – a genuine, open hope. She could not disappoint his faith in her, and somehow her mind and her words rallied to that cause.

'I would build ships,' she began. 'Not merchant ships, but war ships. Large enough and sturdy enough to deter any who think us a soft target. We could have them patrol our waters, even escort our trade vessels. We have the wood and the skill.'

'And who would pay for these ships?' Ahiram asked.

'The city. The palace. The guilds.' An audible grumble arose from the nobles then, but she spoke above it. 'Are you not losing more from the theft of your trade shipments? What man among you does not invest in guards and strongboxes? Yet you are willing to leave your city undefended, for any foreigner to pillage as he wishes.'

The sounds of discontent did not abate.

'Or I would aim to speak with these raiders,' she went on. 'I would see whether a deal could be arranged. Some promise of favourable trade so that we may give them enough that they will not steal more. We could make ourselves more valuable as allies than as enemies. Is that not what we have done with Egypt?' The noise from the benches surged, and again she raised her voice above it. 'Yes, we say that the pharaoh is our patron, but truly we are at his mercy. He leaves us our independence because he likes our gifts. Who else but Tyre produces wine so sweet, or glass so pure, or ivories so intricate?' She pandered to Ahiram's vanity, but she did not look at him. 'Let these raiders see the reward of our friendship, and they may stop harassing our farmers and terrorising our waters.'

She let her words settle upon the men. Among the muddled sound of the hall, it was difficult to tell whether they found any merit in her advice, but the admiration on Shapashuru's face was enough. Zakarbaal was still standing beside her, and he squeezed her hand in a way that made her heart lift with love for him.

'And these gifts, I suppose, would also be provided by the palace? By the guilds?' The benches fell quiet for Ahiram in a way they had not while she was speaking, but Elissa did not let the irritation of that fact cloud her.

'Yes. Who else? As I said, these measures would be an investment against more serious loss.'

'It is interesting that, yet again, the temple asks so much from us – from the palace – while your own wealth lies untouched.' Ahiram leaned down to speak in the king's ear. Elissa could not hear what he said.

'What wealth?' she started. 'How do you expect us to—'

But Zakarbaal interjected. 'It is not the temple that asks. We have given advice only as members of this Council, and in the interests of the city. Is that not our purpose here?'

Elissa warmed to hear him speak as if they were one voice and tightened her grip on his hand.

'Perhaps it is your purpose, Priest, that we should examine.' There was a light in Ahiram's eyes that Elissa did not like. He spoke slowly, as if each word of his was a weighty and important thing. 'You would encourage the king to fritter away his resources on ships and gifts, while all the while yours are allowed to grow and grow. I wonder – perhaps we are all wondering – why you should want your means to surpass those of the king?'

Elissa felt Zakarbaal stiffen. She turned to him and saw that his face was stuck somewhere between surprise and fear. She waited for him to speak, but his lips seemed to hesitate – perhaps knowing that the wrong words would hold more danger than silence.

'That is nonsense.' Elissa spoke for him. 'You have a subtle tongue, Ahiram, and we all know what you are implying. But you are wrong if you think that a single man here would take my husband for a usurper. Where is this wealth you speak of? It seems an obsession to you, but has anyone witnessed it? Has anyone witnessed anything except a priest devoted to his god and to his king? You speak against him to disguise your own failures. The men here are not so blind as you believe.'

She thought she had spoken well, and that her forceful words should leave Ahiram cowed. But his face barely changed. If anything, the light in his eyes glowed brighter, the edges of his mouth curled into the faintest smile. She felt her confidence shrink and retraced the things she had said, looking for something that would make that hated face seem so satisfied. Her mind snagged on that dangerous word. *Usurper.* A dagger in the ears of kings. But they had all known the merchant's meaning. She had only put clearer voice to it. Though perhaps that had been her mistake.

She looked at Zakarbaal but his face was unreadable, his gaze fixed ahead of him. She looked at her brother, whose eyes cast about the room as if he were struggling to catch up with what had been said. *He will not believe it*, she told herself. *No one could believe it.*

But still her chest felt tight, and her husband's hand, clasped in hers, felt strangely limp and cold.

Chapter 24

CARTHAGE

Dido was pleased to have Aeneas return to the hall, whether he sat among his men or ate his meals at her table. Over those evenings, she heard more tales of how the Trojans had finally come to wash up on Libyan sand. Some of the places they had visited were places she too had seen on her way from Tyre, and they compared memories of seas and shores that felt so far away now, so desolate compared to the warmth of the hearth here in Carthage.

Aeneas did not press her for stories of Tyre, and she avoided conversations that would lead him back to Troy or its fall. She was enjoying the new lightness between them and was afraid to test it. *Enjoy things as they are*, she imagined Anna saying. Though she would not admit it aloud, her friend's words had settled into her like rain into soil. *Take joy. Love lightly.*

Over the past days, these words had dripped right through to her heart, to tease at the firm seal around it. Would it really be so deadly a thing to unwrap some small portion? Enough to let in a little joy? She did not need Anna's permission for that, she assured herself. Yet even as she sat on her carved chair, smiling vaguely at the conversation around her, Dido resolved to borrow a fraction of her friend's courage. To open herself to the warmth she felt while Aeneas sat beside her. To take what pleasantness she could from these days and evenings, and not spoil them prematurely with fear for their end.

'I hope that you and your men will join us for the Feast of Ashtart,' she said, as she gathered the last beans from her bowl. 'It is soon approaching, so perhaps you will still be our guests by then.' She smiled, but hurried to move on from the topic of the Trojan departure. 'We have a tradition, each year, that our best hunters go out of the city to seek a lion. If they catch one, we dedicate its skin to the Lady of the Chariot so that she will keep us in her protection. I myself always join the hunt, though I confess I have no great skill. But you must be an experienced hunter, I think. Given the stag you dragged with you when we first met.'

She was pleased to see Aeneas's eyes ignite.

'My father taught me to hunt, yes. I had two hounds at Troy that I trained from pups. Before the war, I would go to the mountains with only them beside me, chasing deer and hares, and lions, too, when the courage was in me. It would be a pleasure to join this hunt of yours. If that is what you propose?' He seemed suddenly to doubt, perhaps to fear that he had overstepped.

But she put a hand on his sleeve. 'Yes, yes! It would be an honour to me. We will gather everyone the day after tomorrow and set out for the prize. May Baal grant us fine weather.'

The skies were not as clear as Dido had hoped, but she wrapped her thickest shawl around her shoulders and gathered the hunters, nevertheless. Some Trojans mingled among her own men, with borrowed spears and nets. When Aeneas arrived, he stood close by her, and stretched out a hand to the slender hounds that paced excitedly and whipped their tails.

'Did Piddaya find you?' she asked, as she leaned down to scratch her favourite dog between the ears.

'Yes, she came to our chamber before I left. Thank you for thinking of Ascanius. He will revel in the company, I'm sure. I have thought that he ought to spend more time apart from me – with other children, I mean.' Aeneas gave a half-smile, but Dido sensed his worry.

'You will be back before dusk. He will hardly have time to miss you. And there is no one I trust better than Piddaya to take care of him.'

'Yes. Yes, of course. He will enjoy his day of excitement, no doubt. And we will enjoy ours.' His half-smile became full, and his eyes caught hers in a way that made her heart quicken.

'We will.'

Though Dido was queen, she would not lead the hunt. It was enough that she was a part of it, and she would only slow down the more experienced trackers. So, when the hunt master called for attention, she fell quiet with everyone else.

'Stay close by me,' Aeneas whispered, leaning towards her. 'We cannot let the Queen of Carthage become lost in the woods.'

Perhaps she would have found these words patronising from another mouth, but they only warmed her. The anticipation of the hunt was thick in the air, stirred up by the winter breeze, by the restless energy of the dogs, by the many hands that gripped their spears and bows, not knowing if or when they would be needed. Even for those with skill and experience, hunting was a dangerous sport, and the nerves of the gathered crowd rebounded between one man and another, filling Dido with the same pregnant charge they all felt.

The order was given to move out. Some of the young men raced away with the keenest hounds, pulled on by the thought that they might be the one to drape a lion's skin over their shoulders. Eventually, each group found their own pace and direction, and no man was left to face the wilds alone. Dido and Aeneas headed into the trees with alert eyes and ears, and a single dog that zigzagged back and forth in front of them with its nose close to the ground.

'We named this one Copper, for her coat,' Dido said affectionately. 'She's still young. But she is fast. I've seen her chase a full-grown hare and close her teeth on its neck.'

Aeneas looked at her with surprise. 'I have not known many women to enjoy the hunt. Perhaps none at all, before you.'

'How many women have opportunity to enjoy it?' Dido asked. 'I never hunted at Tyre. My father taught me a great many things that have served me throughout my life, but he did not teach me to hunt. I thought it strange at times, that Lady Ashtart should be Breaker of Bows while I was not even allowed to hold one. But sport became necessity when we came to Libya. Before we had flocks and granaries, my people needed as much food as we could find, and no hand could afford to be left idle in that pursuit. I am no great huntress,' she hastened to clarify, 'but I can lay a snare and skin a beast if I need to.'

Aeneas did not reply at first, and a part of her hoped that her words had shocked him. Dido had held so much of herself out of reach that she feared the prince's admiration was only for her softer parts, for the Dido who treated Ascanius so sweetly and who sent pretty smiles across the table. But after a moment, Aeneas found his tongue.

'You are a marvel.'

She barely caught his glance before he strode ahead after the hound. But as she followed, she smiled to herself, let his words lift her cheeks before swallowing them down like sweet cakes. By the time she had lengthened her steps enough to catch him, she was breathless.

They were far from the city before they found their first quarry. Dido did not see the creature at all, only heard the cracking of twigs far ahead. But Copper was away before Dido could even put out a hand for Aeneas to stop. The slender hound flashed over the uneven ground, and the two of them had no choice but to chase.

'Copper,' Dido barked when they had lost all sight of her. They stopped with hearts racing and rooted themselves in silence, peering through the trees for a shiver of movement.

'Your hound is fast indeed,' Aeneas said with amusement. 'I hope she can handle herself against whatever she saw.'

That made Dido anxious. 'She will come back to us if it is too large for her. But if it is a hare, or a fox . . . '

'She might chase it all the way to Egypt.'

Dido laughed, far preferring that image to the more fearful ones her mind had conjured. 'She might. As I said, she is still young. And more compelled to serve her instinct than any other demand.'

'May we envy her that.' His smile seemed to twist, and Dido did not know what to say. She read some part of herself in that minute slant of his lip, in the cloud of responsibility that so often came over him. It had no right to follow him here, to these silent woods where there was no one but the two of them. She stepped towards him and reached out a hand. But as her fingers brushed his, she felt a splash of rain. She looked up to find the sky drawn over and dark. Black clouds rolled above them, and the trees that had seemed so open suddenly felt close, as though sky and ground had wrapped around her and Aeneas while they weren't paying attention. Another drop hit Dido's cheek, heavy enough to make her blink.

Aeneas's hand closed around hers. 'We should find shelter.' Even as he spoke, the rain grew heavier, as if Baal were suddenly wringing a cloth on to their heads. A peal of thunder raised the hairs on Dido's arms.

'We are miles from the city.'

'I saw a cave not far behind us. We can wait out the storm there.'

'What about Copper? We cannot leave her.'

'She will find us,' Aeneas said confidently. 'Or take herself back to Carthage.'

Even with her shawl about her shoulders, Dido felt the fat drops of rain seep through her dress, clinging the fine fabric to her skin. It was difficult to argue.

Aeneas kept hold of her hand and led her through the trees, rushing under the pelting rain but glancing back often to make sure she did not stumble. Dido's heart hammered as they ran, and by the time they reached the cave entrance and fell against the dry rock wall, she found herself laughing as she recovered her breath. She felt like a child somehow, with her hair stuck down by rain and sweat and her fine boots all scuffed with dirt. Aeneas looked at her in bemusement, but then he began to laugh too, his chest shuddering beneath his rain-darkened tunic. He bent over to draw a lungful of air, and when he straightened, he looked at her so directly that Dido's back pressed against the rock. She felt trapped in that gaze, but not unpleasantly so. She was captured by it.

Aeneas stepped towards her, and she felt herself tense. Her laughter stopped and she stood, barely breathing, looking into those dark eyes that drew closer and closer. When they were inches from hers, when Aeneas's hand was on the rock beside her, and his hip separated from hers only by the layers of cloth between them, he stopped. He seemed to catch himself, to come up against some invisible barrier. But he did not pull back. So Dido leaned forward and kissed him.

The kiss was long and unrushed. A slim part of Dido knew that she could stop it, or should stop it, but that part was pushed out by the release she felt, the tenderness of his lips against hers, the press of his hand on her waist, until he finally drew away.

Dido could tell that Aeneas was trying to read her. He looked suddenly uncertain, even regretful, and that stung her.

'We should go further in,' he murmured. 'I can still feel the rain.'

Dido hesitated before following him. More than ever, she felt she did not fully understand the energy between them. She felt embraced and rejected all at once, and now she was being asked to enter this other place, this hidden world beyond the world, where she could not be sure what the rules might be, or if there even were any. But there was an appeal in that, too. An uncertainty that thrilled the breathless woman who had run through the rain and kissed a man because she had wanted to. So she stepped inside.

They did not go far, only deep enough to escape the storm. There was no hope of a torch or a fire with the forest now soaked, so they made the most of the grey light slanting in from the cave mouth. Aeneas brushed away the debris of the floor with his boot, clearing an area for them to sit, and unclasped the short cloak from his shoulders to lay it down. He gestured for Dido to sit upon it, but when she did, he chose a spot for himself that left a generous space between them. Another sting.

Dido could feel herself begin to churn with that most detested feeling – embarrassment. She avoided Aeneas's eye as she settled herself, smoothed out her rain-dampened skirt, tucked wayward strands of hair behind her burning ears. Perhaps she had misread everything that had passed between them these past weeks. She had been so concerned with holding off her own feelings that she may have mistaken his. And yet she held the memory of his lips on hers, and she could not believe that he had not wanted it, that he had not been wanting it for as long as she had.

'I'm sorry,' he said softly, and Dido's head snapped up. 'I should not have done that. It was the passion of a moment, nothing more. Forgive me, and we will not speak of it again.'

'Why should you need my forgiveness? It was I who . . . There is nothing to forgive,' she said stiffly.

'I know of your vow.' Aeneas's face was solemn. 'I know that you have sworn not to marry or to love another man. That you mourn still for your first husband.'

'For my husband,' came her natural correction, and yet she knew that this was not only a reflex but a choice, a fresh guard that she was putting before her.

'Yes. I understand. And I have no wish to make you an oath-breaker and bring the anger of your gods upon you. What you have vowed to them will be sacred to me. I will not disrespect it again.'

'I made no vow to the gods,' she said. It was true enough, but said so quickly that she surprised herself. 'The promise was made to myself and to Zakarbaal, my husband.' The difference had not mattered before. Why should it now? But so much time had passed, so much had happened in ten years, that the woman who had sworn those words almost felt like another person. Or perhaps that was only how Dido wanted to see it. Had she not been that same woman until so very recently? It was not the passage of time that had changed her, but the coming of Aeneas. 'My vow is my concern, not yours.'

'It is a piece of you.' Aeneas's gaze was so intent it seemed to dig at her. 'One of many you have held away from me, that I have had to discover from others. Even now, I do not know the truth of your marriage and how it ended. Today is the first time that you have spoken your husband's name. Will you not trust me with your history, even after I have bared so much of myself?' He looked injured, but Dido did not allow herself to soften.

'The story is common knowledge. You could have asked any-one in Carthage, and they would have told you what happened at Tyre.' She imagined him seeking out information about her.

The vow – that was one thing. What else had he learned? She felt exposed by the thought, but she was also flattered.

'I am not seeking a story,' he said. 'I can hear gossip and legends in any port from here to the Black Sea. What I want is to know you. Why do you make that so difficult?'

Dido was quiet, though her heart offered a thousand answers. Because she was afraid. Because she was protecting herself. Because a vow alone was not a strong enough barrier. Because it was easier to be a legend than a flawed and fractured woman. Because, despite all the time that had passed, she still felt ill and angry and vulnerable when she thought about that episode of her life. And because she knew it would be painful to tell that story.

As the silence stretched, Dido could feel Aeneas pulling away from her, preparing to rebuild his own wall and retreat behind it. That was safer for both of them, she knew, and yet she could feel herself screaming with the impulse to stop it, to keep him close, to clasp his rare spirit to hers.

'I did not love Zakarbaal when I married him,' she began in her quietest voice. 'That came later.'

When Dido's story was finished, she sat with her hands on her knees, tightening and releasing her fingers as she waited for Aeneas to speak. She had told all, as honestly as she could bear, from beginning to end. And now she felt as if she were sitting here naked on the floor of the cave.

'You feel guilty.' Aeneas looked at her steadily, and though there was no judgement in his eyes, Dido read it there anyway.

'I did not say that.'

'You did. In all your excuses. Why you had to leave Tyre so quickly. How you had other people depending on you. Did you not think that I, of all people, would understand that?' He paused, but she was too defensive to absorb his sympathy. 'And the belomancy. The arrow.'

'What about the arrow?'

'I understand why you did it. Or I'm trying to. But you think that if you hadn't done it, then none of the rest would have happened.'

'I don't know what would have happened.'

'But you feel guilty. I can feel that you do.'

Dido's heart was pounding, but the sensation was not pleasant as it had been earlier. It was a feeling she could not escape, one that pinned her to her body, to herself and to her past. She wished that Aeneas would stop looking at her, would close his eyes or march out into the storm. She had revealed too much – more than she had intended or realised.

'You must have much that you regret,' she said. 'Things that you wish you had done differently. When Troy fell. When you lost Creusa.'

'Of course. Of course I do,' he said hoarsely. She knew that she had hurt him with those words, that she had turned her own shame on him because it was too much to hold alone. Was this how things were between them? Trading wounds, comparing scars. Was this how it would always be? But even as they wounded one another, she felt herself closer to him than she had ever been. Here in this cave, they were not Queen Dido and Prince Aeneas. They were only themselves, with no audience but each other. Nothing to prove or perform or win or defend. Here, they could wear their pain and be face to face with someone who might understand it.

Dido stood up and moved towards Aeneas. She watched his grieving face shift as his eyes followed her. He stood, too, but there was still a so narrow, so wide gap of cave floor between them.

'I'm sorry,' Dido murmured, as she took the bravest step of her life and waited, trembling, to see what Aeneas would do.

He seemed to be weighing different words in his mind. His mouth twitched, his eyes roved over her. Then he stepped forwards and held her face in his rough hands, put his fingers into her hair so that she shivered.

'I am glad to know you better,' he whispered. And when he kissed her this time, he did not pull back.

Outside the cave, the rain fell and the sky thundered, but Dido no longer heard it. Mouths and bodies collided with no space for the world between, no space for thought or self except the self of that moment. Memory and duty were squeezed out like unwanted voyeurs, sent flying back to the city where they meant something. And Dido's vow went with them, so slickly that she did not feel it leave. Here in the cave, there was only Aeneas's eyes, his lips, his skin burning as hot as hers, his heart pumping vitally beneath her fingertips. Nothing had ever felt so real and yet so apart from reality. She laughed as he kissed her neck, and shuddered as his hands gripped her flesh, and let every thought and feeling pass through her as naturally as a wind through a wood, without examination or doubt or shame. The gates she had guarded within herself were flung open. Their hinges rattled unheeded with each slow, delicious breath. And she knew that she was allowing herself to fill with that most needed and most feared thing, that made her heart heavy and light, that made her head spin while anchoring her to the earth: the deadly, sweet rush of love.

Chapter 25

TYRE

The Council meeting had shaken Zakarbaal. There was a fragility to his smiles now, as if he were afraid the wrong person would see them and take his ease for something more sinister. They did not return to the palace the next week to hear the petitions of the nobles, nor the week after that. There was more than enough work at the temple, and without discussion the two of them seemed to agree that their focus would be better spent there. It was easy to forget what had transpired in the hall when their ears were filled with other people's concerns, and their hands busy with ladles or libations.

Elissa was satisfied by their shared silence on the subject of the palace, that veiled thing that they each stepped around as they spoke of daily matters. She would have left it unbroken if Zakarbaal had only been willing to do the same.

'I keep thinking there is something we must do,' he said one night as they lay in their bed. The room was dark, and though they had said their goodnights some time ago, she knew that her husband was not sleeping. His mind was grinding like a grain quern.

'What do you mean?' she asked eventually.

'Is there not something we could do to assure the king? To make clear that the temple poses no threat to his authority, that we are not courting the favour of the people? That I am no rival to him?'

He avoided the dangerous word that had been spoken in the hall. The word she had spoken while her passion was burning. *Usurper*. Was he afraid to speak it, even here in their private chamber? Or was he saving her from blame?

'The people do favour us,' she said, 'because we provide what the king will not. Are we to shrink ourselves to appease him? That is just what Ahiram wants. To quell our influence because our aims do not suit his. Because we work for the city and not for his purse or standing. Our success puts light on his failures.'

Zakarbaal sighed, and she waited for his voice in the darkness.

'I know all this. Do you think I don't see it? But there is danger in what we are doing, Elissa. I am not saying that we should not serve the people.' He sighed again, deeply, as if he were trying to expel something. 'I fear what is being said in our absence. I think I must return to court.'

She felt a sting. Zakarbaal was not a careless speaker. He did not want her at the court, and this was as plainly as he would say so. She knew it was her imprudent words that had watered this seed of fear in him. But Elissa refused to let it grow in her. She found it uncomfortable, even painful, to look at anything that made her think of her own mistakes, to dwell on things that blew against her vision of how things were or how they ought to be. And it made her angry to talk of reducing what they had built. The palace had not wanted her, so she had proven her worth beyond it. Must she now apologise for that? Was she always to keep her head below her shoulders?

'A king cannot endure enemies in his own city.' Her husband's voice was low. 'If Pygmalion can be convinced that I am such an enemy, or that you are . . .'

'Go to the court, then, if you think you must.' Elissa could not bear for him to finish his thought. If he spoke his greatest fear aloud, she would be forced to look at it.

She waited for him to speak again, and began to regret her sharpness. She reached for his fingers in the space between them, but found only crumpled linen.

Elissa had been on her feet since dawn, and now the sun was on its way to setting. Though Piddaya had brought her water and nuts throughout the day, she had not had time for a proper meal. Lately, it had become more common than not for Piddaya to accompany them to the temple. There was little to be done at the house, for they were barely there. They took their meals from the same broth they prepared for the worshippers, or shared in the sacrificial meat when there was any to be had.

'Will you not come and take some food now?' Piddaya asked.

Elissa could not disappoint her maid's hopeful concern, and nodded wearily.

It was only when she took the weight off her feet that she realised how sore they were. They seemed to expand into their new unused state, and she kicked off her sandals to let them breathe more fully. The broth was the same as usual, made with animal bones and whatever greens could be found, fortified with dried peas and lentils. She drained her bowl ravenously.

'Some more?' Piddaya was already dipping the ladle, and Elissa raised her bowl in surrender. But just as it was refilled, there came a cry from the precinct entrance – a child's voice. Elissa put down the steaming bowl and rammed her feet back into their sandals. By the time she reached the source of the sound, a small crowd had gathered.

A teenage girl was holding up a boy by the crook of his arm. The boy was young and his pale face was creased in agony, but he seemed determined not to cry. His eyes were full of tears and he bit his lip with gapped teeth.

'Princess!' the girl called. She looked relieved, as if she had spotted a friend. 'My brother needs help. Please.'

'What's the matter with him?' Elissa could already guess the source of the boy's pain. His right foot hovered above the ground and he leaned against his sister to stop himself from falling.

'He stepped on our hearth, the clumsy fool. I've told him not to chase the dog.' Even as she scolded him, her eyes were filled with worry, and she looked at him with a love Elissa recognised, even if it felt distant to her now.

'Why did you not take him to the temple of Eshmun?' Of the city's pantheon, it was Eshmun who favoured the healing arts.

'I do not know the priests there,' the girl said simply. 'Please, Princess. I thought that someone here could help him. He barely made the walk. He can't go to the other temple now.'

'No, of course not. Come. Can he make it to the bench here?' She turned to clear a path for the boy, but most of the crowd had already drifted away, their curiosity sated or perhaps disappointed. Elissa glanced across the precinct, looking for Zakarbaal, but he must have been occupied inside the temple. A burnt foot was a new challenge, and her first thought was to consult with her husband. Luckily, Piddaya had stayed close by her.

'Could you fetch a bowl of water? The largest you can find. And some salve, if we have it – ask one of the attendants. And some cloth for dressing.' Her mind was racing, but she kept her voice calm and authoritative, so as to protect the confidence that the children clearly had in her. They looked grateful, and the girl helped her brother awkwardly on to the bench while they waited for Piddaya to return. Elissa crouched down to observe the boy's foot more closely – a nasty collage of pink and red and black.

'I wouldn't worry. I've seen worse,' she lied.

Between them, she and Piddaya did their best to bathe and wrap the foot. In truth, Piddaya did most of the work, while Elissa tried to distract the boy from his pain, and his sister from her fear. She told them stories from her childhood in the palace – not all that exciting, she granted, but the children were wide-eyed to hear them. She told them grander tales, too, ones her father had told her of the kings that had come before him, of marvellous and miraculous happenings, of the gods and their quarrels. The boy's foot had long been seen to, but she went on anyway, enjoying the rapt attention of those young faces.

When the sun had finally given up its hold on the sky, Zakar-baal appeared beside the bench. 'We should be getting home,' he said.

'You go.' Elissa smiled to reassure him. 'Piddaya and I will follow soon. I promise.'

She knew he would not have left her if Piddaya were not there too. He looked exhausted, and she was glad when he nodded.

'I won't be long.' She reached towards his hand and their fingers touched briefly. Then he left, and she turned to the children. 'First, we must make sure that you can get home, mustn't we?'

The boy grinned back at her, though the lines of pain had come back to his face now that her stories had ended.

'Do your parents know you are here?'

'They're not in the city,' the girl said. 'They stayed on the mainland to guard the flock. But they wanted us here because it was safer, they said. My sister looks after us.' Suddenly, her eyes brightened. 'You might know her! She danced at the Great Awakening, with a snowdrop in her hair. She said she wasn't far from you in the line. Do you remember her?'

'Yes, I think so,' Elissa lied again.

'I could run back to the place we're staying and fetch her. Then we can carry my brother back between us. It isn't far.' The girl was already on her feet.

'Are you sure? It doesn't seem safe for you to go alone.'

'I do it all the time.' She had her hands on her hips. 'And I'm fast.'

Elissa didn't want to dent the girl's obvious pride with further doubt, so she let her go. She smiled a little to watch her run off, remembering her own determination at a similar age.

She and Piddaya sat with the boy until his reinforced escort arrived. Elissa spoke with the elder sister briefly, flattered by her breathy excitement as she reminisced on the dance.

'You were wonderful. You and your husband. The city is blessed to have you. And thank you for all you've done for my brother.'

'It wasn't much,' Elissa admitted. 'Just get him home now. And try to keep him away from any more fires.' She smiled playfully, but the girl's nod had gravity.

'I will.' She hesitated. 'Please don't think that I don't look out for him. I'm trying. Honestly, I am.'

'I know that,' Elissa said gently, though in truth she knew little about the girl's situation. 'You love him. That's what matters.'

She could not know that, either, but she felt it in the way the two girls led their brother carefully out of the precinct. The sight left a tingle in her chest as she tipped out the bowl of water and put the salve back in the storehouse.

She and Piddaya walked the short way home, with a lamp from the temple to guide them. When they reached the house, Elissa was surprised to see no light from within.

'He has already gone to bed,' she said. It was unlike her husband not to at least leave a porch lamp for her.

Piddaya set about bringing some light to the downstairs, and Elissa went on up towards the bedroom, still carrying the lamp from the temple. Even if Zakarbaal were asleep, she would give him a kiss. They never ended the day without one, and he never objected to her waking him for that purpose. The stairs creaked loudly beneath her – that was usually enough to stir him.

She found the door to their bedroom open, and stumbled over something at the threshold. She crouched with her lamp, and saw that it was a round bottle of perfume. It belonged on the table beside the door, and as she put it back there, her hand lingered. Her husband was a fastidious man. It was odd, then, that he had not replaced it himself.

An uneasy feeling stirred. She let the bottle go.

'Zakarbaal?' Her voice came as a whisper, hardly loud enough to be heard. And yet she felt unable to raise it. She swallowed her fear and approached the bed.

It was empty.

She held the lamp a moment, watching the flame quiver. Then she took it to each corner of the room, looking for . . . For what? For her husband, curled up in a corner, or sitting alone in the dark? He was not here. She went back to the stairway.

'Zakarbaal?' Her voice was loosened by panic.

'Mistress? Did you call me?'

'My husband is not in bed. He's not downstairs?' There was a hope in the question, but Piddaya shook her head.

Elissa went to the other chambers on that floor and the floor above – rooms they never used. They were all empty. As she descended to the ground floor, she realised her legs were shaking.

'He must have gone back to the temple,' she declared.

'But we just came from there. Would we not have seen him?'

'He went another way, perhaps.'

'What other way?'

Elissa closed her eyes, as if to shut Piddaya out.

'We'll go back and look for him,' she said calmly.

They went to the temple, and he was not there. They went to the attendants in their sleeping quarters, but none had seen him since sunset. Elissa tried to recruit them to look for her husband, but they seemed unwilling to be directed by her without the authority of a priest.

She left in frustration, but did not return home. She and Piddaya walked all the streets surrounding the temple and their house. They knocked on doors and shone their lamps down dark passages. Somehow the pounding of her already aching feet was a comfort to Elissa, as if constant movement meant continual progress, as if Zakarbaal could not be lost while they were looking for him.

Their circles took them wider and wider, until they were close to the palace walls. That was when Elissa's unease spiked again. She did not fear dark corners and silent streets, for she did not truly expect to find her husband there. But the palace held a different potential, one she did not feel ready to confront. If he was there, it was not by his own decision – he would have told her of his plans to go. His exhausted face, seen hours ago, flashed into her mind, and she forced it out again. She didn't want to think about the fears that had laid upon her husband these past weeks, the fears she had chosen to dismiss in him, and bury in herself. As if ignorance could make them less real.

Though her mind was in flight, her legs were leading her on towards the palace gate. It was closed, and the two guards watched her with indifference.

'Has Zakarbaal, priest of Melqart, been summoned to the palace?'

Their faces remained unchanged in the torchlight.

'Has he been brought here?'

She heard the desperation creep into her voice, and ground her teeth. 'Will you not answer me?'

Perhaps their silence was an answer, but it was not one that she liked.

'If he is here, I demand to see him. I am sister to King Pygmalion.'

'We know who you are.'

The other guard – the older – turned his head as if in warn-ing, and they returned to their silence.

'Let's go home now,' Piddaya urged. 'Perhaps your husband will be there, or perhaps he will return tomorrow.'

Elissa wanted to argue, but she had no other plan. Not at this hour, with her eyes straining and her feet burning and her heart throbbing with fear.

It was only when she returned to the house, and to her dark bedroom, that she noticed the broken lock on her dowry chest. She lifted the lid and, though the chest was as full as ever, the fine cloths were ruffled and out of order, as if they had been tossed about and stuffed back inside.

Someone has been in my house.

The knowledge was like a dagger; it had been pricking her skin ever since she had found the perfume bottle, and now it was driven deep. If they were thieves, why was nothing miss-ing? She swept a frantic hand through the fabric, until it found the red ruby fillet. Somehow, it was a relief to clasp it, as if she had found her husband in the chest. But with that feeling, she knew she was already considering the possibility that he had been taken from her. The hardness of those ruby studs beneath her fingertips was like a bridge to him, one she was desperate to hang on to. What she could not know was whether it was a bridge that spanned this world, or entered the world below.

Elissa was up before dawn the next day, having barely slept in the room that felt so violated, in the bed that felt so wide and cold without her husband. She woke Piddaya and they went first to the temple, and then to the harbour, and to the other harbour, and to the morning markets, speaking with everyone they passed. How could a person disappear without witness? And yet it seemed that Zakarbaal had.

All the time they were searching for him, all the times she said his name and waited in hope for some stranger to decide whether they might have seen him, Elissa felt she was holding her emotions on a leash. She could not let dread overcome her, even if her throat was so full of it she thought she would suffocate. She forced herself to keep moving. *There is no standing still.* Even after all these years, the memory of her father's voice was enough to keep her focused.

They went to the palace again. The gates were still closed, and though the guards had changed, they held the same silence. More and more, she became convinced that this was where her husband must be, if he was anywhere at all. She wanted to hammer on the gate, scream Zakarbaal's name until her voice was raw. But she leashed that instinct too. *You must be wily, Little Jackal. Know when to guard yourself.*

That night, she sat with Piddaya by the hearth, staring at the flames and yet not seeing them at all. Elissa would not utter her deepest fear – she could barely allow her inner self to give it shape – and yet she knew that Piddaya knew. The maid put a hand on hers, and then an arm around her shoulder, pulling her close. It surprised Elissa, but she let herself be held. They had never been tender like this. Their relationship was a practical one, though not uncaring. But Piddaya knew that what she needed in this moment was not to feel alone. She realised, with sluggish clarity, that Piddaya often knew what she needed before she knew it herself.

'Thank you,' she said quietly, without explaining what she was thankful for.

Piddaya did not answer, but went on holding her just as before.

Chapter 26

TYRE

Again, dawn drew Elissa back to the temple. Though her rational mind had given up hope that she would find Zakarbaal there, another part of her felt it was only natural. How many hours had they spent together in the precinct? Months. Years. The place felt infused with him, as if one could not exist without the other. And that was a comfort.

There were already some worshippers hovering about, and when she began to cross the precinct, they drifted towards her.

'I have prayed for you, Princess,' one said.

'May you find your husband. Melqart save him,' said another.

She hated the sympathy in their faces. It tore at her as she passed, threatening to expose something raw. She swallowed and kept her own face unbroken. The news of Zakarbaal's disappearance was well known by now. She felt as if she had spoken to every citizen in her search for him. And yet it was a private thing – this crushing fear she felt. He was not lost to them like he was lost to her.

Though she walked with purpose, in truth she had none. She found herself by the storehouse and stopped, realising she did not know where she was going. The door was open and she could hear someone inside, so she stepped towards the sound for lack of a better direction.

One of the attendants was on his knees, scooping handfuls of grain from the floor, putting them back into an open sack. He turned when he heard her.

'We cannot afford to waste it,' he said.

'What happened here?'

The shelves, usually so orderly, seemed in disarray. There were more open sacks along the wall, spilling their precious contents, and the floor was scattered with other things too – broken pottery and squashed apricots.

The attendant looked about him at the mess, his expression resigned.

'The palace guards came. Yesterday, at dusk. They said they were looking for gold, so they must have been disappointed.'

'Gold?' It seemed almost unbelievable, but then she remembered her dowry chest, and the unknown hands that had plunged through her dresses. She felt her heart begin to race.

'The palace guards?'

The attendant nodded.

It was confirmation of a truth she already knew but hadn't wanted to accept. Her husband had been taken by the palace. Which meant that the king, directly or indirectly, had ordered it. The king that had once been a soft, mewling bundle in her arms, an object for her fierce affection, a little brother who ran to her whenever he grazed his knee and buried his streaming nose in her skirt.

Her chest burned with anger. Anger at Pygmalion, but anger at herself too. She should have hammered on those palace gates the very first night, or bribed the guards, or demanded to be let in and not moved until she was admitted. Well, she would not be stopped now. She was already charging across the precinct. She had lost sight of Piddaya, but she didn't need her. It was easier to be fearless when she had no one else to worry about.

Elissa had only just left the precinct when the guards came into view. She had to rein in her momentum as they stopped in front of her.

'The king invites you to eat with him.'

Her head was spinning so much that she almost laughed. She wanted to spit on their shoes and push past them, but that was her anger trying to rule her. Here was an opportunity to make a different move, and perhaps a more successful one. She cooled herself and took a breath.

'Take me to him.'

Pygmalion had a bearing of agitation masked by repose. He was half-reclined on his personal couch, propped awkwardly on a too-small cushion while he arranged his face to look older and wiser than it was. Elissa sat opposite him on a carved wooden seat, with scrolled arms and inlays of ivory along the frame.

'I am glad to see you, Sister.'

Somehow, his stilted speech made it easier for Elissa to keep calm. She could see him trying so hard to master himself, to be in control. And this only made it clear to her that control was still a thing that might be claimed.

'I would like to see my husband.' She made her first grab.

Pygmalion's face faltered a little, then softened to something imitating sympathy. 'I have heard of your misfortune,' he said, pausing to take a sip from his cup. 'The city is speaking of little else, it seems. A priest gone from his house, and no one can say what has become of him. A tragedy, we all agree.'

Tragedy. That word struck Elissa unexpectedly, and she tried to disguise her wound by picking a pistachio from the platter before her. She rolled it in her fingers, unable to eat it.

'And do you have means?' her brother asked. 'Now that you are without your husband. Has he left you . . . wealth?'

It was an odd question, Elissa thought. But she remembered what the temple attendant had told her: the guards had been searching for gold. She thought of the nonsense that Ahiram had spoken, of the fictitious wealth he claimed her husband had been hoarding. Pygmalion's mask was slipping as he waited for her answer, and beneath his false concern she saw his greed. The awful haze of the past days was coming to new clarity, but a part of her was afraid to look. To look was to know, and to know was to go beyond the place where all realities were still possible.

She squeezed the hard nut between her fingers. 'I have enough,' she said. All answers felt dangerous. Perhaps she should lie and tell him that there was wealth beyond imagining. That he could have it all if he would only tell her where Zakarbaal was. It might be enough to make her brother reveal himself. And once she had found her husband, they would work out what to do together. They could leave Tyre, if it came to that. She would hate that. He would hate it. But they would be safer elsewhere. And they would be together.

She realised that Pygmalion was considering her, perhaps wondering whether to press her about hidden gold. She looked right back at him, a lie formulating on her tongue.

'You should move yourself back to the palace,' he said. 'You could bring your household. And all your belongings. All your treasures. You will not need them, though. We have plenty here to keep you.'

It seemed such an obvious ploy, so clumsy and ill-considered, that Elissa felt some of her ease return.

'Come now, Sister. It would be for the best. A widow should not be alone.'

Widow. That word cut sharper than *tragedy*, and the two together meant death. Pygmalion did not flinch as he said it. For him, it was simple fact, certain knowledge. And now, as much as she had resisted, it was knowledge to Elissa too. It came like a hammer blow to her chest. She sat, hardly breathing, fighting the cold panic that made her want to shudder and scream. Zakarbaal was dead. Likely he had been dead for days, but in her mind he had still lived. It was as if Pygmalion had just cut him down in front of her. And amid her horror was the searing flush of foolishness. She had mollified herself with the sureness that she could outwit her brother. That she was smarter than him, subtler than him. Better than him. And yet, with those fatal words, she realised that she had been playing a game that was already lost, idiotically moving pieces to an end that could never be a victory.

So why did she feel as if she were still playing? Because it was easier to focus on this room, on the next words she would speak, than on the flood rising in her body, the crushing grief she felt closing around her. Because she knew that there was something still to lose. It had only been chance that kept her from returning home with Zakarbaal that night. If she had, would she be dead too? Was her life still held at the whim of her fool brother and the poison dripped into his ear? If she raged now, gave in to the torrent of emotion that wanted so desperately to break over her, if she accused Pygmalion of what she knew had been done, she would close every other door open to her. All that would be left was naked hostility, and where would that lead? She would follow her husband beneath the earth, to spend a cold eternity there.

Don't let yourself be trapped, Little Jackal. Whether urged by self-preservation, or by her need to feel some small amount of control, she ignored the blood pounding in her ears and hid her trembling hands beneath the table. Perhaps the best way to avoid being caught was to pretend that she already was.

'I will come to the palace, Brother.' The words felt fragile as they left her mouth, but sounded remarkably intact. 'It is as you say, I should not be alone. And I would be grateful for your hospitality. I will bring all my belongings – everything I have.' She allowed a little stress to fall on those words. 'Only, you must give me time to arrange my affairs. And to close up my house.'

'I can send men to help with that.'

'No. No, Brother, that will not be necessary. I need some time to grieve and gather myself. Three days is all I ask. And then I will be glad to be here, in the home we once shared.'

She cracked her rigid face into a sad smile and met his eyes. If her appeal to their kinship made him feel guilty, he did not show it. He had a look of satisfaction, almost relief, as if all had gone as he had hoped. That was good, Elissa thought. She needed him to be relaxed. She needed to stall any rashness he might conceive. She needed to buy herself some space to breathe.

As soon as she was through the palace gate, Elissa turned a sharp left and followed the path towards the very edge of the city, to a quiet corner shaded by an olive tree, where a view of the sea glinted over the wall. Here she allowed herself, finally, to collapse. Her legs gave way and she folded on to the dry earth, raking her fingers across it until her nails were cracked and filthy. Her lungs burned as she drew in great shuddering breaths, and hissed them out again. She did not feel her tears but tasted them, warm and salty. She hated that taste, so pointless and defeated, but she could not stop it.

It felt as if the floor had gone out from her life, as if she were falling with no one to reach out and grab her. Zakarbaal had been that person. And she had thought he always would be. Nothing felt so very terrible or impossible when she had known that Zakarbaal was there with his reassuring words, and his hands that made her feel so loved and light and grounded all at once. She imagined him here with her now, kneeling behind her with his weight pressed against her back, his arms wrapping her like a blanket, his breath on her neck as he rocked with her. It was painful to summon the memory of him, and painful to send it away. Neither would bring back the real man who had been her husband. The warmth and the sureness and the ease and the intimate knowledge of one another's souls. All the things they had shared, that now belonged to no one if they could not belong to them both.

She thought of the last time she had seen him, the brief way she had touched his hand, the carelessness of their parting. It was a wound she should not have opened, and she whimpered at the agony of it. How she wished she could return to that moment and dissolve all the world around her, see only his face, hold it in her hand, and kiss him and kiss him. She should have grasped him and never let him go. What might have been different if she had? She might have gone with him and saved him somehow, with some clever trick, or else died beside him. Her pain was so great that for a moment she wished it. There was no pain in death, no rending of two souls who were supposed to face everything together. She craved the simplicity of it.

Suddenly the wall beside her felt so close. The drop beyond so clear in her flailing mind. She pressed her eyelids shut, and saw the jagged rocks she had looked down upon so many times, saw her body upon them as if it were no longer hers. Something she could be parted from, and the grief that wracked it too. She allowed herself to pulse with that image, then forced it away. Zakarbaal would not want her to follow him. His spirit would weep to see hers so soon.

Elissa came back to herself, to the world of persistent life and unhealable sorrow. She pressed her palms into the dirt, as if to remind herself that it was still there. Her heart was thrumming with the knowledge that she was in danger, filling her with the instinct to move, to do, to find a way to keep going. And yet there was something broken between body and mind. She could not will herself to stand. She felt so heavy, so filled with the pain of loss that it seemed as if even the tiniest movement might send a crushing flood of agony. She stayed perfectly still, closed her eyes again, listened to the leaves above her, and felt the wind blow cold against her cheeks.

'Mistress.' The voice was so soft that Elissa thought it might have come from her own mind. She opened her stinging eyes, and saw Piddaya standing in the dappled shade of the tree. 'You cannot stay here, Mistress. Can you stand?'

The maid put out a hand, and though her grip was only light, it felt as if she were pulling Elissa's whole weight. When she swayed, Piddaya steadied her.

'He is dead, then.' The maid didn't expect a reply. She had read it already in her mistress's grief. Elissa was grateful that she did not have to speak the words.

Her grief hung like a sodden cloak, but already she felt stronger with Piddaya's arm around her waist. The maid led her trembling legs over the cobbles and held her up when she felt like dropping. After the longest walk of Elissa's life, they made it back to their empty home.

Chapter 27

TYRE

Elissa sat beside the hearth. She was not cold, but she was shivering. Piddaya had put a shawl over her so she pulled it tight, as if she were swaddling herself. The embrace of the wool was a comfort, but somehow it made her ache too. She let it go.

'Shall I mix some wine, Mistress?'

Unmixed would be better, Elissa thought. Let it be strong and uncompromised by water or sweetness. Let each gulp numb her mind, until she had forgotten where she was or what had happened, until her chest no longer felt like a cliff on the verge of a landslide.

No. That was the coward in her, the child that thought she might hide behind her hands and so stop the world from existing. She had bargained a few days from her brother so that she could have time to think, and she could not do that if she were soaked in wine.

'No wine,' she managed to say.

'Some dates, then? You look so pale, Mistress. You must have something.'

Unfair as it was, she wanted to snap at her maid. Did she think that a little fruit would restore her? Restore anything that had been lost? Her mouth felt dry like ash, and the thought of food sickened her. But the effort of articulating this was one she could not summon, so she let her head nod.

As Piddaya went to the pantry, there was a gentle tap at the front door. Elissa thought she might have imagined it, but it came again, more insistently. It tapped at her frayed nerves, tapped in her reeling brain. She needed it to stop, so she went to the door without calling Piddaya.

She had no expectation as to whom she might find on the other side, but even so, Shapashuru's stooped frame was a surprise.

'Princess,' he said, with voice low. 'Might I come in?' The old man glanced up the street. His usually bright face was grave, his eyes alert.

Elissa stepped back without a word, and he closed the door firmly behind him. With the impetus that had dragged her to the door being spent, Elissa swayed on her feet.

'Oh, come now. You don't look well at all, Princess.' Shapashuru put a guiding hand behind her, and they came back to the hearth together. Once she was sitting down, Elissa swallowed her nausea and forced her mind to focus on the words streaming from the guildmaster's mouth.

'You have learned the truth, then. Your husband is dead.' He looked genuinely grieved, his aged mouth slack with sorrow. 'I had hoped my investigations would lead to another end. Oh yes, Princess, I have looked for him as you have. I have had my sons listening for news. Since the dance, I knew he might meet with danger. And with Ahiram whipping up these rumours of buried gold . . . ' His white head hung low. 'I should have stood up against him. Can you ever forgive me? I did not realise that things would move so quickly. But that brother of yours has a fickle mind. Perhaps I should not say so. Perhaps such words insult the gods, by insulting the man they have graced with kingship. But are the gods to be offended by the truth? I trust Great Melqart is nobler and wiser than that. Surely he is as angered by this senseless death – the death of his own devout priest – as we are. Tyre is his city, as much as it is mine or yours, Princess. And she is being ground to worthless, immoral dust.'

This Shapashuru seemed a different man to the one she knew. He was more vigorous, more acute. His eyes were no longer gently shining but aflame. He was angry – he had said so, and she could see it. His fists were balled in his lap, the sun-spotted skin quivering. The longer she looked at his hands, the more scars she noticed – echoes of a life spent in the pursuit of beauty and perfection. He was a craftsman – a moulder of glass and gleaming faience. But he spoke to her now as a man of state. Perhaps she had underestimated him.

'I sense you have not come here to speak only of my husband's passing.'

'No, Princess. You are right.' He sighed deeply. 'I am sorry to have come at all, to disturb you in your grief. If things were different, I would have given you more time. But we are past that point, I fear.' He reached over and clasped her hands. She flinched a little at the sudden, unexpected contact. 'You must move against your brother. You will have support, I am sure. People still remember the controversy after King Mattan's death. Pygmalion's succession was not legitimate, and his failures have proven it. Tyre will welcome you as its queen.'

'Move against him? You make it sound as if we are playing a game of Hounds and Jackals. As if I might simply remove his piece from the board.' She tried to steady herself against what Shapashuru was saying. If she had felt adrift before, this was like a new storm filling her horizon. She wasn't sure she had the heart to face it.

'You are right,' the guildmaster said. 'It will not be as simple as that. But it may be quick if we act now. The losses will be small.'

And there was the truth, squashed down and softly spoken. People would die. No doubt more than they imagined or intended.

Power was rarely taken without blood. Elissa's father had told her of cities torn apart by civil conflict, whole peoples scorched by years of death and generations of hate. He had told her of the coup her own great-grandfather had orchestrated, the executions carried out to secure his throne, the assassins that had stalked him, even years later.

'I will not start a war. Tyre is crumbling as it is. I will not turn her on herself.'

'That is not what I propose. Not a war, but a coup. A swift action for the city's good. With the right plan, perhaps only Pygmalion need die.'

It felt stark to hear him say it. Despite her anger and the clawing loss that tore at her, Elissa recoiled at the image of her brother's bloodied body. She remembered her childish vow, whispered over his cradle, that she would never let harm come to him. That memory was painful to her now. The memory of her love for him was painful. But Pygmalion's death would do nothing to remove her pain, and it would not bring Zakarbaal back. It would only be another bond severed – another piece of herself gone from the world.

'I can't,' she whispered. 'I won't.'

Shapashuru sat back in his chair and let her hands fall from his. He looked disappointed. But though his disappointment stung Elissa, it was a dull scratch, blunted by her own accept-ance that she could not be what he needed her to be. He was not the first person to have expectations for her, great imagin-ings for her potential. Her father's belief in her had sunk so deep it had become her own. She had lost count of the people who had praised her capabilities. She had devoured their words and allowed them to fuel her, always striving towards the next opportunity to prove them right. But perhaps they had all been wrong. Zakarbaal had died because she couldn't resist reaching, because she wanted people to look at her and to praise her and to confirm what her father had seen. But she knew now that she was not worth their gaze. No one else would die for her.

She sat silent, staring into the flames in the hearth. She thought that Shapashuru would leave – wished he would. She was no help to him or their city. He must know that now.

'What will you do?' he asked softly. It sounded like a pitying question, and she turned her head expecting to see the guildmaster changed back to the kindly old man she knew. But his eyes were still alight. 'You do not want a war. I respect that. What, then, is your plan?'

His faith in her had not waned. She felt it in his steady look, a look she had seen from so many others. People who needed her, who trusted her. And, as always, Elissa drew strength from it. She could not abandon herself while others refused to.

And yet it was so hard to think with this gaping hole in her chest. It was all she could do not to collapse into it. While Zakarbaal had lived, anything had seemed possible. He had made her feel clever and sure. And, just for a moment, she allowed herself to dream that he was still with her. It was a dangerous drug – one liable to pull her into its grip if she were not careful – but she needed it now.

If Zakarbaal were here, she would flee with him, as she had imagined doing when her hope still kept him alive. That vision had not seemed so terrifying when he had been a part of it.

Can I survive this? she asked her own soul.

And Zakarbaal's voice answered: *I see no other way.*

'I will leave Tyre.'

Shapashuru looked surprised, but his attention remained keen. 'Alone?'

Elissa hesitated. She could still feel Zakarbaal's spirit, and it helped her form her answer. 'I will leave with anyone who wishes to come with me. I will take a ship and find new land to settle, where we can build a new Tyre.'

She surprised herself this time. But as she spoke this new future into existence, it somehow felt as if it had always been there.

'Yes.' Shapashuru was nodding. 'I have a ship. A trade ship, large enough for settlers and whatever supplies we can gather.'

'You'll follow me?'

'Further than anyone.'

She felt her cheeks quiver and took a deep breath to keep her throat from tightening.

'There are many who would. Though we must keep our enterprise quiet. Share it only with those we know we can trust. Allow me to spread the word discreetly.'

'We cannot risk discovery.' She agreed. 'All must be prepared before we make our move. Is three days enough time? My brother will keep his distance for now. But he has summoned me to the palace, and once I go, I may be unable to leave again.'

'Three days.' Shapashuru nodded slowly, his mind clearly working. 'I can make us ready.'

'And I will bring all that I can, as everyone should. As much as your ship will carry. Who knows what we shall need to barter for, or for how long we must sustain ourselves. A pity that my husband's famed wealth is not real. Gold would greatly aid us.' She smiled tragically, but as she stamped down the wave of misery she had piqued, an idea occurred to her. 'If they are able, each settler should bring a piece of scrap metal. Anything will do – bronze, copper, tin, lead. Something broken or worthless. Will you tell them, Shapashuru?'

'What is it for?'

'You will see. Or else we will not need it after all, which will be all the better. Just tell them.'

The old man gave her a slanted look, but he did not press her. 'A queen may have her secrets.'

Chapter 28

TYRE

Elissa spent the next three days packing up her house – and making a show of packing up her house. Pygmalion was less likely to disturb her if she was clearly doing just as he had asked her to do.

It felt good to be busy. Or, at least, while her body and mind were focused on preparations for her departure, Elissa's pain was forced to recede into the less used parts of herself, the parts she only remembered when she was still or alone. Her nights were torturous. While she lay awake, she thought again and again of all the moments that had led to Zakarbaal's death, all the times she might have acted differently, spoken differently. And when she slept, her dreams were filled with him. But his face was wrong, or he had no face, or he would walk away from her and refuse to turn. These cruel simulacrums of her husband made her awaken to an ache deeper than if she had not seen him at all.

By the end of the third day, Elissa's belongings were prepared for travel and stacked outside the house. It didn't look like much, now that everything was gathered together. And there was little of real value – her dowry chest filled with fine cloths and garments, dyed in red and purple and yellow; her personal jewellery, which she had fitted within two small ivory boxes; and a crate of silver tableware embossed with flowers and birds. The pile was padded with more practical things, too – food from the pantry, warm wool bedding – and yet it did not look like enough for the founding of a new life, never mind a new city.

'Are we mad to do this?' she asked Piddaya as they stood waiting for the men Shapashuru had promised he would send.

Strands of her maid's hair were stuck to her forehead, dark with sweat. A day of hauling sacks and boxes had left them both exhausted.

'I have never thought you mad,' Piddaya said. 'Though even if I did, I would not say so.' She gave a sideways grin.

'Well, perhaps you should.' Elissa laughed – an unfamiliar sensation after the past days, and perhaps a reflex brought on more by fatigue than amusement. 'Promise me that in future you will tell me if I seem to be losing my mind.'

Her maid nodded, but then her smile dampened. 'I will be sad never to see Tyre again.'

Elissa had avoided saying such things aloud. She knew that if she dwelt too much on what she was leaving behind, she might lose the strength to do it. But in wrestling her own feelings, she had not thought that this scheme of hers would take Piddaya from her home too.

'I told Shapashuru that I would sail with anyone who wished to follow me. You are no exception to that, Piddaya. If you want to stay, I will not force you to leave.' She turned to face her maid fully, and met her unreadable eyes. 'You have been my servant all these years, bound to me since you were a child. But I cannot ask you to leap into the dark with me, not if you don't want to. You can remain here, or we will let you leave the ship at some other port if that is what you wish. Or—'

'I don't want to stay,' Piddaya interrupted. 'I was an orphan when I came to you. You have been my family, and Zakarbaal too. The city will be empty for me when you leave. Tyre will not be Tyre without you in it.'

Elissa loosened with relief. Even for that perilous moment, it had been difficult to imagine a new life without Piddaya beside her. 'You have been family to me, too,' she said, no longer able to look at the woman beside her but instead gazing ahead at the vacant street. 'Especially since . . . Especially now.'

Perhaps her maid heard the waver in her throat, or perhaps she simply knew that no more needed to be said. They fell back into silence.

The sky had begun to lose its light, and Elissa hoped that Shapashuru's men would arrive soon. It had been agreed that their best chance was to leave at dusk. The harbour would be quieter once the fishing boats had come in and the markets had closed. They did not want to draw suspicious or unfriendly attention if they could help it. And though it would be dangerous to sail at night, Shapashuru assured her that his merchant sailors were as experienced as any men on the sea.

Just as Elissa's nerves began to convince her that something was wrong, a small band of men came up the street from the direction of the harbour. Among them, she recognised Shapashuru's two sons.

'Princess,' one of them said as they drew close. 'All your things are prepared?' He surveyed the pile of boxes and took one from the top. He frowned. 'This one is empty, my lady.'

'All is as it should be. Leave nothing behind, please.' She forgave his sceptical look. No doubt he thought her mind addled by grief, but he said nothing more.

It wasn't until the men began to carry off their loads that he spoke again. 'And you, my lady? Are you prepared? Best you follow us to the ship and keep close.'

Elissa hesitated. 'Piddaya, you go with them. See that all our things are put aboard. And the other thing – will you see to that, too?'

Her maid looked unsure. 'I can see to it, just as you told me. But ought you not to come with us?'

'There is something I must do first. Go, please.' Something had shifted in the relationship between maid and mistress over the past days, and Elissa did not want to command her. She hoped their trust in one another would be enough. 'I will follow you soon.'

Shapashuru's son looked between them, waiting with a sack of barley at his feet.

'We'll watch for you,' Piddaya said.

And that was cue enough for the young man to swing the sack over his shoulder and follow the group that was slowly making progress towards the harbour.

It was easy to leave the house behind. Elissa did not even look back as she hurried away from it. Though she had not allowed herself to understand it consciously, the building had held an unease for her since Zakarbaal's disappearance. It was a place tainted by events she would never fully know or want to imagine. Later, when she was far away and her mind had time to look back on these frantic days, she would miss the bed. She would regret not touching its carved frame one last time, not taking a moment to appreciate that place where she and Zakarbaal had grown their love, and talked into the night, and slept easily beside one another.

Instead, her heart carried her to the temple. This was the place she and Zakarbaal had built their lives together. It was the place she had asked him to be her husband, the place she had fallen in love with his generous spirit and felt so proud to see him at his work and to join her effort to his. It was the place in which they had tended their stems until each was wrapped around the other, supporting and supported, so close that they seemed two blooms of one plant. It was the last place she had seen Zakarbaal alive.

She realised that she could not leave Tyre without being in that space again. She went to the bench where she had sat as her husband said goodbye, where his fingers had brushed hers so briefly. Her hands tingled with the memory, almost pleasantly, but at the same time her chest felt as if it were crushing her from within, squeezing her heart and her lungs until it was a struggle to breathe. She wished that she could remember Zakarbaal without this smothering pain. But she would not shy away from it. To feel pain was to know that she had loved him, and so she let it sit upon her, sink into her flesh. It would be with her forever, she knew, and that was a precious comfort.

The precinct was empty of worshippers, with the sun now melting into the horizon, so Elissa visited each corner in peace, soaking up the moments she recalled there, packing them away for her journey. She had no urn of ashes to carry away with her, no body to bury. Shapashuru had made enquiries, but no trace of her husband had been found after his disappearance. Elissa told herself that this was better, that if Zakarbaal was nowhere, then he could be anywhere – anywhere that she was. And so she gathered up his spirit, each fragment of him held in memory.

As she crossed in front of the temple doors yet another time, Elissa realised there was something else she ought to take with her. She had packed no divine figurines – ironically, the priest's house had no homely shrine, for the temple had been their shrine all these years. She imagined Zakarbaal chiding her for remembering blankets and jewellery but not his own life's purpose. There was no place more filled with risk than the sea, and she could not ask people to follow her across it without Melqart's protection.

Women could not enter the inner chamber of the temple, where the cult images were honoured. And even if she were willing to commit that sacrilege, she didn't have the boldness to remove something from the god's own sanctum. Instead, she went to the storehouse where the more humble figurines were kept, the ones sold by the temple or used in public rites. It was not yet locked for the night, so she walked right in.

The mess she had discovered on last entering the storehouse had been wholly cleared, and the shelves looked fuller than they had of late. *Good*, she thought. Elissa had told herself again and again that she had no choice but to flee her city, and yet guilt pricked her still. She worried for the people, and for the legacy that she and Zakarbaal would leave at the temple. *Let it survive without us*. She made the silent prayer as her eyes moved over the higher shelves, deciding which godly image might best serve her new people.

There, leaning against a stack of folded cloth, was a bronze figure of Melqart, tall as her forearm. It shone faintly, reflecting the light of a lamp on the table, and seemed alive in a way the others did not. She reached for it and let its weight sit in her hands. This was the one. But as she was about to leave, she spotted a stack of libation bowls, bronze like the statue. Must she not have means to honour Melqart, and serve him pleasing wine and fragrant oil? She took a few bowls from the stack, and balanced them in the crook of her arm.

'Princess Elissa. What are you doing here?'

The voice made her start. She turned, already knowing to whom it belonged. Azmilkar, one of the priests under her husband.

'I'm leaving Tyre.'

It sounded more like a confession than it needed to, and Elissa knew it made her sound guilty. But wasn't she? It was bad enough that she was abandoning the temple and the people who relied upon it, but here she was, stealing from it too. The statue slipped in her arms, and she squirmed to rebalance it.

'I'm sorry.' She swallowed, but kept her head high. 'There are people sailing with me. People who look to me. I must give them all that I am able. And we need Melqart's favour.'

She had expected Azmilkar's face to darken with disapproval – betrayal, even. She cringed, waiting for his eyes to shame her, for his voice to call out for the other priests.

But he spoke softly. 'Of course you must go. Tyre is no longer safe for you.' He looked at the bronze cradled in her arms, and around at the shelves of the storehouse. 'You and your husband have made this temple what it is. There is little here that was not by your getting. You think I will deny you the Rising God's blessings?' He reached around the shelves, taking painted cups, ivory figurines, a box of sweet incense, a string of polished turquoise beads. All this he put gently into a hemp bag, and pushed it into her hand. 'If I could spare you more, I would.'

Elissa looked at the young man curiously. She had never spoken with him much before, not beyond the practicalities of temple life, and she regretted it.

'And will you be safe here?' she asked. 'The ship leaves tonight, but there is still time. Come with me, if that is what you want.'

Azmilkar shook his head with a rueful smile. 'My place is here. I have been announced as the new Head Priest.' He looked a little awkward as he dipped his head in humility. 'My father is delighted. And for myself, I intend to continue the honourable work of my predecessor.'

Elissa's chest filled with a prickling warmth, to know that this man would be stepping into her husband's shadow. She nodded slowly. 'Look after her,' she said.

'The temple?'

'Tyre.'

Azmilkar reflected her serious gaze, and when she left the storehouse, she felt lighter somehow, despite the full bag now weighing her down.

Chapter 29

TYRE

Elissa walked alone to the harbour under a darkening blue-grey sky and an early smattering of stars. Even now, after all she knew and all that had happened, she felt safe on these streets. Tyre was still her home, for these last hours at least. Azmilkar had given her a lamp, but she hardly needed it. She could find her way by the moon alone, by the shapes of the black buildings, by the feel of the stones beneath her feet.

Piddaya was waiting near the harbour entrance, by the top of the sloping path that led down to the ships. Her hands were anxiously scrunched in the folds of her skirt, and she threw one of them up when she spotted Elissa.

'Mistress!' It was a whispered shout, and she came running with a flush of relief on her face. 'What's this?' she asked, eyeing the heavy bag. 'Did we leave something behind?'

'These are gifts. From the temple.'

The maid only nodded and tried to take the bag.

'I can manage it. You've done enough today. Everything is arranged? The boxes? Was there enough—'

'More than enough. It's all done. Come on now, we mustn't linger. I think you'll have quite the surprise when you get down there.'

Piddaya was not wrong. Instead of one merchant ship waiting to sail – as Shapashuru had said – there were five. And all along the beach and jetties, there milled a great crowd of people, more than Elissa could count as her eyes scanned across them. Men, mostly, but women and children too. The realisation made her chest close a little tighter. That this many people trusted her to lead them across the sea, to lead their families, was an honour. But it was a grave responsibility too. She had not anticipated that she would have so many fates bonded to hers, and she felt the weight of them. The bag dragging at her arm was like a balance, and she clasped the rough hemp tightly in her fingers. They would need all the aid that gods and men were willing to grant.

By the time Shapashuru found her in the dark, she had recomposed herself.

'I did not expect so many,' she said, keeping her voice level.

'Yes, ah . . . Perhaps I should have warned you. Once the whispers began, there was no stopping them. I could not accept one man and deny another without fair reason. And they are good people, each one of them. Brave and hardworking people. They know what they have entered into. And they know the risks. Is it not encouraging? It is a testament to your reputation, my queen.'

Queen. This was not the first time that Shapashuru had used the word. Three days ago, when she had first heard it from him, she had let it drift by her. It had seemed like an unserious novelty then, or a distorted echo from a life she had once imagined. But now, as she stood facing the ships, it started to feel like something that might be real. Her old self-belief, so cowed in grief, began to flex its weary limbs. *Could she do this?* That question was past asking. Streams of Tyrians were climbing the gangplanks. *How would she do this?* By doing just what all these people had dared to do. By trusting in her wits.

'We should leave as soon as possible.'

Shapashuru nodded. 'The captains have their orders. Everything is loaded. As soon as everyone is on deck, we will raise the anchors.'

It was bright on the ship, almost dazzlingly so. Men stood around with torches illuminating their varied expressions – some tense, others excited, many hovering between. Elissa wondered how her own face might read and tried to smooth it. Let them see confidence or nothing at all.

If it had not been so bright, they might have seen the guards sooner. But they emerged from the darkness straight on to the jetty, as if they had sprung from the water.

'These ships are forbidden to sail,' a tall guard called loudly to the deck, with his fist tight around his spear. 'Princess Elissa. Guildmaster Shapashuru. You will be escorted to the palace immediately. No other man shall move.'

She counted twelve guards. They were well outnumbered by the men on the ships, yet the tall one spoke with the full expectation of being obeyed. She could ignore them, Elissa thought. The ships were full and ready. But their anchors were still buried. In the time it took to raise them, the guards would be aboard, and their glinting weapons with them.

This was what she had feared. But fear could be a worthy defence when properly heeded.

'I will disembark,' she called in a clear voice.

Shapashuru's hand gripped her shawl. 'My queen—'

'Stay here,' she murmured. 'Have the anchors raised.'

He pulled tighter.

'Trust me,' she whispered, then walked down to the guards. 'Gentlemen,' she said, as her slippered feet stepped from the gangplank. 'I trust my brother, the king, is well?'

This pleasantry seemed to throw them, and the tall guard cleared his throat. 'You will be escorted to the palace immediately,' he repeated, but made no move towards her. 'The guildmaster too.' One of the other guards moved at that, but she put up a hand.

'Yes,' she said, so softly that the men had to be still to hear her. 'You have your orders. I understand. That is what the king has asked for. But it is not what he truly wants.' Elissa's heart was hammering, but she smiled as softly as she spoke. 'What he wants' – she paused to pass her eyes over the men, to make sure their attention was on her – 'is my husband's treasure. You've heard of it, I see.'

A few faces shifted in the torchlight.

'It is true that the priest Zakarbaal gathered a great wealth of gold, and that I have inherited it as his widow.' She found it surprisingly easy to speak of her husband, perhaps because she was not really speaking of him. This was another man, a false ghost of her own invention. 'My brother has sought this gold, as you know. He wants more than anything to seize his hands upon it. That is why he sent you here tonight. That is why he summons me to the palace. I, myself, hold no value. Nor any other person here. But the gold . . . What reward do you think he would give to the men who recovered it?'

She let the question hang and turned to call up to the ship.

'Piddaya. Have my husband's treasure brought to the jetty.'

She could not see her maid's face amid the torches, but she knew she was there.

It was not long before four young men with thick arms came creaking down the gangplank, with two great wooden crates carried between them. The crates landed on the jetty with a heavy metallic clatter, and Elissa tried not to reveal her satisfaction at the sound.

Before any guards could move, she spoke in her soft voice again. 'I offer you the treasure of Zakarbaal. Take it to my brother, and see what favour comes to those who please the king. But in return' – she met the eyes of the tall guard, the one who seemed likely to hold authority over the others – 'you will let us sail. The offer is more than fair. A pain to me, in truth, since I am forced to give up this great inheritance. But I will not see blood spilled into the harbour. And that is the alternative.' She sent a warning with her eyes and set herself solid. The guards were well armed, but they faced five ships of men. They could not know what weapons were aboard, but she gave them space to imagine.

The tall guard watched her carefully. 'This is the whole treasure?'

'All the gold my husband had gathered. You have my word. And if it is false, may Ashtart strike me down.'

It was a game, she told herself. A game of words and of nerves. And she would win it.

'The king demands that you are brought to the palace. That is my order.'

'He summons me because he seeks the gold. I offer you a swifter solution. Or else, if you do not want to take it, I will go with you and have these men throw the treasure off the jetty. And we will explain together why the king must now dredge his gold from the harbour floor.'

The guard paused. He eyed the men behind her, perhaps judging how quickly they might act. When he looked at her again, he seemed to have reached a decision.

'I leave you with your prize,' she said.

Elissa turned and strode up the gangplank, and felt it move as the young men followed her. She tried not to look like she was hurrying, but as soon as she was on deck, she made motions for the ship to move off. The gangplanks were taken in, and the guards did nothing to stop it. They were already examining the crates, lifting them to judge their weight. She saw one man put the tip of his spear against one of the lids, trying to prise the nailed wood open. She gripped the ship rail.

She had hoped they would carry the crates straight to the palace and allow Pygmalion to open his own gift. She had imagined her brother's face as the wood was lifted away to reveal a convincing clatter of worthless scrap, and a heavy bed of sand beneath. Was she wrong to enjoy that image? If so, she was being punished for it now, as her stomach churned and she urged the ship to move.

Slowly, languidly, it responded. She heard the sloshing of the black water, felt the shift of the deck, and steadied herself against it. This was her first time aboard a ship as large as this one, but she gave none of her mind to appreciating the new experience. Her focus was on the guards and the crates. And only when she was sure they were getting smaller did she allow herself to breathe.

In the days of wandering, when their old home was behind them and their new one not even in their imaginations, the first place that Elissa and her people landed was on the shore of Cyprus. And the first person that Elissa met was Anna.

The sea had suited Elissa surprisingly well given her lack of previous exposure, and she had now been so long upon it that she had to adjust to being back on land. The world swayed as she made her way across the beach, legs stumbling over the sand. Piddaya, the poor thing, had not settled so well to life aboard the ship. She looked thinner, after only a short journey from Tyre's shore to this one. Her maid had struggled to keep any food down, and even when she did not eat, her fair face was tinged a queasy green. The smell of the livestock they had brought with them on the ships had likely not helped. As soon as the gangplanks were down, Piddaya had run to the sand and knelt down to let it run through her fingers, sucking in great gasps of island air. Elissa might almost have been amused if she had not felt so guilty. She wondered whether her maid already regretted following her across the sea.

It was easier to pity Piddaya, to worry about the others who had followed her from Tyre, than to think of her own feelings. They were too great, too tangled, to be confronted in those early days of her wandering. Later, when time had made them less suffocating, she would allow herself to pause and to remember. But for now, allowing herself to think of what she had lost in Tyre felt like reaching into a pit that might reach back, that might drag her into the dark with no way to pull herself out. She avoided that gaping emptiness by keeping her mind full, and her hands and mouth busy, whenever she could. The days aboard the ship were long but she had filled them, even if she could find nothing to do but study the wide horizon.

They had passed other harbours along their route north. They might have landed at Sidon or Byblos, or continued on to discover what remained of ravaged Ugarit, but Elissa was glad to have put a larger portion of sea between her and her brother. And Kition had a familiarity of sorts. The land did not look greatly different from the one they had left – the sand felt the same beneath her feet, and the trees had a shape and texture that she found comforting. Their green branches waved at the edge of the beach offering shade, and Elissa was keen to accept.

She had not yet made it off the beach, however, when a movement of people caught her eye. Away to her left, a group emerged from the trees. Her first instinct was fear, but it was quickly replaced by curiosity. They were only women, she realised, in light dresses that blew about them in the breeze, with their hair worn long and loose. Elissa stood and watched as they walked towards her own people still milling about the boats. Her feet turned away from the treeline and started back down the beach.

By the time she reached them, the women were arranged in a line, facing out towards the sea but with their eyes demurely downcast. Only one of them showed animation, and she was raising her voice loud enough for the gathering crowd of Tyrians to hear her.

' . . . and so it is a custom among our people that a bride must earn her own dowry before she can be allowed to marry. And by tradition, she does this by selling herself to any man who will pay for her, only for one night. A stranger is best, a sailor or a trader, such as you fine men are' – the young woman took a moment to share her appealing smile across the audience – 'for he will leave our shore and make no further claim on the woman, nor cause any violence through jealousy.'

Elissa saw some of her men nodding as they listened, clearly convinced by the sense of the explanation. She had heard of similar customs among certain cults of Ashtart, but they had always felt like vague tales to her and not something she would ever witness. Now here these women stood, draped in cloth that gave more than a suggestion of what might lie beneath. They seemed so youthful in their bearing, glancing up prettily at the watching men with locks of hair spilling unheeded over their bare shoulders. But somehow they did not seem like maids. Their figures were too voluptuous, their skin pleasantly dappled by years under the sun. And there was something in their expressions, in the artful curl of their lips and the bright light of their eyes, that told Elissa she was watching a performance.

'It would shame these girls to put a price on their virginity,' the young woman with the loud voice went on. 'And so they must rely upon the goodness and generosity of a stranger to offer a worthy price. And you'll remember I told you that these are all unmarried girls, unknown to men. Their beauty is ripe and sweet, and may be sold only once. Is that not a jewel worth purchasing? And surely its price must be worthy of a dowry. You, sir.' Suddenly, the woman was pointing at one of the men in the crowd. 'What might you expect for a dowry? What worth?'

The man looked flustered to be asked, and stuttered his answer. 'Oh, ah . . . a dish of bronze?'

The woman looked unimpressed.

'Two dishes?'

The woman's eyes, so expressive beneath her fringe of dark curls, were pitying. 'Not all men are wealthy. It is true. But I cannot believe that none among you can afford a proper price. Look again upon the beauty of these girls' – she swept an elegant hand in their direction – 'and return with your most worthy offering. We shall not move from the shore. Take your time – though have a care that your favourite is not plucked by another before you make your choice.' She smiled, and for a moment all was still. Then the first men began to hurry toward the ships.

'Stop.' Elissa was pleased at the extent to which her own voice travelled.

She felt the men around her pause, and noted the wrinkle of annoyance that came upon the young woman's face.

'What is your name?' Elissa asked.

The woman hesitated, then announced confidently, 'My mother named me Anna.' She gave a neat bow, but never allowed her eyes to break away.

'I would ask for the names of these girls,' Elissa said, looking down the line, 'but perhaps I should only ask what they are called today. Tomorrow it may change, I think. A fresh crop of virgins with the same faces. Or do you change your game, I wonder? Not virgins, perhaps, but tragic widows. Lonely Amazons? Yes, I can see that one working.'

'Who are you?' The woman stared at her.

'A liar and a cheat, when I need to be. And therefore able to spot another.' Elissa felt a wave of confidence from the satisfaction of seeing through the woman's charade, and she let it run through her. 'But more formally, you are speaking with Princess Elissa of Tyre. These people follow me.'

The woman – Anna, if that was in fact her name – could not hide her surprise. Her eyes widened a little, and her annoyance seemed to drop away. 'Indeed.' Anna looked her interrupter up and down. 'They are wise to follow one so quick as you. But tell me, Princess Elissa of Tyre, are you a tyrant as well as a leader? Or will you allow your people to decide for themselves whether they would like to purchase what I am selling? All men desire a little fantasy. There was no harm in my game.' She flashed her delicious smile again.

'No great harm, perhaps.' Elissa regarded the woman carefully, and let her words ring out across the beach. 'But I am charged with founding a new city. One better than that we have left behind us. When one of my men chooses a woman to lie with, I expect that he shall bear a duty towards her, that they will be bonded until death and raise children together, and be fine examples to others in their city.'

She didn't quite know where this decree had come from, but as she spoke the words they felt right. She would build a city secured by the ties of duty, where no one was left behind or made to care for themselves as people in Tyre had been. Families were the foundation of that, she thought. She had known for herself, through joy and through grief, the strength of the marriage bond. But there was something else pulling out these words. A discomfort at the disposability of these women, the light way in which they were given up, as if they were only passing pleasures and not whole people with hearts and histories and futures. She did not like the eagerness of her men, who would happily take these women today and sail away from them tomorrow. Was she not a woman, too? Was she as flimsy to them, or might she become so with only a small tilt of the light? There was little that truly separated her from the line of girls on the beach, only the privilege of her birth and a fragile respect she had nurtured. If she were to succeed as a woman leading men, she had to preserve the dignity of all women.

'So, I make you an offer,' she called out to the women arranged on the shore. 'If one of my men desires to lie with you, I shall pay a dowry for you to be wed. You may come aboard our ships and sail with us to the founding of our new city. You will have as much share of our fortunes as any Tyrian, and enjoy the protection of your husband and of my sovereignty.' She smiled at the brilliance of her idea, so freshly formed. Many of the people brave enough to follow her from Tyre had been young men, without the cares of wives or children, and with a reckless spirit for adventure. They were too many, in truth. She had worried on this fact, knowing that there were no wives for them, and without wives no children. How could such a people last? But now she saw that the gods had all in hand. Here was their providence. 'Accept my offer and join us.'

The women looked uncertain. They turned to one another with sceptical faces, and the most unimpressed among them was Anna's.

'What a strange assumption you have made,' she said loudly. 'That any woman here should be so desperate to leave this shore and her current occupation. Do we look destitute and in need of rescue? We each have a means here to earn our own wealth. What purpose would a husband serve us?'

Elissa rallied. 'I do not demand that you come with me. It is an offer, no more than that. But I shall not allow any of my men to lie with any of you women without committing to the bond of marriage. That is the protection that I offer you.'

Some of the women seemed to soften with interest, but Anna's expression was still hard.

'You call it protection. I call it control. What if a woman should want to join you without such a marriage? Or without any marriage at all? Would you have her then?'

Again, Elissa was pushed back by Anna's words. And she was humbled to feel some drag of truth in them. She was not sure she had ever met a woman who argued as firmly as she did herself.

'I . . . Yes, I would accept her. I will force no woman to enter a marriage if she does not wish to.'

'And how will you protect her, once she is aboard your ships? What if a man should decide to take his pleasure without paying for it? Then she will be without husband or payment.'

Elissa hurtled on, spurred by a boiling need to prove herself. 'Any man accused of rape shall be thrown overboard.'

The words came loudly, and she hoped that their force made them credible. In truth, she was not sure that she could go through with such a threat, but she needed her audience – her own people, and the Cyprian women too – to believe that she would. Elissa's heart was beating uncomfortably, and her mouth was dry.

Anna considered her for a moment, seeming to hold her in appraisal as if she were a piece of cloth at the market. Then she went to speak with the other women.

The Tyrian ships rested in Kition's broad bay for only a few hours, long enough for Elissa's people to gather fresh water and stretch their limbs on the sand. She ordered them to keep their distance from the town, knowing of its trade ties with Tyre. Her instinct told her that there was a danger in making themselves more noted here than necessary.

By the time they were ready to sail again, a dozen of the Cyprian women had decided that they would come aboard the ships. Anna was the only one among them who refused the offer of a dowry.

In those first days, Elissa often felt Anna's eyes upon her. When she was standing beside the rudder, speaking with the captain, or up at the bow of the ship looking out over the waters ahead, she could always sense when the other woman was near. She might have placed her on one of the other boats, but in truth she did not yet know whether she should trust Anna, nor any of the other women they had gathered from the Cyprian beach. And she was aware, too, that she had not yet earned their trust in turn. She had made a promise to protect them, and she was best able to do that if they were within her sight. So she had taken half the newcomers aboard her own ship, and put half under Shapashuru's supervision aboard another.

The price of her caution was that she now felt, even more than she had before, that her worthiness to lead was being scrutinised at every moment. Anna's direct gaze made her self-conscious, as if the woman were waiting for her to prove herself – or, more likely, the opposite. But in the weaker part of her heart, Elissa felt that was what everyone was waiting for, all these people who had followed her across the sea. A man could lead by sheer force of character, or by birthright, or by besting his enemies. A woman might do all this, and yet one mistake could undo her in the hearts of her followers, satisfy their doubts that she had ever truly deserved their faith. It was no great phenomenon for a man to gain a following and hold on to it, but a woman could not afford to falter. She had to be exceptional.

While they were at sea, though, there was little for her to do. She had to trust in her captains, her navigators. Even the boys who climbed the rigging to look out from the top of the mast had more worth than she did. Yet even as Elissa struggled to know her current purpose, she knew she must continue to look like she had one. She remained always on deck, always standing for as many hours as she was able. Always visible, always available. What else could she offer?

Elissa had been long enough at sea that as soon as the weather began to turn, she felt it. It was in the clouds, the subtle darkening of the sky and the water beneath, the wind that whipped a little sharper, the rain that fell so faintly you almost thought you had imagined it. They had sailed through such turns before, but when she looked across at the captain with his sun-leathered hand on the rudder, she could see his concern.

She strode across the deck, feeling the trace of Anna's eyes and many more beside.

'Should we land again on Cyprus?' she asked the captain. They had been following the island's long coast, but had intended to sail onward to a port in Anatolia. 'Or will the weather hold?'

'The wind is already turning against us. We will go on as we can until we reach a bay. If we try to anchor here, we will break upon the rocks.'

Elissa looked towards the land and saw the clear truth of his words. Only unfriendly cliffs and black rocks that revealed their heads as the surf swirled around them. She nodded and turned back towards the wide deck, where anxious faces awaited her.

'All is well. We will make our landing on Cyprus as soon as we can. And until then, we shall ask the gods to hear us. Come, let us pour an offering to the Lord of Storms. Piddaya,' she called, 'please fetch a jar of wine from below.'

They sailed on as the storm swelled around them, rolling the ship's deck and their stomachs with it. Elissa poured out the libations herself, though as much wine was spilled by accident. Those around her were on their knees or crouched low, clinging to rails and ropes where any were available. The crew ran between them, putting their hands to where they were needed, while the captain roared his orders above the wind.

Elissa, crouching too once the libations were done with, did not see the change in the coastline, but she heard the change in the orders. A bay had been spotted, and the men strained to lead the ship towards it. Even then, with land in the imagination if not in sight, every minute seemed to stretch to an age, every toss and howl of the storm made Elissa's gut clench. She understood now why seafarers were such religious men.

All five ships made it to the bay, storm-lashed but undamaged as far as Elissa's inexperienced eye could tell. The people that spilled out of them were shaken and animated, stretching out the tension from their limbs, chattering with relief, laughing as they ran to embrace friends from other boats.

'I have survived much worse,' the captain said, after he had finally left his deck and come to stand beside Elissa on the beach. 'But these people are not sailors. They fear the sea because they do not know its moods. They will hesitate before they go upon the waves again. Pay that some mind.'

Elissa took his words with gravity. She must give her people some time to recover their nerve. The bay was sheltered from the worst of the wind, and the rain was no heavier than a whipped mist. So she set about directing her men to their tasks. Beside places to rest and food to eat, she would have them prepare a smoky fire. Though their supplies would last well enough for the time being, Elissa could not neglect an opportunity to trade for more. The smoke would announce their presence and attract any curious parties who might have farms or flocks hereabouts.

By the time the sun was balancing on the horizon, the only locals who had been drawn to their camp were a small family – a man, his wife and their two children. The man was tall and lean, with a slight hunch about the shoulders that only served to make him appear taller as he loomed over Elissa's unimposing frame. She smiled broadly and greeted him with words of welcome.

'I am Elissa, leader of these people you see. Come, allow your family to sit with us a while. We have lentil stew to share and fine goods to trade. Perhaps your wife would like a new shawl? We have the best cloth from Tyre. Metals, ivories and glass too.' She realised she was beginning to sound like a street seller and slowed herself. 'But here, take a place beside the fire first. And a bowl of stew before the sun is gone.'

Once the family all had bowls in hand, Elissa sat beside the tall man and spoke again. 'Do you live close by? Is there a settlement here?'

'A small one, yes. A few in fact, scattered along this coast. But my house is set apart. I go between the villages here and offer my services, such as they are needed.'

'And what are your services?'

'I am a priest. At Sidon I was a servant to the Lord of Storms, Lord of the Sky, Lord of the North – whatever title your people give him. To me he is Baal, and I serve him still.'

'He whom we call Baal Zaphon.' She nodded. 'You are of Sidon? We share a homeland, then, for our ships sailed from Tyre. How did you come to be on Cyprus?'

If the man was pleased to find fellow Canaanites upon his shore, he did not show it. He sighed and took a spoonful of his lentils, chewing slowly as if he were in no hurry to answer her question. 'Sidon is a great city. Full of ambitious people. And I was one of them for many years, before I realised that I had not enough gold or connections to rise any higher than I already had. The temple of Baal had but one Head Priest, and I could never hope to be him, nor to be content with brushing floors or washing blood from altars, or refilling oil and incense for the rest of my days.' He put down his spoon to scratch at his beard. The hairs were wiry and dark, but Elissa saw threads of silver too. 'I convinced my wife that we could find better prospects elsewhere. And so here we are.' He glanced over at his wife, who said nothing as she turned her eyes down to her bowl.

'And how are your prospects now?' Elissa asked delicately.

'Different than they were.' He gave a closed smile as he chewed another mouthful of lentils, but his eyes were stony in the firelight.

'We should have been glad to know you earlier today,' she said lightly, hoping to flatter the man out of his discontent. 'We were caught in violent winds and making our prayers to Baal without a priest to lead us.'

The man's mouth stopped, and she saw him swallow.

'You have no priest?' He looked across the crowd of Tyrians gathered about the fire. 'So many of you, and no priest among you?'

Elissa felt suddenly as if she were being criticised. She had not known who or how many would choose to join her until they were there waiting in the dark by the ships. And it was true that no priests had joined her – though she knew there were some temple attendants among her followers. She had not given the fact much thought before, but now it felt like such an oversight, a glaring way in which she had failed. As the winds had blown across the deck and tilted the ship like a one-wheeled cart, she had tried desperately to give her people courage, to do as she had seen her husband do a thousand times and invoke powers much greater than her own. It had worked to a degree, but she knew she was no priest. And as much as they might trust her in other ways, her people knew it too.

'You are not merchants,' the man observed, looking again at the people he could see in the fire's light. 'You have families with you. And animals. No, I think you must be colonists. Tyre is seeking to extend herself.'

'Not colonists, no. We have not been sent away by Tyre, but rather . . . Well, we have left of our own will. On our own journey. We are settlers. Though we do not yet know where we will stop our wandering and build our city.'

The man's face had become animated, and he straightened his shoulders. 'A new city cannot live without a priest. Who will sanctify your temple? Who will lead your festivals? And bury your dead? I feel as if the gods have brought your people to my shore. Or brought me to them. A priest without a temple, and a people without a priest. And I a Canaanite as you are.' His eyes were set on her now.

'I do not know your name,' Elissa said, in part to gain some space to think.

'Hashmun.'

It was true that a city needed a priest. And today she had learned that her people needed one, too. In the darkest moments, a priest could offer hope and a precious grain of control over the uncontrollable. As she glanced about the fire, she noticed that some of her people had taken an interest in her conversation with the stranger. None had blamed her for the fearful turn in the weather, or for bringing them across the sea without a priest to protect them. But they might blame her if she turned away an opportunity to recruit a servant of Baal, a man who could appease the Lord of Storms. It could make the difference between persuading them back on to the ships and camping on this sand indefinitely. It could cement her as their trusted leader, or deplete the fragile faith they held in her.

'You would leave Cyprus and sail with us?' she asked. 'We are bound for further lands than this, if the winds will allow it. In truth we do not know where we will found our city, but I would welcome a priest to join us, if that is your meaning.'

To her surprise, Hashmun paused and drew himself back a little. 'To leave this land where I have built a living and a reputation would be no small sacrifice. It would be a risk, certainly, to sail with you to unknown places.'

Strange, Elissa thought, that he should be suddenly so attached to Cyprus, a place which had only seemed bitter to him before. She understood his game as soon as he began to play it.

'I would need assurances,' Hashmun went on, 'for myself and for my family. I would be your Head Priest, I assume? With all the dignity owed to such a position. And my son' – he threw a look to the gangly boy who was wiping stew off his chin – 'he would inherit the priesthood after me. And his children after him.' This was not a question but a demand. Hashmun knew how to leverage her need of a priest to his best gain. And Elissa could already see that this was a game she would not win. She regretted bemoaning the winds that had forced them to shore, but the truth was the truth. Her people needed to feel safe before they would sail again, and Hashmun was just the man to deliver that sense of security.

'Pray to Baal,' she instructed, determined not to let her authority fall below his. 'Ask him to change the winds and make the skies fair for sailing. Prove you have his favour, and you will win the priesthood. For you and your descendants.' That point seemed important to him, so she granted it. Such roles were often passed down within families. But nonetheless, she did feel a resistance within herself, a silent balk at the thought of handing the honour of Head Priest to this stranger, when she would give all the world for it still to belong to her husband.

For several days, the Tyrians slept and ate and prayed on the beach. Hashmun led the rites with a commitment and sincerity that impressed Elissa. He was pious, yes, but he also knew how to bring people together, how to combine the faith of many into something greater. She saw how he calmed fears even by his presence, by his slow resonant words and impressive stature. And she told herself that she could not resent the way her people looked to him. Even a queen could not be all things. She needed others around her who would spread the weight of responsibility.

The winds were slow to change, but no one seemed to mind. The days were mild and the breeze pleasant while they were stood on firm ground. Eventually some of the local herdsmen came to trade, and there was roasted meat each night from the sacrifices. Away from the shore, the land stretched out in swathes of green, and the children would occupy themselves looking for fruits ripe enough to pick. They came back with sticky mouths and baskets full of plump treasures.

On the fourth evening, Elissa sat beside the fire with a full belly and a heart that, for the first time since her final days in Tyre, was beginning to untighten. She believed now that she had done well by her people in recruiting Hashmun, and well by allowing them these easy days upon the shore, and well by keeping their faith for as long as she so far had. Though her mind continued to be pulled back to Tyre and to her husband and to all the evil that had happened, she found those thoughts less agonising than she had before. Perhaps because her new path felt surer. And because, as much as she missed Zakarbaal, and longed so much to speak with him and share all that she was experiencing, she knew also that he would be proud of her. That was a different pain, she thought, blinking away tears, and swallowing her grief in the hope that no one had noted it. But she would not give it up for anything. Only keep it within herself.

'The sky is clearer tonight,' Piddaya said, as she leaned all her weight back on her arms and stared up into the dark. 'I can see so many stars! Maybe the ships will be able to sail tomorrow.'

Elissa did not reply, but looked up for herself. The inky sky was awash with glittering specks of light, and only a few sluggish clouds blocked their view. The moon shone like a pearl.

'Though I was thinking,' Piddaya said more slowly, 'now that we're here and we've got to know the land a little, perhaps we don't have to leave at all. I mean, we can carry on sailing, of course we can. But maybe we don't need to.' She let her quiet words settle for a moment, and Elissa could feel her maid's face turned on her. 'Where will we go that is better than this? There is food here, and good trade, and we are not so very far from our homeland. It just feels . . . I don't know. Familiar. Or at least like we could make it familiar. Everyone has seemed so comfortable these past days.'

Elissa looked at her now and saw the shy hope in her maid's eyes. Compared to the unpredictability of the sea, the groundlessness, the claustrophobia of the narrow decks, remaining here on this shore was a tempting option. It was not the plan that Elissa had imagined for her people, but that plan was still so vague, so difficult to picture with any confidence. Here, they had sand beneath their feet and could step into the same tide that had lately lapped beneath the walls of Tyre. Piddaya was right – there was a comfort in that.

'Is that what the people want?' Elissa asked in a low tone. 'Have they said so? That they would rather stay and build a city here than journey onwards?'

Despite her attempted discretion, the conversation apparently reached the ears of Hashmun. He turned and spoke before Piddaya could answer.

'You would have different risks to contend with, I think, if you chose to remain on Cyprus,' the priest said, leaning towards Elissa's mat. 'I have learned enough of your departure from Tyre to know that you have enemies there. And news travels easily between this island and the coast of Canaan. Your brother will soon know that you are here, if he does not already.'

His words sent a finger of cold down Elissa's spine. They forced her to revisit a fear she had put away: that Pygmalion would try to pursue her across the sea. She had told herself that her caution at Kition had been overmeasured, that if they had sighted no unfriendly ships by now, then none would appear. But it was more wish than sense, perhaps. *Put yourself into the mind of your opponent*, she heard her father say. The manner of her leaving had embarrassed Pygmalion, and that was a dangerous thing.

'My brother may harass us,' she acknowledged, trying the weight of that reality in her mind, testing whether it was enough to sway her. 'Or he may let us be. Or we may travel elsewhere and find new enemies.' Elissa knew these were pointless words, without a certainty among them. But if she had wanted to be certain, she would have stayed in Tyre. In certain fear and certain anger. The world beyond would always be uncertain. And that was what she had chosen, and what all those who followed her had chosen.

'I will think on it,' she said. 'The night is no time for decisions. We will see what the morning sky brings. And perhaps we will consult the gods, too, if our new priest is trained in the ways of reading signs.' She glanced at Hashmun, who bowed his head.

'I know the ways.' He did not acknowledge that she had accepted him as her priest, but she saw from the brief meeting of their eyes that he had noted it.

'Good. Now, my knees are as stiff as old hinges.' She straightened out her legs and flexed her numb feet in the sand. 'I will go for a walk before bed.'

'I'll come with you,' Piddaya offered.

'There's no need. I'm only going to the treeline. Stay and finish your cup.'

She wanted time alone, and Piddaya knew her well enough to understand that. So Elissa walked away from the fire and towards the dark shadows of the trees, shivering a little as the warmth seeped out of her skin. She drew her shawl tight and strode without hurry, looking up at the stars she had been waiting to see while wishing that the clouds had kept them hidden for a few nights more. If the ships could not sail, there was no decision to be made, and she could remain with one foot on the shore and one in the sea. But she knew that the winds had turned, and that she would have to choose whether to follow them.

Though some chatter carried across the sand, Elissa enjoyed the relative quiet of the trees. She stepped between them, relieved in a way to be out of sight, to not have to worry about whose eyes might be on her and what they might see. When she was among her people, she felt the weight of those looks, the weight of her queenship. It was an attention she had sought and paid for most dearly, and which she would never take for granted. But out here in the dark, she could return to being only Elissa, and that had its own value.

As she rounded a dense huddle of trees, she saw a lamp flicker ahead. She tried to turn, but the bearer had already seen her. Of all the people to disturb her moment of solitude, she sighed inwardly that it should be Anna.

'I'll not disturb you,' the woman said, as if reading what Elissa hoped she had hidden from her face.

'No. It is no disturbance,' Elissa muttered awkwardly, stepping further into the light from the lamp. Its brightness gave her an excuse not to look at Anna directly. 'I hope that you have been comfortable since our landing here. And your . . . companions as well. I know you likely imagined we would have travelled further by now.'

'It is true I did not expect to come ashore again on my own island.' She flashed a smile that Elissa caught. 'But that is the way of the waves. There was nothing else to be done. And it seems we shall be able to set sail again soon.' There was the curl of a question that Elissa did not feel she could answer, but she was relieved that the woman seemed content with her decisions. It was strange, really, that she should care so much what Anna thought, given that she barely knew her.

'The winds are changing,' was Elissa's noncommittal response. After a long moment of silence, she said, 'I will let you get back to the camp.'

Anna nodded and moved to slip past her, but stopped abruptly. She pulled Elissa's wrist hard.

'What are you—?'

But as she turned, she saw what the other woman had seen. An aging man, long-haired and lean, with his wiry arm outstretched. At its end, she saw the black point of a knife. He stood a few feet from them, half-obscured by the trees.

'You're her,' he said. There was a waver in his voice that he tried to conceal. 'The princess from Tyre.' Though he addressed Elissa, he glanced between both women. 'I heard about you. Traitorous bitch. And I saw your ships. And I thought, what might that king in Tyre pay to know that you were dead?'

Fear stabbed Elissa's chest. But with it came a surge of anger. After what had happened between her and Pygmalion, how had she come out the traitor? She boiled at that word, and could summon no others while it rang in her brain.

'And you're quite sure, are you, that you have the right woman?' Anna's voice was light, almost melodious. It pulled Elissa from her own self-regarding mind. 'There are two here before you. Will you kill us both to be sure? Do you have that in you, do you think?' She had dropped Elissa's wrist and had her lamp-free hand at her waist instead, toying with her belt as if she were bored by the conversation.

'You don't look the right sort,' the man said scornfully as he glanced over Anna's loose hair and unembellished dress. There was a fragment of doubt in his eyes, though. 'This one's got jewels on her head. Looks like a princess to me. So you just go on your way, why don't you?' He flicked his knife towards the beach. 'Before I decide I'm not so sure after all.'

Anna's feet did not move, but her hand came away from her belt, and Elissa saw that she held her own knife – smaller than the man's, but slender and deadly. 'I think you ought to leave us now,' she said flatly.

The man looked at the blade as if he was deciding whether it was real, and then at Anna as if deciding whether she would have the courage to use it. One or the other must have left him unconvinced, for he turned back to Elissa and lunged.

Two things happened very quickly. Anna threw her lamp at the man, making him flinch backwards. And then the entire scene went dark.

Elissa instinctively dropped to the floor and began to scramble across the stony ground, away from where she had just seen the man standing. Behind her there were grunts and cries, and she realised that some of them belonged to Anna. She turned around but could see so little between the black trees. She crawled back towards the scuffle, reaching out a terrified hand in front of her until it found the loose cloth of Anna's dress. The woman was still. The grunts had stopped. For an awful moment, Elissa thought that Anna might be dead, but then she felt her body shuddering beneath the cloth.

'We must get to the beach,' Elissa whispered with the little breath her fear had left her. 'Come, keep close to me.' She crawled in what she thought was the right direction, though everything had been turned around in the darkness and confusion. She kept one hand clasped on a fold of Anna's dress, and together they made their way to the beach.

In the moonlight, they stopped. Elissa looked for signs that Anna was injured, but aside from a scratch on her face she could see none. Then she looked down at Anna's hand, which still held the knife, which had gripped it even as they crawled. It was covered in blood.

'Are you cut?' Elissa asked.

Seeing her concern, Anna raised her hand and stared at it. 'I think I killed him,' she rasped.

'You had a knife,' Elissa said stupidly. 'Where did you . . . How did you . . . ?'

'I always carry it. I tell all the girls to carry one. But I've never used it. Not until now.' The woman spoke as if she were half in a dream, and yet the fear in her eyes was sharp.

'You saved my life,' Elissa said. 'That man would have killed me.'

They were simple facts, but they seemed to shift something in Anna.

'Yes. He would have killed you.' She nodded slowly and swallowed with some effort. 'I couldn't let him do that.'

Anna still held the knife, as if she could not let it go. Elissa peeled it gently from her fingers and set it down on the sand.

'Thank you, Anna. I owe you my life from today. I hope that I can prove it worth saving.' She wasn't sure that the woman was truly hearing her words, and in the moonlight she saw that she had begun to shiver. Elissa folded herself around her, held her tight and rubbed her bare arms. 'Thank you,' she whispered. 'Thank you. Thank you.'

By morning, the skies were clear and the winds favourable. Elissa did not ask Hashmun to consult the entrails or the smoke or the holy oil. She knew now the best course for her and her people. To found their new city in Tyre's shadow would be a mistake. The further they went, the more opportunity they would have to build their own legacy.

Her people had seen her return to the campfire the night before, with Anna propped up beside her. They knew that something had happened. That she was afraid. But she could not allow them to think that fear was her only reason for dragging them back on to the waves. In time, they would see that this was their proper fate. When Elissa had built them a city they loved, when she had proven that their faith was worth stretching a little further. And when that time came to pass, she hoped that her old enemies would have forgotten her – or that she would have travelled far enough to be out of their reach.

It was the wind that brought them to Libya's unending shore. After Cyprus, they had come to the Anatolian coast, then continued further west through the sea of many islands, and followed the merchant routes beyond until they came to Sicily. They had stopped here and there, to trade or to rest, but always Elissa's people were willing to board again and press further towards the unknown edges of the world. Once Sicily had shrunk from their sight, Elissa worried that they had consigned themselves to the open sea, that they ought to turn back towards the certainty of a coast to follow. But the winds bore them onwards so peacefully, so directly, that it felt as if turning back would be to go against the fortune laid by gods and nature. Even so, the blank horizon made her anxious, and when the first blur of the headland appeared, Elissa was so relieved that she cried out. It felt like the fulfilment of a promise, and as the ships continued on and found the embrace of a wide and sheltered harbour, she had to blink the tears from her eyes.

Why should this shore feel different to those they had passed before? Elissa struggled to find the reason that her heart pulsed so keenly. Perhaps it was the sheer distance they had travelled, the longing to end their time upon the sea. Or the feeling that she had finally put enough water between her and her brother. Perhaps it was the instinctive appeal of the coastline, with a promontory that jutted out boldly into the gulf to remind her of Tyre's little island. Whatever the reason, she stepped from the ship with determination.

Elissa watched as her people spilled from their decks on to the sand, then turned her gaze inland. Beyond the beach, the earth was alive with trees and shrubs. A green land meant they might grow crops, graze animals. She let the sight fill her eyes and felt the promise grow in her heart.

'We have dropped all anchors, my lady.' The captain's voice interrupted her imagination just as it began to carry her away. 'This must be some part of Libya that we have landed in. My ship has never come so far.' His weathered face was more animated than she had seen it in their travels together. She was pleased to see her own excitement reflected. 'I assume you mean to make use of the harbour for a time. For tonight, at least?'

'At least.' She turned to take in more of the wide landscape, but something caught her attention. 'Do you know what tongue they speak in Libya?'

'No, my lady. I can't say that I do.'

'I will try Egyptian, then.'

She had seen the men as they emerged from the thin line of trees. Now they were almost on the beach, with spears held but not raised. Elissa strode towards them with an open expression that needed no translation, crushing her fear as her sandals crunched over the sand.

'Greetings to you,' she said, as confidently as she could in a language in which she was long out of practice. Her father had insisted that she learn Egyptian when she was a girl, but her occasions for conversation since then had been rare. As she summoned the words, it felt as if her mind were grinding coarse flour. 'We are from Tyre, in the land of Canaan. We have sailed here across the sea. I am Elissa, queen of these people.'

An inelegant introduction, but she was relieved to see the men's faces move with understanding.

'Greetings to you, Queen Elissa from Tyre.' The man at the front was well-built, with black hair braided so that it fell in front of his ears. His bare shoulders were dark and smooth, reflecting the sun's lustre as he adjusted his pose. 'I am Iarbas, leader of the Auseans. Do you bring goods to trade?'

She was a little surprised by his directness, but kept her face smooth. It was natural that he should assume they were merchants – many before him had done the same. And it was better than being taken for marauders.

'We have much to trade.' She smiled broadly and gestured towards the anchored ships. 'Our boats are filled with cloth, with metal, with oil and wine. Come, I will show you.' Perhaps it was foolish to advertise so eagerly the precious things they carried, but instinct told her that trade was a route to friendship. And if they needed to secure anything in this unknown place, it was that.

She took a step as if to lead the men on to the beach, but Iarbas raised a hand. 'There is time for trade later. First, you and your people will eat with us.' His face, serious and discerning until now, relaxed into a grin. 'You may bring some wine from your ships, if you like.'

Elissa found that the Tyrians outnumbered their hosts by some margin, and yet somehow enough bread was found for every belly, and dates, too, and creamy white cheese from the large flock of sheep and goats that ranged through the surrounding scrub. Elissa was generous with the wine, and could feel the value of her investment as the two peoples mellowed into one another's company. Many had no common tongue they could call on, but food and smiles were enough to make strangers less strange. As Elissa ate her portion, she found herself impressed by the ease and contentment in which the Libyans seemed to live. If these people could thrive in this land, there was hope that her Tyrians might too.

Once hunger was sated, and while there were still some hours of light in the sky, Elissa ordered her people to bring goods from the ships – those most likely to delight foreign eyes. She could not have been more pleased with the response, and smiled proudly as the Auseans admired their dyed fabrics, their delicate ivories, their shining silver and glass and faience. Exchanges were made, and the Auseans seemed even more well-disposed towards their visitors than they had been before.

'It is rare that we find trade ships passing this shore,' Iarbas said, as he and Elissa sat beneath the shade of his canopy tent. 'Our flocks keep us, and we can gain all we need from the land. But find me a man who does not love beauty and variety.' He caught her with his easy smile, and she returned it.

'Of course. The world holds many beautiful things. And our people have made a reputation by trading them. Even the pharaoh in Egypt does not have craftsmen to outmatch us.' She spoke with pride for Tyre, a world she had left behind, feeling herself walk its streets again, with the smell of the dying vats pinching her nose and the heat from the furnaces sending sweat down her back. There was a sadness beneath the memory, but she chased it away. Had she not brought Tyre's craftsmen with her? The knowledge of creating beautiful things was not lost to them. She only needed a place where they could begin their wonders again.

'You may trade with us as often as your ships can sail. You will always find eager customers here in the summer months, though you may have to find us further along the coast. We go where our flocks lead us – or rather, where their greedy mouths lead them.' There was his smile again, so endearing that Elissa could quite forget they had met mere hours ago.

She laughed with him, but did not let the flash of opportunity escape her.

'We could set up a trading post here,' she said casually. 'That way, you will always be able to find us, should you wish to trade. We'd have our workshops and bring other goods from abroad on our ships.'

'Yes, you could.' Iarbas's face was thoughtful. 'We Auseans would welcome it, I think. And other tribes too may come to trade.'

'But we would need land, of course. If our people were to remain here. Somewhere close to the water. We can trade for whatever area you are willing to grant us, from the goods you have seen today. Would that suit?'

Her words, at first so keen that they spilled from her mouth, trailed to silence. Iarbas was looking at her with bemusement, and she worried suddenly that her Egyptian was not as sure as she had thought. His lips seemed to twist between a smile and a question before he eventually replied.

'Any man in Libya – any woman – is entitled to the land bounded by their oxhide.'

It was Elissa's turn to be confused. When she did not answer, Iarbas pointed to the tent above their heads – a large animal skin stretched between wooden poles.

Elissa nodded as she gathered his meaning, and looked about at the Ausean camp. Every man, every family, lived their life beneath the shade of an oxhide, kept their bed and belongings within its shelter. She turned Iarbas's words in her mind, and ignored the irritating feeling that she had amused him in some way she did not understand.

'I do not have an oxhide.'

'Then I will give you one. No trade necessary,' he added graciously. The smile had dropped from his mouth and he spoke with sincerity. 'Accept it as a gift, from a host to his guest.'

He left her at his tent while he went to procure the spare hide. When he returned, Elissa was on her feet, rocking with anticipation.

'Shall I help you to pitch it?' Iarbas asked.

'No, thank you. I shall take it away from your camp, so that we are not too crowded. My people and I appreciate the hospitality you have granted us. Truly. From today, the Tyrians will count the Auseans as friends.'

Even as she walked from the camp, Elissa could feel her mind folding in ways that might strain her new alliance. Trickery was not a firm bed for growing trust, and yet the cleverness of her idea had already seduced her. It returned her mind to a place that promised satisfaction, that distracted from the fears and sorrows of her recent reality. It was the call of a game she could play and win.

Many of her people were back at the beach, so she went to them there. A group of young men were throwing stones into the sand, cheering as theirs landed close to the target or knocked an opponent's further away.

She approached one man who stood spectating at the edge. 'Your knife. Is it sharp?'

The man took the blade from his belt. 'As sharp as any. You may borrow it, my lady, if you like.' He held it out uncertainly, as a puzzled wrinkle divided his brow.

'No,' she said. 'There is something you might do for me, though. Do you have a steady hand?'

Elissa recruited not only him but also five others from the stone-throwers. Craftsmen and sailors whose fingers were rough and well trained. The light was beginning to leave the sky, so they had to move quickly. She led them to where she had dragged the oxhide, a low hill overlooking the bay where their ships were anchored.

'If you want to serve your queen and secure a home for yourselves and all who have sailed with us, this is what I ask: cut this hide as finely as you can. Turn it into threads so slender that I might weave with them, and I will win you a new Tyre.'

The next morning, when Elissa did not approach the Ausean camp, Iarbas came looking for her. She was waiting for him at the hill where she had set her cutters to work.

'Will you grant me this land?' she asked, as he drew near.

He frowned. 'What land? I thought you understood me yesterday. It is not something to be traded.'

But Elissa barely heard his answer. She was wound tight after a night of anticipation.

'Look,' she said breathlessly. 'It is bounded by an oxhide. Shall that not entitle me to it?' She gestured to the narrow ground that separated them, and his attention followed. Between their feet ran a strip of hide, barely visible among the stones and grass, and at each of its ends was laid another strip, and beyond that another one, stretching away from them in both directions as if it were Libya's longest and least nourished snake.

Iarbas stared at the ground for some time.

'I have surrounded the whole hill,' Elissa declared. 'And a little more besides. And I have not broken from your custom.'

It was a liberty if not a lie, and Elissa felt her self-satisfaction flicker as Iarbas's face remained tilted to the ground. She could not read his expression, and began to feel that her cleverness was misjudged, that it was a risk she should not have taken. She ought not to have played this game with a man she did not know.

A noise came from Iarbas, something like a growl to Elissa's anxious ears. But as it went on, she realised that he was laughing. He finally looked up, but said nothing at all. Only laughed and laughed.

Elissa had thought that Iarbas was laughing with her. It was a relief to see him take her little trick in good humour, to appreciate together the art of her manipulation. It was only later that she realised the heart of the joke had passed her by.

In Tyre, which still felt to Elissa as if it were the measuring stick of the entire world, there was never enough space. Portions of land on that tiny island had been bartered and argued over for as long as she knew. Buildings grew upwards instead of out because that was the only direction open to them. But here in Libya, there was no shortage of land. You could walk for days in any direction and find nothing but pasture and a wide horizon. In this growing light, Elissa saw her oxhide trick as Iarbas must have seen it – striving for every inch she could gain in a place where a mile was worth no more than the shrubs that covered it.

'The land is not mine to sell,' Iarbas said to her later as they sat together beneath his tent once more. 'It belongs to no one, so you may do as you like with it. As long as the Auseans can move our flocks freely, and can trade our goods for yours, then we are happy.'

'If you will not ask a price for the land, then I will pay you a tithe. A measure of the grain we grow each season, if that would appeal to you.' Her delight at securing the land had been flattened not only by Iarbas's laughter, but by the uneasy feeling that she had stolen something valuable. The Auseans might not think it so now, but minds could change and friendship could sour. If her new city grew fat, would her neighbours' generosity turn to envy? Better to link their prosperity to hers.

'If that is what you wish, then I will not reject it.' Iarbas looked at her appraisingly. 'You are a strange woman, I think. You promise me grain you have not even begun to sow. How will you support so many here?' His concern sounded genuine. 'Our people do not sit at one place and wait for seeds to grow. We follow the paths of the seasons, wherever pasture and trade lead us. Perhaps you would fare better by doing the same.'

'You are a wanderer.' Elissa smiled warmly. 'But your way is not mine.'

Iarbas laughed at that, but Elissa did not know why.

'Do you not know the name my people have given you?' he asked her. 'Since you have come to us from so far across the sea? They call you Dido.'

'Dido? What does it mean?'

'Queen Dido, they call you. The one who journeys. The wandering queen.'

The loss of Zakarbaal had soaked into Elissa like paint into fresh plaster. In the year since his death, she and her grief had hardened together, an indelible pattern that could never shift now that it had set. So much else had changed in that time, and so quickly, that she had barely noticed her heart becoming fixed, sealing itself with loss and with love so closely that one feeling was now impossible to separate from the other.

Other things became fixed in that first year, too. Her people, following the custom begun by the Auseans, had come to find pride in calling her Queen Dido. And Elissa had found appeal in it too. Her new name had a peculiar power, she realised. It allowed her to put distance between her public self and the woman who had been bereaved and defeated at Tyre, to screen the fragilities that Elissa had carried – still carried – from eyes that needed so much to see and believe in Dido's strength. She knew, too, that when her people called her Wanderer, they were forging their own identities with hers, making legend of that fearful time when they were upon the sea without a home. Dido was a name that bound them all, a name that served her and those who followed her, but in her private soul she held another title. Her days of wandering were over, but she was now and always would be the Widow Queen.

Their city had grown out of the earth just as their crops did. Every day a new wall was laid, a new house daubed with plaster.

There were difficulties, of course, mistakes and reconsiderations. For all the expertise that the displaced Tyrians possessed, who among them had ever planned a city? In their old home they had improved and repaired, made simple things beautiful or built upon walls that had stood for a hundred years. Here, they broke new ground with every turn of the hoe, and each man earned his citizenship with sweat and blisters.

Even Dido's hands were kept busy. If they did not hold a tool or a rope, then they tapped upon her belt, as her mind reached for solutions to problems they had not even met yet. Always she had to keep ahead, leading the way. A hundred lives or more were pinned to hers, and she would preserve them to the very limit of her ability.

They had spent their first months with the Auseans as intermittent neighbours, as the tribe moved its flocks around the wide region of the coast. It had been a reassurance in some way, to have this reminder that a people could survive here in this new world. But it had also made Dido self-conscious, to have another group of eyes waiting to scrutinise her progress. The Auseans were not her people, so why should she need so badly to prove herself? Perhaps because Iarbas had doubted her, because, even as the first building began to rise and the first crops began to push out of the soil, she had caught him looking at her sometimes, with an expression somewhere between concern and surprise. It was the surprise that she chased, the recognition that a woman might achieve as much as a man, or more. That she might be her father's true successor after all.

After a winter journeying south to Lake Triton, the Auseans had returned to settle their camp beside the city again. Their sheep came filled with lambs, and their mouths with stories from inland. As soon as the tribesmen were spotted, the Tyrians put down their work and set out to greet them, and Dido was first among them.

'The winter has suited you well,' she said when Iarbas was close enough to hear her. He smiled at that, but she could already see his eyes on the city behind her. She felt her satisfaction swell as he drank it in.

'And you, too. Can this be the same place we left? You Canaanites build faster than a spider spins its web.'

They held a feast that night, to knit themselves back together with friends who had been long away. Beneath a clear sky, the Auseans displayed their antelope hides and ostrich feathers – trophies of their travels – while the Tyrians poured out beer and sang songs that made Dido blush. She was glad at least that Iarbas could not understand them, especially when he sat so close beside her. She found herself praying that he would not ask her to translate.

'And what have you called this city of yours?' he enquired, as the flute players struck up a new melody. 'It must have a name. What place shall I speak of, when I am asked where I gained my sash?' He played with the tasselled end that hung from his waist. It was the first thing he had bartered from her.

'I have not named it. We only call it Carthage.'

'And what does that mean?'

'The New City.'

She did not explain its true meaning, the one she felt when she spoke it, and that she knew her people felt too. It was their New Tyre.

'It is as good a name as any. *Carthage.*' He seemed to be tasting the word on his tongue, and nodded his head slowly. 'Perhaps it needs no other.'

Dido found herself smiling, and not from politeness. Iarbas's opinion had come to mean a great deal.

'Your city is your testament, Queen Dido,' he said, leaning closer so that he did not have to shout above the music. 'She is as impressive as you are.'

Dido let the words hang without reply. They warmed the deepest part of her, and she was content to sit in that feeling.

'Will you walk with me?' Iarbas asked eventually. 'I have had enough of beer and songs this evening.'

Dido did not need convincing. The noise was beginning to rattle her head, and she rose from the mat so quickly that she had to steady herself. Iarbas offered his arm and she took it gladly. A brief thought crossed her mind that she ought to have someone accompany them, but that was a rule for maids and wives. Not for a queen, and not for Dido the widow. So she walked freely, comfortable in the knowledge that she had never once doubted Iarbas as an honourable man.

They did not hurry in any direction, but meandered their steps towards the shadows of the city, then veered away to see what light the moon cast across the sea. Everything felt beautiful, even though she could barely see her feet beneath her. There was a sheen of contentedness over every silhouetted tree.

'Perhaps you know why I wanted to speak with you alone,' Iarbas said softly as they came towards a cliff edge.

Dido felt her limbs seize, and suddenly Iarbas's arm felt as if it were locked around hers. She freed herself awkwardly.

'Dido? Elissa?'

The way he spoke her name only confirmed her fear. Noble Iarbas, whose tongue was always prone to lightness, was speaking with the tenderness of a lover. Her own voice felt so shrivelled that she could not get a word out.

'I have been waiting all winter to speak with you again, and to make my proposal. I knew even as I set out for the lake that I could never find another woman I so admired. And I do not know how we will come together, or what it may mean for our peoples, but tonight has given me hope for that. What matters is whether you can accept me as your husband.'

His face was only half-revealed to her in the moonlight, but what she saw of it held a patient hope, and an earnestness that made her quiver.

'I cannot,' she managed to say.

'You cannot accept me?'

'I cannot marry. I cannot take you as my husband, nor any man. I'm sorry.' She choked on the last word, and stepped away so that she could take a great breath into her lungs. Her chest was tight, squeezing her from the inside. It was as if the hammer blow of Zakarbaal's death had struck her again, and dislodged her grief from the quiet place in which she had sealed it. She wished that she had seen this possibility before it came, that she had known how to prepare herself. Now Iarbas's proposal hit her with full force, and she could only say what felt most true and sure. She could not marry again. She realised that she had already made that promise with herself, in the time that had passed since her husband's death. Perhaps on the very day she knew he was gone. Her heart had belonged to Zakarbaal, and it had gone with him to wherever his spirit rested. So how could she give it to another? But it was more than fidelity that pinned her chest. It was dread fear. That if she gave her love again, she might lose it again. Love and loss – for Dido, one was chained with the other. And she could not feel that way a second time. She could not take another husband that she would one day have to mourn. In that moment, marriage to Iarbas – a good man, a man she could surely love – felt as if it were a greater risk than throwing herself from the cliff.

'Elissa?' He did not sound hurt but afraid, and his hand touched her shoulder. It should have steadied her, but she only felt her legs crumple. 'Come. Sit down.'

They sank on to the stony ground together.

'I'm sorry,' she said again. 'I cannot do it. I wish that you had not admired me. Or that you could admire me only as a friend, or as a leader. As I admire you.'

'I do. I do admire you, Elissa, in all those ways. That is why I know we would make a good match.'

'Please don't. Don't call me by that name. I am Dido now. I cannot return to the past and be the girl that I was. I wish that you had known her, but you met me as a widow. And I can be nothing else now.'

He took a moment to absorb those words. 'There is no shame in loving again.' He leaned towards her, but she only shrank away. 'I do not know the ways of Canaan, but in Libya a widow is not something to be shut away. There is a tribe I know, south of Triton, who honour their women with a band around the ankle for each time they are married. They wear them with pride, for the more bands they wear, the more loved they have been.'

'It is not shame that prevents me, Iarbas.' She could feel tears stinging in her eyes, and felt embarrassed that he might hear them in her voice.

'You still grieve for your husband.' His face flattened with acceptance, and that gave Dido some relief. 'I understand. I have asked too soon.'

'No. Time will not change things,' she said firmly. 'My grief will not end. And I will never marry. That is the truth, as plainly as I can tell it. Please do not go away from me with hope I cannot fulfil.'

She could feel his eyes searching hers, perhaps looking for a truth he preferred. But she looked back at him fiercely, pleading with him in the scant silver light to understand what she was telling him, to not think her cruel or unfeeling or superior. This was the most honest self that she had ever shown him, and she needed him to see it. She was afraid, yes, but not only for her heart. Dido knew the delicate balance of what she had created for herself here in Carthage, and the price she had paid for her tender grip on power. She would reverse that trade in an instant if it would return Zakarbaal to her. But Iarbas was not Zakarbaal, and no other man could be. For her to take a husband would be to risk everything she had gained, to share or even to lose her power as queen. And in some way, that was its own betrayal. Though she did not speak this other fear aloud, she let it fix her resolve as she stared into Iarbas's black eyes. For some time, there was only the whisper of leaves between them.

'It is not for me to argue with your heart. I have heard what you have said.'

'And you accept it?' Even now, she was not sure he believed her.

'What else can I do?' His expression was sad – an emotion Dido had rarely seen on him. But in a moment it had blown away, and he smiled softly. 'Shall we go back to the feast?'

As soon as they had returned to their mats and the competing songs of the Carthaginians and the Auseans, Dido felt a hundred eyes upon her. Speculation, imagined or real, buzzed in her ears until they grew hot. She was sure that each person could see Iarbas's disappointment, her own discomfort, even as they hid their feelings with good humour. Had her people already guessed the nature of the conversation that had passed? Would the mouths of the city be full of it tomorrow?

She hated that thought, but realised that the marriageable status of Carthage's queen would always be fertile ground for gossip. With dread, she imagined that curious talk spreading abroad, imagined it drawing other men – curious, ambitious, power-hungry men – who would bring their proposals just like Iarbas. Not every man would understand her rejection as graciously as he had. Her chest began to tighten once more as the vision spread out before her. She saw herself having to defend her widowhood again and again, to explain to unfeeling ears that her heart was closed, that it could not be reopened by gifts or sweet words or political advantage.

She picked up her cup with a shaking hand, and drank until she had found her solution. Tomorrow, she would address her court. She would inform her advisors of her decision never to remarry. She would make a vow to herself and to her husband, with the court as witness, so that they understood her seriousness. She would swear her fidelity to Zakarbaal – because she owed that to him, because in her heart he already had it, and because she knew that a promise to a man, even a dead one, would mean more to other men than any promise she might make to herself. And within days, her small city would know her intention. They would no longer have cause to speculate each time she allowed a man to share her company. In time, the news would spread more widely, and save her the disturbance of suitors.

Already, Dido felt safer. By this decision, long settled in her own mind but now solidifying into something the world would see and respect, she could shrink the boundaries of her life. Not to limit, but to preserve herself. She would remain Dido the queen, Dido the widow, and her heart would have firm edges to hold it, to stop it spilling out in ways that had become terrifying to her in her grief. Now, always and forever, she would be wife of Zakarbaal and mother of Carthage.

Chapter 30

CARTHAGE

Dido reminded herself of what Anna had said about loving lightly, but as she lay with her limbs curled against Aeneas, it seemed impossible. It was as good as telling a starving man not to enjoy his food too well. Now that she had opened herself to the feeling, it was as if there were a great cataract inside her – one which she had no hope nor desire to stop. She let herself drown in it, breathed it happily into her lungs.

They had stayed in the cave all night, trapped first by the storm, and then by the darkness, but above all by the closeness they had found in one another. Beneath his cloak and her shawl they had twined their bodies, pressing skin against skin with no place for the cold to enter. Now the sun had risen, but Dido could not bear to peel herself away, either from the warmth of their improvised bed or from the intimacy of the cave. The world outside was so wide and so complicated. She wished that it could go on without them, at least for a while longer. But even through the haze of love, Dido's thoughts found their way to Carthage and to her people, imagining their worry for their lost queen. And though she resented that her mind could not allow her to be selfish even for this one day, she felt guilty.

'We should get back to the city,' she said with a cracked voice. She pushed herself up before her will could leave her and began to re-pin her dress. As she raised her hands to her disarranged hair, she felt a jolt in her chest. Her fillet was missing. She twisted about, looking for it on the cave floor. As the squeeze in her chest became uncomfortable, Aeneas produced the slip of red cloth from somewhere beneath him.

She snatched it a little too quickly, and, realising it, smiled generously in compensation. 'Thank you.' But her eyes were straight back on the fillet, as she smoothed it between her fingers.

'A gift from Zakarbaal?' It was barely a question. When Dido looked up, there was sympathy in Aeneas's eyes. 'I had guessed as much. Why else should a queen so wealthy wear a fillet with tattered ends and one ruby missing? I mean no offence, of course,' he added quickly, reaching to take her hands even as they held the precious cloth. 'When we met, I gifted you a diadem you would never wear. But I know the reason now. Because I know you.'

He regarded her gently, as if she were suddenly made of glass. There was understanding and acceptance in his look, and she knew she did not need to explain anything further.

'I thought I had lost it for a moment.' Though she smiled again, her chest was knotted, and she tried to push the feeling away.

The walk back to the city took less time than Dido expected, and less than she would have liked. The forest was still and peaceful, with birds chattering between the branches, and the puddles of last night's rain dazzling in the morning light. Sunshine was never more beautiful than after a storm.

She and Aeneas spoke easily, laughed freely. Everything was smoother between them now. Dido felt herself springing with new energy, but when they came to the city boundary, she regretted that she had let herself be carried along so quickly. She regretted, too, that she had not stopped to kiss Aeneas again while they were still in the shelter of the woods. Here, with her own buildings looming towards her, she felt strangely exposed. And as they continued walking, she saw people appear from their houses or workshops, faces turning in their direction, voices shouting in relief that the queen had returned.

She tried to smile at those she saw, but her cheeks hovered uncertainly. She could see them taking in her arrival and the companion beside her, their eyes passing over the two of them in scrutiny. Was it judgement that she felt from them? Or merely intrigue? Neither felt comfortable, and she wished that she had a mirror to view herself. Had her uncombed hair betrayed her? Did her crumpled dress tell secrets she would rather keep? No one but she and Aeneas could know what had happened in the cave – her rational mind knew that – but truth and knowledge were not really what mattered, after all.

It was opinion and rumour that she feared, that she could already feel sprouting in the minds of her citizens. She cursed herself for not imagining how things would look, for not thinking up some clever way to avoid this awkward parade into the city. So much that had happened since yesterday's storm had not been planned, not sagely weighed or decided. She had allowed herself to be carried by feeling, to live and love more freely than she had dared to in a decade. It had been easier to take each step while she was not looking at the path ahead. And she could not say that she regretted any she had taken. But the city was not the forest. She could not trail blindly, or hide away in a cave outside the world. Here she was Queen Dido once more, and she needed to take control.

As she stepped through the boundary gate with Aeneas beside her, Dido resolved to fix a confident smile. She passed it around to all who watched her, and at the same time reached out to take Aeneas's hand. He did not resist, but let his fingers settle firmly around hers. She felt her chest warm, and her smile became more natural. She might not have planned such a thing, but it felt so right that she could almost convince herself she had – and that was enough to convince her people. She knew now that in their eyes – and in her own heart – Aeneas had become her husband.

Dido had got ahead of rumour, but that did not mean that no whispers reached her ears. Whether directly in her crowded hall or in low tones from Anna, she heard what people were saying. The Widow Queen had finally been wooed. She and the prince had gone out for the hunt, and he had brought her back as his prize.

These whispers irritated Dido more than she would show. Her own people spoke as if she were no more than a slender doe. The two of them had gone into the woods together, so why should Aeneas be the catcher and she the thing to be caught? In the cave, they had met as equals, each drawn towards the other. But that was not the story that delighted tongues and ears. She was vexed that words passed about so carelessly could sour her new happiness, but she could not remove them from her thoughts. In the meeting of two hearts and bodies, why should a man be treated as if he has won something, and a woman as if she has given something up?

She sat in her hall with Aeneas in the chair beside her, with Ascanius on her knee, with the spoils of the hunt – such as had been claimed before the coming of the storm – roasted and laid on silver plates before them, and wished she could enjoy the blessing of that moment. She thought of Zakarbaal, of a conversation years ago, and knew that it was her drive to win that made her so discomfited. The whispers of the hall scratched at her pride, but she reminded herself of what her husband had said to her then. Love was a victory. Happiness was a victory, even when quiet and private. And whatever people thought or said, she could hold on to that.

Was it strange that she should use a memory of her first husband to smooth her feelings now? Since she had awoken in the cave, with Aeneas's warmth at her back, her chest had seemed to snag each time she thought of Zakarbaal. He was still there within her, not pushed out by the flood of all she had felt this past day. There was not a deluge in the world that could displace him. But she no longer knew what she should owe to him. She had broken a vow he had never asked her to make. Would he curse her for that? Blame her because her heart had mended and changed over ten long years? Because she no longer needed the protective limits she had prescribed for herself, not as she had when his loss was all she could feel? No. The man she had loved would not haunt her for taking happiness into her hands. His spirit would not poison her dreams with guilt. To be so vindictive in death, he would have needed some seed of it in life.

As Dido reasoned these things to herself, she felt the knot in her chest loosen. Since taking her seat in the hall – at this celebration of the hunt that had brought her and Aeneas to one another, this wedding feast that was never called such – she had been expecting some voice to rise up from the benches and ask if her vow was forgotten. But no voice had come. And perhaps that was as it should be. Who had she betrayed, if not herself and not Zakarbaal? If she had broken anything, it was only an idea of her own creation: the Widow Queen. When Dido had made her vow, her people had not objected. Even though her refusal to marry made their city's future fragile, by denying it the security of blood heirs. She had felt her people's trust then. And they did not object now, as she led them upon a new path. For all their whispers, their gossip and their jests, they had never questioned her course. And she loved them for that. She had redefined herself before – at Tyre, at sea, here in Libya. And she was free to do so again. Who had any right to stop her?

It felt to Dido as if the palace had become a timeless place. She could not say what the hour was, how lately the sun had risen or set, whether this was the third or fourth or fifth night since she had opened herself to Aeneas. They spent much time in her chamber that was now theirs. She could not tire of his warmth, or the feel of his skin, or the weight of his limbs overlapping with hers. It had been so many years since she had known that comfort, so long that she had been able to convince herself she didn't need or want it. She had told herself that it would not feel the same with anyone but Zakarbaal, that she would rather have none of that joy than a poor and torturous shadow of what she had lost. But Aeneas was not a shade. He was so real and so necessary that she ached to touch him, to be with him and to know that his greatest desire was to be with her.

'We ought to eat.' Dido sighed and kissed the tender skin on the underside of Aeneas's forearm.

He smiled at the graze of her lips and opened his eyes. 'We should check on Ascanius first.'

'Or bring him to the hall, and we shall all eat together.' Dido pulled herself from the warm bed and tied her dress with a sash. She reached for her ivory comb and began to run it through her hair, smiling as the fine teeth snagged. Each tangle felt like a record of love enjoyed. Only when every knot had been worked smooth did she replace her fillet.

Aeneas was putting on his sandals when there came a gentle tap at the door. Dido crossed the chamber to open it.

'I'm sorry to disturb you, Mistress. But he's got himself in such a state, and he just kept asking for you.'

Ascanius's plump face was red and wet with tears. Dido's look of sympathy was enough to make him cry out, and he rushed forward to bury himself in her skirt.

'No need to apologise.' She smiled to reassure the nurse. She could tell the girl was still nervous around her, having only come to work at the palace these past days. She was a niece of Piddaya's husband, and well-experienced despite her young years. 'We were just coming to find you,' she said brightly, putting a hand on Ascanius's head. 'Weren't we?' She turned to Aeneas, who had appeared beside her.

He knelt down to peel Ascanius away from Dido's dress and take him into his own arms. 'Time for some food,' he growled softly, tickling his son around the ribs. 'I'm so hungry I think I could eat a whole bull.'

'No, you couldn't.' Ascanius giggled, his little body squirming.

'At least half of one. And you can have the other half.'

By now the tears had vanished from Ascanius's eyes as if they'd never been there.

The hall was mostly empty when they entered, but the faces that looked up from their cups seemed pleased to see them. Dido saw one or two eyebrows raised and tried not to imagine the comments that might be whispered out of earshot. Her union with Aeneas was still the court's latest and most unavoidable gossip, but it would soon become no more than an unremarkable fact.

They ate a simple meal of fresh bread and dried fruits, but each bite seemed delicious to Dido, and she savoured the flavours on her tongue. Ascanius chattered away about the places his nurse had taken him that day, and about how she had promised to take him to see the ships come and go from the harbour. He loved the swirling of the water as they dropped and raised their anchors, Dido knew, and the excitement of seeing what would be carried across the gangplank. Despite his earlier upset, he seemed generally content, and that was a relief to her. She would hate for him to feel as if she had taken his father away from him. No, all three of them belonged to one another now.

As she dipped the last piece of bread in her wine, she saw the shipmaster rise from his bench and approach their table.

'It is a pleasure to see you looking so well, my queen.' He turned and bowed his head toward Aeneas too before going on. 'I'm sorry to disturb your meal, but I have news to report. We finished our repairs on the Trojan ship this morning. Her hull is strong and ready, should she need to sail.' His voice trailed off a little, and his eyes glanced from one face to another. 'I thought that you would want to know.'

'Yes,' Dido stuttered. 'Yes, I do. Thank you.' She inclined her head graciously, and the shipmaster backed away towards his companions.

Dido sat stiffly, her hand hovering while the soaked piece of bread turned her fingertips purple. Her thoughts raced but her tongue was glued to her teeth. Somehow, the ship had ceased to exist in her mind until this moment, as if it had dissolved when Aeneas's lips met hers. Suddenly she was so conscious of him sitting beside her, of his silence, which hung as heavily as hers. Had he understood the shipmaster? Aeneas's Canaanite had improved in his time at Carthage, but when they were alone, they often still spoke in Akkadian. She swallowed away the dryness in her throat.

'Winter is a bad season for sailing.' He spoke before she could. 'I am grateful to your shipwrights, of course. But I shall

254

let the ship rest in your harbour. If you can accommodate her.' His fingers pried at a fig, but he did not eat any of it.

'Yes. Winter is a bad season for sailing.' She nodded sedately, but felt her chest flush with relief. The understanding that she had assumed between them took a truer form with these few words. It felt solid now, something she could trust. If any part of her had still been holding on to Anna's advice, to the self-protection of loving lightly, this was permission to let go. Aeneas was staying. He loved her enough for that, and she loved him enough to drop her heart into his hands.

Chapter 31

CARTHAGE

Dido wondered whether she had found every scar on Aeneas's body. She did not count them, but they were many. Some she could not fail to notice, like the one on his hip – a wide and jagged tear, dark and mottled where the skin had knitted over with time. She knew that the injury pained him still, that the cold of winter made the joint stiff, that he walked with a limp that was only perceptible once you knew to look for it.

Other scars were less obvious, delicate nicks or dimples that she found as she ran her fingers over him. Each one held a story. Sometimes Aeneas would tell her a detail from the war, a moment that had marked him, but she never pressed for them. She knew that it was their pain, in part, that had drawn them to one another, but she did not want their love to be defined by it. They were more to each other than two wounded creatures.

Dido lay, staring at the ceiling of her chamber, listening to Aeneas's steady breaths beside her.

'Tell me about the palace at Troy,' she said. 'Was it like this one?' She knew that she was skirting dangerous territory, but he answered her lightly.

'It was larger. And older.' He rolled over on to his side and she mirrored him, admiring the graceful way his hair fell to frame his face. 'We lived on the highest level of the citadel. From my window, I could see the city spread out below, and the wide coast and the shining sea.' He smiled with the memory. 'Troy had stood for hundreds of years by the time I was born. We told the stories of our ancestors by the hearthside, and my kin numbered so many that we could not all be seated in the hall at once.' His eyes dimmed a little before he went on. 'The palace was a sprawl, but beautiful. Courtyards and kitchens and shrines, chambers built upon chambers so that there was a place for everyone. King Priam had many sons, you see. Each time one of them married, I thought I might lose the precious space I had been granted.'

She frowned in surprise. 'But you were a prince.'

'A prince, yes. But not of the royal line – or, at least, very far down it. My father was cousin to Priam. I was never destined to accede to the throne, and Priam did not let me forget it.'

Dido heard the creep of bitterness and looked at him quizzically.

'Oh, he treated me well enough, but only as far as kinship required. And he was happy for me to lead his men on to the battlefield. Yes, I proved my place when war came to Troy. I was second only to my cousin Hector when spears needed to be raised and men's hearts threatened to give way. But even in those years, the king never paid me true respect. Perhaps he was ashamed to see me prove my worth when his own son had brought ruin to our people.'

Dido knew that part of the story – she could hardly have failed to hear it from the surviving Trojans. A prince of Troy had gone abroad and brought back another man's wife. And how many had suffered for that one act?

'The line of Priam is destroyed.' Aeneas's voice was sombre, but there was another edge to it, something he was holding back. Dido wondered if it were satisfaction, but she knew that his heart was not cold enough for that. Perhaps it was only recognition of the strange and twisting nature of fate. 'My blood, Ascanius's blood, is the only royal line that the Trojans have now. I carried that knowledge with me when we left our city, and . . . I hardly dare say this. You may think me awful and selfish. But I think that it drove me on. It helped me to survive my grief, to be the strength my people needed. To know that there was no one before me now, no one to look down on me and no one to heed but myself. To know that I could build a new city, a new Troy, and serve it as its king.'

Dido watched his face and could almost see that vision living inside him. Even as he hesitated to speak it, he was lifted by it. She did not think him awful. Had she not harboured selfish desires? But nonetheless, a part of her was shaken by what he had said. Her destiny to build and to rule, to gain more than others would grant her and prove she was worthy of it, had come to pass. Aeneas's had been lost at sea.

She smiled to assure them both. 'And you have found Carthage instead.'

Perhaps it was not the right thing to say. She looked into his eyes but could read little from them.

'I have found Carthage instead.'

'It is close to noon, I think,' Dido said briskly, breaking from Aeneas's gaze to look at the window. 'I should go to the hall. My people will think I have forgotten them.'

Dido knew she had been neglecting the matters of the city, that the throne she had worked so hard for had sat empty while she indulged desire over duty. But had ten years' service not earned her a few days of unburdened happiness? She told herself that it had, that her people would agree. Now she must return to their sight and give them her ears again.

'I shall see you at dinner, then.' Aeneas was lying on his back, his voice as flat as he was.

Dido hesitated. 'Come with me. To the hall.'

'You have business to attend to. Carthage needs its queen. She has no need of me.'

'Are you so certain?' She extended a hand to brush his cheek, but he did not turn his head. 'The Trojans follow you. They trust you. And you know what they need. You are as much a leader as I am. Come and take your place beside me. I would value your guidance.'

The last part was a lie, perhaps. Had she not spent a decade ruling alone? She needed no one to guide her thoughts or her judgements, beside what she already gained from her advisors. But she knew that Aeneas needed to feel like more than her pet. He needed purpose.

'Alright,' he agreed.

It was only when Dido entered the hall and felt a queue of faces turn upon the two of them that she fully realised what her invitation to Aeneas meant – or, perhaps more importantly, how it would appear. She had given him more than herself now. She had given him a portion of her power, a slice of the city she had built. Perhaps that had been inevitable; perhaps the people had been expecting it since they first saw her pass through the gates with her hand in his. But the murmurs that buzzed through the hall made her feel as if a new threshold had been crossed, and new opinions kicked up like dust.

Dido veiled her self-consciousness and swept towards her throne with a smile, taking her seat with grace and nodding as cups of weak barley beer were brought for her and Aeneas. Her face felt warm as she realised how many stood waiting to speak with her. Had they been coming to the hall each day, only to leave in disappointment? Or resentment? She could not allow these thoughts to cloud her head. She was here now, and she would remain until everyone had been heard.

She had to stop herself from sighing, however, when she saw that the first in the queue was her Head Priest. He could be trying at the best of times.

'Lord Hashmun.' She invited him forward with her eyes. 'You have something you wish to discuss?'

The priest approached the throne, with his head half-bowed. Since their first meeting on the shore of Cyprus, his hair had turned from black streaked with grey to quite the inverse. This, and the way that he leaned on his priest's staff, made him look more venerable than his years might warrant.

'Queen Dido,' he said without hurry. 'And how am I to address the one beside you?'

'He is Prince Aeneas, as you surely know. He has been at Carthage more than a month now.'

'Prince? Or should I call him King?'

She tensed at that. Perhaps it was natural that the husband of a queen should be a king. But there was a danger in the word, a fear that her own title might be outranked by it. It was a wrinkle that had not occurred to her before this moment, and she hastened to smooth it.

'He is Prince Aeneas, still.' Dido turned to Aeneas, and thought she saw a hardness in his brow. But he nodded. 'Surely you did not seek my audience to discuss such a small thing as this, Lord Hashmun? Come, be brief for there are others waiting.'

The priest ruffled at that, but made her wait on his pause. 'The Feast of Ashtart is close upon us, and I thought that our queen might have concern for its preparations.'

'Indeed, I do. Have I not already given allocations for the sacrifices? You may take ten rams from the royal flock. Those with the whitest fleeces and the strongest limbs, such as will please the Lady of the Chariot.'

'And the musicians? The dancers?'

'The same who performed for Baal, only two moons past. These are matters for the temple, Hashmun.' She lowered her voice, in part to hide her frustration.

But his only grew louder. 'And shall we expect you at the feast? Will we hear your prayers spoken over the smoking altars? We have not welcomed you at the temple of late.'

Dido's blood was hot now. *It has been a week*, she wanted to scream. A single week in which she had trusted the city to its own management, and yet Hashmun spoke as if her throne were layered with dust, as if the people should barely remember her name. She knew that his empty questions were not for her ears, but for the crowd that waited behind him. Dido could see no better remedy than to let them hear her voice instead.

'Carthage will honour the goddess with pleasing gifts and song,' she said, her words echoing through the hall. 'I will join with every citizen in calling the Mighty One to our protection, and raise my voice as piously as I ever have. You can be sure of that.' She let her gaze return directly to Hashmun, and it seemed he had run out of questions to ask. He stepped away without a bow, and Dido tried to cool herself. She had known the priest's nature when she'd first encountered him – or the seeds of it, at least. Ambitious and grasping, but competent and charismatic enough that his usefulness had outweighed any misgivings. Over the years, she had thought again on her decision – the first time, when they had argued so fiercely about the dedication of the temple – but it was a dangerous thing to disrobe a man who had proven his favour with the gods. So Hashmun had sat for ten years like a well-bedded thorn in her flesh. But what was one thorn to a queen?

As the next citizen approached, Dido pressed herself into her throne.

'My lady. I hoped we could discuss the repairs to the west wall . . . '

As each report or concern was laid out to her, Dido listened with her usual attentiveness, asked diligent questions, gave her solutions. There were no catastrophes to face, no petitions that she had not heard some version of before. So why did it feel that something had changed since her return from the hunt? Yes, Aeneas sat beside her. She looked to him from time to time, invited his contribution, translated the details he did not understand. It would be an insult to make him sit there without acknowledgement. And the petitioners looked at him too. Some, mostly Trojans, addressed him directly, while others let their eyes flit back and forth. Most spoke only to Dido. But even these petitioners seemed to approach her differently, to ask their questions more doubtfully. Had her abrasiveness towards Hashmun unsettled them? No, there was something more subtle happening in the hall. Something she could not put her hand upon until she was lying in her bed that night.

She somehow felt as if she had been thrown back into the past, to a time before the trust of her people was given as granted. They had doubted her then because she had not yet proven herself. And because their new leader came in that most unlikely and untested form, lacking the unearned assumptions of precedent. In short, because she was a woman.

But what had begun as a barrier had become a strength. Without a husband or children, she lacked the frames that ought to define her, the identities that might rival that of devoted queen. Her chastity made her immutable, dependable. And as the years passed, it almost seemed that her people had forgotten she was a woman at all. Neither did they see her as a man. Instead she could fill out a new shape in their minds, without mould or boundary. She was exactly as they needed her to be.

Now her love for Aeneas had frayed that illusion. It had exposed her womanhood, and reminded them that she was made for more than politics, that she could desire and be desired. She had felt it in the hall, even if her people did not know it themselves. They regarded her differently now. In their eyes, she had become vulnerable, flawed, corruptible. No longer just their queen, but something more and something less.

She had become human.

Chapter 32

CARTHAGE

It seemed to Dido as if that winter were the shortest of her life. Weeks and months spilled by as she and Aeneas and Ascanius stitched themselves into one another's lives. There was barely an hour that she did not spend with one of them, and the warmest moments were when all three could enjoy time together. They walked along the beach or visited the hounds in the kennel. They watched sunsets and gazed at constellations, or simply followed Ascanius as he trundled his wooden goat around the palace courtyards.

Fatherhood glowed in Aeneas like the hearth in a home. It brought out his best nature, made him soft and light – so much that Dido struggled to imagine the warrior she knew he had been. These hands that raised Ascanius into the air and tickled his ribs until he squealed were surely not made for violence. That self was behind Aeneas now, and the way was clear for any future he should desire. Dido had made that possible. She had given him a home and taken away his cares. His people were safe. His heart was unburdened. The future, their future together, was so open and hopeful that it was almost frightening in its potential. More than once, Dido had found herself imagining the father that Aeneas might be if he could have more children. Had he thought the same? If he had, he had never shared it.

Dido did not ask the gods to give her a child. She had made those prayers many years ago, when her love for

Zakarbaal swelled so high that she longed for another vessel to pour herself into. And she had stopped making those prayers when their denial became too painful. Now, a decade and more later and at the other end of the world, they had been answered. Ascanius was not a child of her body, but her love for him was so natural that she was sure this was how mothers felt. It seemed as if they had been meant to find one another, she a woman without a child and he a child without a mother. His arrival at Carthage had been as much a gift as the arrival of his father, and now Dido's life had a completeness which she had long given up hope of finding. Before Aeneas, before Ascanius, she had made herself feel full by shrinking to fit the space her grief had left for her. Now she felt herself extending, expanding, with every day that passed that winter.

Aeneas continued to sit beside her in the hall, and to listen each day as the petitions were brought. He was different there, with none of the glow that she loved in him. Ruling was a serious business, of course, but he seemed to endure those hours, to wear his care more heavily than needed. The freedom of his tongue disappeared, as if he were afraid to speak his mind, or to speak it and be ignored. And perhaps there was some truth to that fear. Their co-ruling had not been tested by disagreement, but if it were, she knew that her words would have more power with her people. How could it be any different?

Spring came around so quickly that Dido was taken by surprise on the day that Iarbas appeared in her hall. His face gave her a jolted feeling, as if she had tripped, and she grasped the wooden arms of her throne.

'Lord Iarbas.' Why did her voice sound so frail? She cleared her throat. 'You have returned from Lake Triton.'

'I have. Were you not expecting me to?' He gave a hint of a smile, but his attention was preoccupied with the scene before him. She could see his expression shift in confusion, and Dido felt herself grow hot as if he had discovered a secret.

'Was your winter prosperous?'

He did not seem to hear her question. 'Who is this?'

Iarbas's eyes were on Aeneas. He could mean no one else. And yet Dido's tongue felt stuck, and she hesitated as if she did not understand.

'I am Prince Aeneas of Troy. Consort to Queen Dido.' Aeneas straightened himself on his chair, while Dido felt like withdrawing into hers. *Consort*. She had never heard him use the word before, and sensed his hesitation as he said it. She winced as she watched Iarbas's face adjust.

'Consort.' His eyes were on her, pinning her with questions he did not speak. She saw incredulity in them. And hurt. She looked down. 'You must be new to your position, Prince Aeneas, since I have only been away for a season. And yet you seem . . . well settled.'

Dido felt Aeneas turn to her, but she kept her eyes on the table in front of them.

'I am,' he said levelly. 'And grateful to be, after what my people have suffered to reach this place. Queen Dido has been a most generous host to us.'

'I see that.'

Dido glanced up. She could see the tightness of Iarbas's mouth. He almost looked like a different man to the friend she had known all these years. She reached for words to say, but this hall was not the place to explain herself. She could already see the curiosity of those watching, and hear their murmurs – or imagine that she had. She let her gaze sink back to the table.

'You must have impressed her very well indeed, I think, for her to be so generous. It seems that she has given you more than a place to shelter. Why, she has given you her very self. And a throne in her hall. And broken her own vow to do it. You

267

must teach me your charms, Prince Aeneas.' Iarbas's voice kept a strained lightness, but he did not smile.

'I have not charmed her.' Aeneas sounded unsure, as if he were still measuring the man before him. But Dido heard a creep of anger too. 'I came across this shore as she did. And I have made my home here with her.'

'Oh, you have made it? You built these walls, then? And grew the food that you are eating and tended the vines that made your drink? I was mistaken when I believed that you were simply taking the scraps that fell at Queen Dido's feet.'

Aeneas stood up so violently that the heavy table shifted. 'Who are you to speak to me?'

'I am Iarbas of the Auseans. Well known in Carthage to anyone who has been here for more than a winter. And a friend to your curiously silent wife.'

Dido felt the prick of his words, even as he called himself her friend. More deeply because of it. He was calling her a coward, and in that moment she was. She felt his gaze inviting her to speak, to defend either him or else the man sitting beside her. But she could not look up.

Iarbas went on. 'I see that I have disturbed the harmony of this hall, so I will return to my camp.'

Dido tried too late to catch his eye, then sat stiff in her chair as he turned and strode towards the door. The swish of his sash made her heart clench with guilt. But as much as she hated that feeling, she hated the burn in her cheeks more. She flushed it away with self-justification, with pride shaped into reason. After all, what crime had she committed?

That evening Dido went to the Ausean camp, and almost resorted to begging before Iarbas would speak with her.

'You still have a tongue, then. I thought perhaps your new husband had taken it. Does he know you are here?'

'I need no permission from him, if that is what you imply.'

'I imply nothing. I simply wish to understand this man who has convinced you to break your vow.'

His eyes were sharp, but it was a look she knew. She had felt it from him so many times over the years of their friendship, whenever she confused him or surprised him. He had only ever wanted to know her better, but this time she could see his hurt as he studied her.

'He did not convince me, Iarbas. I felt a change in myself. I cannot explain it. I wish for both our sakes that I could, so that you will not hate me or call me inconstant. There are things between him and me that run so deeply, I . . . There are no excuses for the pull of love. I cannot control it.'

'Since when has Queen Dido allowed something to be out of her control?'

She almost smiled at that, because he knew her so well, because it was so true and so baffling even to herself. Her love for Aeneas was not something she could control, and that only made it feel truer and rarer. But she knew, too, that it had put her against her own self, her vow and her values. She had been willing to overlook that – had wanted to, needed to – but now Iarbas had dragged it before both of them. She felt exposed by his opinion, and she realised that his admiration for her meant more than she had ever recognised. She swallowed, hardly able to meet his eye, and gripped her skirt with trembling hands.

'I do not hate you, Dido. But you have hurt me with this. And whether it is only the shallowness of my pride or some-thing deeper, I will have to see in time. But I do not hate you. Cannot hate you.' His voice was soft, almost defeated, and it made Dido sink to hear it. She wished it could be sharp again. Defeat sounded too close to disappointment. 'Perhaps for now, though, I will find it difficult to be your friend. Will you forgive me for that?'

'There is nothing for me to forgive.' Her chest was painful, but she kept her voice steady. 'I only wait for the time when I can call you my friend again.'

'I will stay out of the city for now. For my sake and for yours. Tell your husband that I will not insult him in his hall again.' Iarbas's voice had regained its natural grace, but Dido could tell from his eyes that he still tasted bitterness.

Chapter 33

CARTHAGE

'How long will you allow the Libyans to press at our gates?'

Hashmun's voice had become a persistent disturber of Dido's hall, such that she could not go a day without hearing it.

'Are you content to do nothing, Queen Dido, while these foreigners beset us? Your loyal citizens have made generous allowance for your new . . . situation.' He turned his eyes towards Aeneas with no attempt at subtlety. 'They have been patient while city projects slowed and have shared their winter stores with your Trojan guests.'

'Our guests,' Dido corrected. 'And now our fellow citizens. Who will refill the stores and help our city to grow even greater, in time.'

Hashmun ruffled at the interruption, but he continued as forcefully as before. 'The Libyans are not our citizens. Yet you pay them a tithe we can hardly afford and allow them to intimidate us within our own walls.'

'Intimidate? The Auseans are and always have been our friends and neighbours. They pose no threat to us.'

'Can you be so sure? How many here witnessed the ire of their prince, Iarbas?' Hashmun turned to address the hall with his hand grasped tightly around his priest's staff. 'Your marriage has angered him. And now he holds his camp outside the city but does not enter. Who can say what he is plotting? If I may speak freely before the court' – he had never hesitated to do so before, Dido thought – 'I think that you trust the foreigners too easily, my queen.'

Dido's lip twisted with distaste. 'And I think you forget that we are the foreigners here in Libya. That we pay a fair tithe for land that was generously granted, and that has proven bountiful. Iarbas remains our ally. I have spoken with him myself and I can assure you and all the people of Carthage that all is well. Or do you not trust the judgement of your queen?'

She kept her eyes on Hashmun, but with all her other senses she tried to feel the breath of the hall. Were the people satisfied by her words? Was there more she could say to assure them? She tried not to let herself be clouded by her irritation with Hashmun. His ambition was what had allowed her to recruit him, and he had found the power he sought in his years as Carthage's Head Priest. But often it seemed that it was not enough for him. That he was determined to take some of hers as well.

'A woman's willingness to trust is something to be admired,' he said loudly. 'She looks for peace and she finds it. But I wonder, if this is so, whether she might also be blind to danger?'

There was a ripple of whispers from those watching, and Dido felt her skin prickle in anger. He had stuck in his lever at her sex, because he could find no other angle to pry. She might do all and be all, but she could never close that opening, not to those who were determined to use it against her. But if Hashmun believed even a part of what he said, then he did not know her at all. Dido had navigated danger her whole life. She watched for it always, set her snares before it even approached. Despite her anger, she almost wanted to laugh. Was Hashmun so ignorant of her history? And the history of her ancestors? Her own great-grandfather had been a priest, just as he was. A priest who had overthrown a king. That story was so familiar to her it was written in her very blood.

She steepled her fingers, just as her father used to do. 'You have brought your concern, Lord Hashmun. And your queen has heard it. Be assured that she is vigilant, always, to the threats within this city.' She looked at him pointedly and waited for him to look away.

'As you say.' The priest bowed his silver head, and flexed his fingers on his staff as if he might say something more. But he backed away and allowed the next citizen to make his petition.

By that evening, Dido had still not shaken the interaction from her thoughts.

'Hashmun is wrong to underestimate me,' she murmured in Aeneas's ear as he hunched over his steaming bowl of stew. 'He has watched me build Carthage from nothing. He has seen how willingly the people follow me, how they left their very homes for the promise of what I could offer them. How can he think to pit himself against that? If he challenges my authority, he must know that he will lose.' She was speaking aloud the arguments she had been making to herself all afternoon.

Aeneas listened without expression as he chewed on his beans. 'Perhaps he does not view things the same way that you do,' he offered quietly. He paused, and Dido thought he might say no more than that, but then he continued. 'I have overheard him, several times, when the wine is on his tongue. He says that the people follow you for respect of your father. He says that they trust you because they trusted your husband. That you are queen because of your ties to them.'

Dido knew that her priest had grown bold of late, yet this surprised her. It heated her already simmering anger, but at the same time she felt the unpleasant tingle of doubt.

'He cannot be serious,' she whispered. 'Zakarbaal has been dead ten years, and my father even longer. Hashmun harms himself with such ridiculous words.'

'He is wrong,' Aeneas agreed. 'I have seen with my own eyes the faith you have earned from your people. But . . . ' He hesitated. 'There is no shame in lineage. These ties make you stronger. There is a truth in that. The Trojans would not have followed me if my father were not cousin to the king. Yet I have proven myself also, on the battlefield if nowhere else.'

'It is different for you,' Dido said instinctively. 'If men speak of your father, it is no damage to you. He adds his reputation to yours. But men are not used to seeing a woman stand for herself. They may look at the scaffold that built me and think it is all that I am, that there is nothing lasting beneath, that I am only a fading ripple from men's stones. Hashmun knows that. He is determined to make my people doubt me.'

Dido watched Aeneas's face but it remained impassive, and that only made her skin burn hotter. He returned to his stew and Dido leaned back in her chair. She felt insane, as if what she said held no truth. Perhaps it did not. Perhaps she was only irritated and paranoid.

She thought of Shapashuru then. The memory of his kindly face was usually a comfort to her, but now it twisted at her fraying confidence. The guildmaster had been her first follower, the first to pour his faith into her. But he had admired her, at least in the beginning, because she had reminded him of her father. Perhaps all that she had gained since had been founded upon that. Perhaps any other claim was a delusion. She wished that Shapashuru were still living. He had passed away barely two years after they had landed in Libya. She wished that he could see now what his faith had helped to build, and assure her that she had proven herself not only as Mattan's daughter, but as something more, something separate.

On the chair beside Dido, drinking quietly until now, sat Anna.

'Hashmun is only saying what he wishes were true.' Her friend's voice came softly, but close enough to Dido's ear that she started. 'I never knew your father. Nor your husband in Tyre. I'm sure that they were great men. Noble, admirable men. You have told me as much. But who are they to me?' Dido saw her friend's mouth curl, but her eyes were arrestingly serious. 'I chose to follow you. Elissa of Tyre. Dido of Carthage. Whoever you are and whoever you will be. I knew my leader when I saw her.'

Chapter 34

CARTHAGE

'What do they want from me?' Dido paced in frustration, squeezing her hands on her waist. Her generous chamber somehow felt small, and she wished that she could run out to the cliffs and shout into the wind. 'Have I changed, truly? Am I less of a queen than I was before I knew Aeneas? Or is Hashmun only leading people to embrace doubts they have always held? I cannot be any more than I am, Anna.'

She stopped and spun on her heel to face her friend.

'You are more than enough. And your people know that. Hashmun is trying to start a fire with damp wood.' Anna perched on the edge of the bed. 'A reminder can do no harm, though. Go out into the city, speak with them as you always have. Begin a new building project – the people cannot deny what they see with their own eyes. Without Dido, there would be no Carthage. Don't let them forget that.'

Dido nodded, trying to take in the truth of Anna's words. A few months ago, she would have waved them away. Why tell her what she already knew? But now these words were needed. So much had happened that Dido had thought impossible. So much had changed in her perfectly controlled world that she had begun to doubt that it was hers at all. And she had allowed Hashmun's rattling to affect her in a way it never would have before.

'You're right.' She sighed. 'Thank you. Yes, I only need to remind them.' Dido took in a few breaths and waited for her nerves to settle. But in her stomach, there was still an uncomfortable squirm. 'It just feels so unfair, Anna. Like a game I can play and play, but never finally win. Where the best I can hope for is not to lose. It's as if there must always be some piece missing, some sacrifice I do not even know I am making.'

She knew what she wanted to say, but her words were so unclear, and she could see in her friend's face that she was reaching to understand. Dido's head had been circling these past weeks, and she knew that if she could pick out the grit of what was bothering her, it would help.

'When Zakarbaal died, I felt I had lost everything,' she began slowly. 'It was only with time that I realised that wasn't true. He was gone, and yet I had gained much since his death, things I had given up hope of gaining. Real power. The trust of so many. And it almost seemed as if I had made a trade – one I didn't ask for, one I would never have made willingly.' Her words were quick now, as she rushed to absolve herself. 'If the choice were clear before me, I would not have taken it. I would not have given up my husband and his love for anything the gods could offer me. But . . . ' She swallowed hard. The thought was so strong in her mind. Why was it difficult to say? 'When I lost my husband, I gained a kingdom, and everything my father had promised me. Everything I had so sorely wanted, because I had been shaped for it. And I felt so guilty when I realised that truth. But it is true, nonetheless.'

'You did not wish for it, Elissa. One followed from the other, but that is something decided by fate, not by you.'

Dido clung to those words. 'Yes. My actions, my choices – perhaps they played some part. But I could not have known it then. And now . . . '

'And now?'

'I feel as if somehow Aeneas has been sent to me. But is he a gift or a test? He seems a second chance. To regain the love that I lost. To make the trade again, in knowledge of what it means. Do you see? It explains why my fillet weighs so heavy, why the people are losing their faith. The gods will not allow me to have both love and power. I must always lose one for the other.'

'I do not think that is true.' Anna looked at her thoughtfully. 'Your father had both love and power. Many men do. Why should the gods treat you so cruelly?'

'Perhaps it is not the gods, then, only the way of the world.'

Anna shook her head. 'I have seen enough of the world to know that you deserve your portion of everything it can offer. More than your portion, if you have the will to take it.'

Dido sank on to the bed and they sat quietly for a moment, as she wondered whether she could believe that. Then Anna spoke again.

'If you could make it so that Aeneas had never come to Carthage, would you? You are afraid to lose what you have built. You are afraid to waste what was bought with Zakarbaal's death. So would you rather that chance were not in your hands? Would you erase all that has happened these last months, if your kingdom could be secure again and your mind free of doubts? Would you make that trade?'

Dido hesitated before she spoke, but the answer rose without interrogation. 'No. I would not.'

Dido went into the city, just as Anna had suggested. She made herself visible, every day, so that her citizens could not forget who she was to them, nor accuse her of neglecting them for love's sweet comfort. She went to the temple, too, for piety and for pride – to show Hashmun that she would never shy away from facing him.

The Awakening festival was approaching, and though the anticipation of it always made her grief kick like a mule, she oversaw the preparations with exactitude. She chose the performers herself, selected the most faultless beasts for sacrifice. And all the while, she imagined how this festival would be different. How she would not have to lead the dance opposite Hashmun, as she had for every year of Carthage's short history. That arrangement had been far from ideal, since the rite demanded a married couple. But the people had insisted that their queen must lead the dance, and who else was there to lead the men? It was not usual, either, to perform the sacred dance every year – at Tyre it had been only every seven, for the Great Awakening – and yet when they were building their new home, and praying over fields that had never shown so much as a shoot, it felt right to call upon Melqart by any methods they knew. And each year since their first improvised Awakening the Rising God had made the land green, so perhaps he did not scorn their unconventional rites. But still, this year would be different. This year Dido would keep her steps in time with Aeneas instead. Their true and powerful bond would call upon the god with new vigour, and Melqart would awaken to the stamping of two lovers. No doubt this prospect occupied Hashmun's thoughts, too, and aggravated his ambitious will. He was being pushed out – no longer the undisputed first man of Carthage. And perhaps she would have had some sympathy for him if he were not so determined to tear her down.

Dido was pleased with herself when she returned from the temple on the fifth day. She had felt so hopeless when she spoke with Anna, and now she could not understand why. Already things felt more sure. There was no trade to be made, knowingly or unknowingly. She flew into her chamber as if carried by a strong wind, and found Aeneas tying his boots.

'I am going to the shore with Ascanius,' he said flatly.

'Oh, I—'

'I hoped that you would come with us, but I cannot spend my life waiting to see when you will return. Ascanius was upset that we could not go yesterday.' There was a bluntness to his voice that bruised her.

'I'm here now. I'll join you.'

He shook his head heavily and sighed.

'I was busy at the temple. You know that the Awakening is close, and there is much to do. You ought to have come with me,' she tried, unsure whether he wanted to be more occupied himself or only to scold her for being so. 'You will be expected to lead the men in the rite, and it would be well for you to see what is being prepared.'

'The rite for Melqart?' He looked surprised.

'Of course.'

'How can I perform rites for a god I do not know? And before your whole city?'

'It is your city, too,' she reminded him.

'But not my god.'

Dido had not expected this from him. Suddenly, her visions for the festival, and her thoughts of how good it would feel to perform the sacred dance again with someone she loved, after so many years, were crumbling.

'Melqart belongs to Carthage,' she said, 'just as he belonged to Tyre. He belongs to all who benefit from his blessings. And we will give rites to your Trojan gods, too. Only tell us the ways and the calendar.'

'Another generous crumb from Queen Dido's table.' The way he spoke her title felt as if he were tarnishing it. The bruise Dido felt, ignorable before, sharpened to a pinch. 'My people will see to their own gods.' Aeneas looked away from her and pulled his leather laces tightly.

She wanted to argue with him, but his coldness stopped her tongue. He moved past her to leave the chamber, but their eyes did not meet.

Iarbas's words had dug into Aeneas. That much was clear. Her generosity, so gratefully accepted since the storm had washed his people to Libya, was now something to be resented, only because another man had made him feel small. Dido could not bring herself to pity his injured pride while she felt so angry. She had never treated him like a dog at her table. She had only known him and loved him as her equal – what other way was there for love to be? And was it really so offensive to him that she should want him to share in the traditions of the city? Traditions that meant so much to her own fractured heart? He had enough of her history to know that the Awakening, for her, was more than a civic duty. She had caught him in a bitter mood, she told herself, but it was not the first time. For weeks now, even before Iarbas's return, she had felt a creeping sullenness from Aeneas.

She sat on her bed, gripping the coverlet so that she would not go after him. They only hurt one another when their tempers were high. But as she waited for her anger to cool, an immovable thought planted itself in Dido's mind. Zakarbaal would never have spoken to her in that way. And she would never have held herself back from speaking with him for fear of where it could lead. Aeneas was not Zakarbaal. One husband could never fit the hole left by another. Dido knew that, of course. But she could not help measuring Aeneas against a ghost. A ghost who could not hurt or disappoint her, whom she was determined to remember above all else by the warmth of his love. Her first marriage had not been perfect. But it had been blessed enough that its shine threw all flaws into darkness. Why would she hold on to the small moments of hurt, when large ones had carved themselves so deeply?

There was more than one ghost in her new marriage. Did Aeneas measure her against Creusa, she wondered? Did he think of his first wife as often as she thought of Zakarbaal?

Had he loved her as deeply? Sometimes Dido imagined that there were four of them in that marriage bed, two living and two dead. Two dead spouses carried all the way across the sea, from Tyre, from Troy. And to her and to Aeneas, only one ghost could ever be truly known or knowable, while the other remained as a cold hole in the bond between the living. Dido wondered whether time would ever change this, but in her heart she already knew the answer. Their spouses were dead, but would never fully be gone. Creusa and Zakarbaal had disappeared, but their spirits still lingered in the consciences of those who had left them behind. They had been mourned but could never be buried.

Dido let these thoughts blow through her, and drew in a steadying breath. She had not fallen in love with Aeneas because loving him was simple. She loved him because he carried as much with him as she did, because it made her feel safe and seen to be loved by someone who knew what it was to survive. She reminded herself that Aeneas deserved a love untainted by comparison and deceiving memory, a marriage where the dead were not placed above the living. They both deserved that.

When he returned from the shore, she would take him into her arms and say she was sorry, even if she wasn't. She would shelter their love, and make him smile when his dark moods pulled at him. She would soothe her own pains with greater pleasures. She would cling to her new marriage with as much determination as she clung to her city. And she would have both, or give all of herself trying.

Chapter 35

CARTHAGE

The coldness between Dido and Aeneas did not take long to melt. It could not survive the warmth of their bed, and it was by kisses and caresses that they mended themselves back together. Dido was relieved to feel that closeness again, and she avoided any subject that might chase it away. The Awakening, above all. If Aeneas was not to dance, then she knew she must go to Hashmun and ask him to take up the role, and that alone was a distasteful thought. So she put it out of her mind, and as the day of the festival grew ever closer, she pretended not to see it.

On the morning before the Awakening, Aeneas rose quickly from their bed.

'Will you teach me the steps today? For the rite of Melqart?' He asked it as casually as that, as if he'd meant to dance all along. And though Dido took a moment to adjust, her relief was stronger than her surprise.

'Of course,' she croaked, with her throat still dry from sleep. 'They are not so complicated. It is a matter of feeling the rhythm, above all. You will see when we practise.' She could not help beaming at him, and threw off the covers so she could dress.

Aeneas was a beautiful dancer – his legs quick and strong, his arms poised so gracefully. Dido was proud to watch him, and when they faced one another at the festival, her chest swelled so much that it was almost painful. She was filled up with the music and with the stamping of her people and with the memories that were tied to that moment, and when she looked at Aeneas, it seemed there was no space left for the love she felt. It spilled over and flowed all around her and made the very air intoxicating.

After the dance came the feast, and Dido sipped her wine with trembling fingers. Aeneas drank more quickly and was already on his third cup when the roasted quail were served.

'I have tasted the grapes of Carthage many times this winter,' he said thoughtfully as he stared into the dark liquid of his cup. 'And I have tried the wines you trade for. So much of the world can be drunk here.'

He smiled, and Dido took his words as praise.

'And yet,' he went on, 'I have found no vintage quite like those I drank at Troy. So strange.' His voice slurred a little. Dido could not tell if he seemed sad or only reflective. 'Is it not strange, my love? That every shore should have its own flavour? We might sail for years and never taste the same twice. If I had sailed to Italy and not Libya, what wine would be in my cup now? Would it be like the wine of my homeland, or some new flavour I have never tried? Perhaps I may find out one day.'

Italy. Why should he talk of that place? Why should it even be in his mind? The very name unsettled Dido in a way she did not want to examine.

'I can instruct my merchants to sail further. To bring wines from the lands close to Troy. If it would please you to taste them again, it will be done.'

'No. What is one wine from another? Truly?' Aeneas's eyes cleared as he shook away his musings. He put down his cup to stab a knife into the quail before him. 'Do not trouble your merchants. You must not be determined to provide for me so completely.' He smiled affably, but that did not put her at ease. 'If my yearning calls for it, I will sail myself.'

He took a large bite of quail, and it seemed that the conversation was ended. But Dido did not eat. She sat with Aeneas's words still in her mind, his talk of sailing away to Italy, to Troy. These were passing notions, not plans. She told herself that as she watched him slice another piece of quail from the bone. But to hear him form the words so easily put a heavy stone in her belly. It was a possibility she had never imagined, for herself or for him. Why should they ever need to leave this shore when all the world could be brought to them? She felt an uncomfortable shift as she realised that her mind and his were not as inseparable as she would like to imagine. That he might have visions for the future that were not her visions, and that might not include her at all.

Dido felt the exhilaration of the festival slipping away, being leached into the cold night as she sat alone among the crowd. Love was a mesh that had brought her and Aeneas together, but it was not a mirror. And with all her will, she could not make it one.

Dido's stomach sat uncomfortably for weeks. She told Aeneas that she loved him, that she could not imagine her life without him, just so that she could hear those words returned. Sometimes he echoed her, and other times he only smiled. Sometimes he was distracted and far away, and seemed not to hear her at all.

She continued her commitment to the city, to making herself seen and heard, and though she asked Aeneas to join her at her duties, he declined more often than he accepted. He preferred to spend time with Ascanius or with his men. Each evening, he would begin at her table, pouring his wine from the same jug as she did, but by the end of the night, he would be talking with Trojans in some dim corner. He came to bed later and later, until Dido began falling asleep with the mattress cold beside her.

'I saw Aeneas at the harbour,' Anna said one morning as she came to sit with Dido before the daily petitions were heard. There was a hesitancy in her voice that made Dido feel somehow embarrassed.

She rushed to smooth her friend's concern. 'He goes there often,' she said lightly. 'Ascanius likes to watch the ships.'

'Ascanius was not with him.'

Why did Anna speak so gently? Dido felt her stomach clench with a dread she did not allow herself to understand.

'He was examining the Trojan ship.'

There it was. The punch to the gut that instinct had anticipated. But even half-braced, she felt winded by it. Dido kept her face still, unable to turn and meet Anna's pitying eyes.

'It is his ship,' she murmured. 'It is well that he should maintain it.'

'Elissa.'

Dido swallowed to stop her throat from closing. 'What do you expect me to do, Anna?' Her words were barely audible.

'Expect? Do what you want to do. Whatever you need to do. You must speak with him, at least. Go to him now. I will handle the petitioners. Perhaps he intends nothing, but you must know. Go, please.'

Her friend almost pulled her out of her throne, but Dido let her weight resist.

'I cannot go now. My people have a right to be heard.' Her eyes stung and her heart hammered painfully. She dug her fingertips into the arms of her throne until the nail beds burned. 'Leave me, Anna. Please.' She held her gaze steady, and eventually Anna gave in.

'Come to me later, when you have spoken with him. Whatever happens between you.'

Dido let her head twitch, and that was enough to send Anna away. Even when she was alone, she could not let her fear overwhelm her. She had to be whole for her people. She took a long drink of wine and clenched her hands to stop them shaking. When the first petitioner was admitted to the hall, Queen Dido was ready.

Chapter 36

CARTHAGE

Dido gave half of herself to the petitions, while the other half wheeled higher and higher on anxious thoughts. By the time she was able to rush to her chamber, her legs were trembling. She sat on the bed in strained stillness, trying to centre herself as the world span. She did not know anything yet. Only what Anna had seen. And only what her heart feared. She could not *know* anything until Aeneas returned.

And yet it is in the place between fearing and knowing where the darkest thoughts are given room to grow. Dido felt their vines twisting, entangling her. She could not escape the image of Creusa, Aeneas's first wife, lost and alone as Troy burned, her shadowy face terrified, receding into the dark. Dido should have trusted the chill she felt at that story, should have known from that abandonment that Aeneas would always favour blood over any other bond. That he would hold legacy higher than love.

They could still build a legacy together, couldn't they? She and Aeneas and Ascanius. Perhaps other children would come. Would that stop his ship from sailing? If she could press Aeneas's hand to her swollen belly and promise him a child?

Was her childlessness what pushed him towards his ship? That thought made her shudder with something more agonising than sadness. If a wife was only a path to children, what could she be to him? What had she ever been?

Suddenly, by thoughts and fears alone, all that had been tended between her and Aeneas seemed ripped out by the roots. It had no ground to hold it, only dry dust. Dido had risked so much for the promise of love, for a chance to regain even a fraction of what she had lost. She had jeopardised her power, neglected her city, abandoned her principles and trampled her vow. And even now, she would do it again, if Aeneas would only walk through their chamber door and tell her that all her fears were empty and that he would never leave.

When he appeared, she remained on the bed. She felt as if her legs would not hold her, and she refused to collapse at his feet and sob and beg. He was silent as he crossed the chamber to hang his cloak.

'You have been at the harbour.'

'Yes.'

'At your ship.'

He stopped at that, but did not turn to her. His hands stayed upon the cloak, straightening its folds with drawn-out care.

'You are leaving.' She had meant it as a question, but her voice was too fragile and it fell away. She looked at him, waiting for a response, a denial. But the longer the silence hung the thicker it became, until Dido was choked by it.

'I was going to speak with you tonight,' Aeneas said. 'Now. As soon as your petitions were done.'

A lie. Dido was a subtle player. She knew when moves were made in secret, and the advantage it gave. Aeneas would have told her nothing if she had not challenged him, if Anna had not seen him. She felt herself burning at that thought, that he might have slipped away from her as if she were some clueless fool.

'You meant to deceive me. To allow me to believe that all was still well, and run away like a thief.'

'As you did? From Tyre?'

That jolted her.

'It would be bold to think I could deceive a deceiver,' Aeneas said.

Dido frowned and her mouth dropped open.

'Is that not what you are? Have you not boasted to me of your tricks? How you fooled your brother, how you won your piece of land? Do not pretend now that you are above deception, Dido.'

'Only when it was necessary,' she stuttered. 'Never from cowardice. And never against those I loved. You could have spoken with me.' Her voice dropped low. 'You can speak with me now.' She locked her gaze with his, sending the most honest part of her soul out into the space between them. 'Please, my love. Do not run from me.'

Aeneas sighed. With submission. With relief. Dido could not tell. He came towards the bed, and when he sat close beside her, he seemed so much softer. Her heart flickered with cautious hope.

'I had a dream some nights ago,' Aeneas began. 'My aged father came to me, his face torn with worry. His clothes were soiled by smoke and ash, just as they were when we fled our home. But he seemed younger, stronger than he had been at his death. He asked me why I lingered here at Carthage, why I had not gone to Italy as he'd advised. He asked why I deprived my son of his kingdom.' Aeneas's voice was strained. 'He held our household gods in his arms and he begged me to take them, to preserve our line and the legacy of Troy. When I woke, I was afraid. A part of me wanted to forget this dream, and another part wanted to sleep and find my father again, to see his face and have him guide me.'

Dido was quiet. She knew he was earnest in this, at least. Her own father had visited her dreams many times, and Zakarbaal too. Each time, she felt she had been given a gift, a part of them come back to her – even as she woke to the pain of fresh grief.

'I cannot forget the vision of him, and the things he said to me,' Aeneas went on. 'There is truth in them. I am forgetting my purpose and betraying the will of my gods, the promises I made to my people. I survived the fall of my city so that I could build it again, for Ascanius and all the generations after him. I am selfish to stay here, Dido.'

'You are selfish to leave,' she bit back. 'Ascanius is happy here. He already has a kingdom. I will make him my heir, if that is what you want for him.' She said it rashly, but she meant it. His talk of Ascanius had lit a new fire as she realised all that she would lose if Aeneas set sail. The child had nestled himself into her heart, and to have him ripped away now would be unbearable. Her tone became pleading, but she could not help it. 'He has already lost one mother, Aeneas. Do not put him through that again.'

'He only had one mother to lose.'

Dido felt the lash of those words as if they had cut her across the cheek. Perhaps Aeneas did not intend to be so cold, for he reached out a hand over the coverlet. But Dido flinched from it.

'And what of your duty to me? I am your wife, Aeneas. Such a thing cannot be forgotten or cast aside.' Creusa's shadowy face flashed in her thoughts, and she drove it out. 'Your father died before he knew me and the life we would make together. Perhaps if he were here now, he would counsel you to honour your commitment as my husband.'

'Is that what I am?' His voice was suddenly quiet. 'I made no vows to you, Dido.'

For a moment, she was too surprised to speak. She felt a sickening pulse in her neck, as if she had been caught in a mistake. 'How can you say that? You have sat beside me every day and shared my bed every night. You have called me your wife with your own tongue.' It was true she had never demanded vows of him, or given them in turn. But a marriage was not made by vows. It was made by living. That understanding had never felt slippery until now.

'I called you my wife for ease, yes. What else should I call you? My friend? My host? My generous patron?' He spat the last suggestion. His voice was bolder now, robust in his self-defence. 'If I called you my lover, it would shame you more than me.'

'How courteous,' she said sharply. 'To wrap my reputation so delicately while you tread your boot across my heart.' It made her feel strong to speak strong words. She clung to that like a mast in a storm, even as she felt herself being torn apart. 'Wife or not. That is only a word. You cannot deny what we both know and what we have both felt. Love, Aeneas.' That soft word seared on her tongue. 'You have loved me, and I have loved you.' She spoke plainly, so that he could not diminish these facts with subtlety. 'How much have I given you, all for love? A home and half a kingdom. And I have never asked you for anything in return.'

'Do you think that is what I want? To give nothing? To be nothing and have nothing except what you have gifted me? Things I never asked you for?' His voice was as piercing and as furious as hers. And she was glad for that. Love could not survive in apathy.

'No, Aeneas.' She reached out and took his hand from the coverlet, pulled it to her even as he resisted. 'You want to impress yourself upon the world. To prove your place within it. I know that. Because you and I are two edges of one blade. I know you.' She raised her hand to his face and held his bearded cheek. 'My love. You could never be nothing, no matter who stands beside you. Your light is too strong for that.' She tried to smile, and almost leaned in to kiss him, but held herself back. 'I only meant that I am your wife in my heart. That I have proven my love and my commitment. Have I not earned your love in return, and the right to call you my husband, by all that I have shared with you?'

He looked at her, but his eyes were so empty. There was a slant of pity in his lip that made her hand drop. 'You want my love because it is owed to you? That is not how love works, Dido. It is not a debt to be paid. And if it were, we should not call it love.'

Dido's neck pulsed again. It sent shivers across her shoulders, hot waves up to her cheeks. She willed herself to argue, but nothing would come. What Aeneas said was true, and so painful that it paralysed her.

'I don't understand what you wanted from me,' she murmured. 'Or what else I could have done. Should I have made you king instead of my consort? Kept a looser grip on my power, or cleared more room for yours? If you are leaving because you cannot love me, then tell me so and cure me of my delusion. But I think you cannot stay at Carthage because your pride will not allow you to share her.'

'Even if you gave me the whole city, it would not be mine.' He sighed, and they were still so close she felt the force of his breath. 'Carthage will always be yours, Dido. That is why I cannot stay, if you must have one reason. It is not because I cannot love you, but because every day I feel myself disappear within this city's shadow. I feel the memory of Troy dissolve. And I cannot allow it. I am the guardian of that memory, of a people divided across the lands of the living and of the dead. Our legacy – the legacy of my father and my grandfather, and of my son and his sons – can find no place here. My gods call me to find a home of our own. How can we serve them here, where they do not even have a shrine?'

'I would have built you a shrine. A hundred shrines, if you had asked for them.'

Aeneas shook his head. 'I do not want to ask you. That is the very problem. Can you not see that?'

'And do you not see your own inconsistency? You do not want what you have not asked me for, and you will not ask for what you want. How was I ever to please you, Aeneas? I have loved you and I have protected you, and I have tried in every way to make you happy. To build a happiness we both could share. But you have allowed me to spend myself on a game you knew I could not win.' Her voice was dark, frayed. 'You tell me you must leave for duty's sake. For your people and for piety. But I know it is pride that drives you. I have felt its pull, and I see it in you. But no feeling or instinct has ever been stronger to me than love.'

'And would you give up your kingdom, then? If love means as much as you say. Would you abandon Carthage and follow me across the sea? That is what you are asking of me, Dido. To give up my city for yours. But would you do the same?'

Her heart leapt to answer. *Yes.* That was her instinct. She would give up anything to mend this pain, to chase away the grief of separation, the fear of being alone again. But even as she drew a breath, another side of herself rose to argue. Why should she give up what she had worked for? And how could he ask her to do it? To give up the real home she had built for one that only existed in Aeneas's imagination. To abandon her people, or else drag them back on to the treacherous sea and ask them to leave behind all that they had made here with their own blistered hands.

'It is not the same,' she rasped.

'It is to me.'

A colossal heaviness weighed Dido to the bed, made it torturous to raise her eyes to his. The pain that had begun in her heart had spread itself like fire, and the whole careful structure she had built, to raise up their love, to shelter it, to strengthen it, to screen its widening cracks, was collapsing in the flames. She had staked herself on that monument, and even as it burned she could not leave it, but only rage at Aeneas for lighting the fire.

'You have put a wound in me, Aeneas. And I cannot . . . I do not know how to survive it. Those I've loved have left me before, but never by their own will. Never so needlessly, and never in a way to make me regret the love I gave.' Burning tears spilled from her eyes, and she felt her voice splintering. 'Did you think that you would break away and leave me intact? No. No, you knew the harm you were doing. That is why you were sneaking to your ship. You hoped not to see what you were leaving behind. You are a coward, Aeneas.' She saw that word bite him, and felt strengthened to know she could still affect him. 'Well, you see it now. I hope you see it for the rest of your years. How you cut Queen Dido and left her to die.'

She spoke it like a curse, and fixed him with her gaze as if pressing the memory of that look on to his soul.

'To die? I have not killed you, Dido.'

'Whichever of us wields the knife, the crime is yours.'

His face became gravely still, but in his eyes she saw a spark of something that satisfied her. Surprise. Guilt. Terror.

'You want to hurt me so badly? That you would spend your own life to do it?' He spoke as if he were disappointed, even sceptical. But she knew that she had pricked him. Like a bee that leaves its sting in the flesh, and dies for the effort. It was her final recourse. Her most unbending argument to make him stay. Desperation had drawn it out of her, but drastic words were all she had now. She could not sit in silence as he left her. Surely that would be the greater madness?

'I wish you a long life, Dido. I wish you love, even if I can no longer give it. But I cannot stay here and fulfil your heart while my own suffers. And I cannot stay because you have made me too afraid to leave. I have my own destiny. And I will pursue it.'

His voice was so restrained. Not like the real Aeneas at all. He did not mean what he said. It was easy to tell herself that, to create space in her mind for new arguments, for reasons that he was being untrue to himself or unfair to her. She scrambled for clever words that might convince him, ones stronger even than those she had already spoken. But as she tried to close her tongue around them, she felt the bed shift as Aeneas stood up. He was going towards the door, and she was still weighted to the bed. She raged at her leaden legs, but by the time they obeyed her, he had gone.

For a moment her ears rang with the silence. She was torn between following him and sinking into the floor. Her heart was so tight that she gripped her chest, clawed her nails on the purple fabric. Through the turmoil of her thoughts, a cold realisation began to emerge. She did not want to look at it, and shook her head so violently that she felt sick. Dido fell back on to the bed, clung to the carved post and pressed her forehead against it. But the dread knowledge was still there, and she could not drive it out.

She could make her arguments. She could be clever and she could be determined. She could even be right, and soothe herself with that fact. But a victory of words would not win Aeneas's love. He had already gone too far from her, in his mind and in his heart if not yet in his ship. And she could not drag him back or make him stay. She could not force him to love her.

As the room span, she tried to stand again, to do something other than feel the pain of what she had realised. But it was as if the floor were falling out beneath her. She felt herself fall with it, stomach dropping, and in that moment it was not this floor but the floor of the hall back in Tyre, crumbling as she watched her father collapse toward it. It was that same hall in which she had turned the false tablet over and over in her disbelieving hands. It was the bedroom she had shared with Zakarbaal, on that day when she could not find him in it. It was the floor where she had sat opposite her brother and felt the hammer blow that still, after ten long years, had not healed. Her chamber here in Carthage, here in the present, was compacted with every defeat of her past, every theft, every humiliation, every crushing loss she could not control.

How could Aeneas understand the depth of the wound that he had reopened? And how had Dido been so foolish as to let him do it?

Chapter 37

CARTHAGE

Dido did not go to see Anna as her friend had asked. How could she tell another person what had happened in that chamber? The man she loved, for whom she had given so much and risked so much, did not love her. Not enough to deserve the word, and not enough to stay. The embarrassment of the fact burned her like a brand to the flesh. She could not bear to speak, or to be looked at. Already, she imagined rumours spreading through the city, of the Trojan ship laden and ready, and the foolish queen who had let her heart lead her so blindly. Dido the trickster, so wily and so clever, had been outplayed. Her father's voice came to her unbidden – *What move will you make now, Little Jackal?* – and she felt her stomach turn.

She took a jug of wine from her chamber and carried it with trembling arms through the passages of her own palace, keeping close to the shadowed corners, hurrying quickly to avoid the eye of any servant or courtier. She felt as if the wound of Aeneas's departure were a shameful mark that they would see, a gaping hole for them to gawk at. She would rather walk through these courtyards naked than feel the pity of people she had rebuilt the world for, or hear their maddening whispers. She went as quickly as she could, breaths rasping in panic and in pain. She had to get out. To have space for her feelings to spill over, without spectators for her grief.

She left through the city gates with a sideways nod to the guard. Ahead of her, crowded on the blurred horizon, lay the Ausean camp.

The sight of it sent another blow to her gut, and she stumbled to steer her path away. The thought of Iarbas filled Dido's mouth with an awful metallic bitterness, as if she were being forced to chew copper beads. She remembered the hurt on her friend's face, the disappointment in his voice. Things she could bear while she clutched happiness to her breast and convinced herself it was worth the price paid. But now that happiness had fallen through her fingers, and when she thought of Iarbas, she was left with her bare humiliation, her needling guilt, and a regret that made her wince.

Dido hugged the wine jug to her chest and followed the path her instinct had set, away from the scrutiny of the city and out to the private sanctuary of the grove. Zakarbaal's spirit waited for her there. She needed to be close to him. It was the only balm for the wound that was splitting her from side to side. She needed to remind herself of the love she had had, the real and true love that could not be taken from her, not while mind and memory preserved it. She needed to remember that she was deserving of it, or had been once. And she needed to apologise, too. For thinking that she could build it again with false shadows. For breaking the vow she had made to Zakarbaal and to herself.

By the time she reached the grove, dusk was closing around her and an owl was hooting somewhere out of sight. It was a bad omen to hear that call with no reply. Iarbas had taught her that. The owls of this land were bound to their mate for life, and she shivered to hear this one hoot into the silence. An apt sign for the gods to send, but she could not tell if it was meant in sympathy or judgement.

Dido knelt among the trees and listened to their whisper. She breathed with it and urged her heart to calm, the strangled feeling to leave her throat. She struggled to command her fingers, and scooped out a rough hole in the earth so that she could pour some wine for Zakarbaal's spirit. She had done so a thousand times since landing in Libya, but this time the ground seemed to resist her, and the dirt that forced itself beneath her nails made her sick. She took up the jug and splashed some wine on to the earthy altar, but as it spilled it looked thick and dark like blood, and glistened briefly upon the surface before being drunk thirstily down. She poured again, and again it seemed the sweet wine had turned to gore, so much so that she thought she could smell its iron tang. In horror, she dropped the jug and let the rest of the wine glug out into the soil.

Another omen. Clearer than the first. But as her revulsion subsided, she began to accept what she had seen, to allow it to bed into her fractured mind. It settled with peculiar ease. Should an omen of death not be a terrifying thing? Why, then, did it make her lighter? She felt as if some tight cord had been released, and though tears raced down her cheeks, they did not burn as they had before. They dropped on to the wine-stained earth as if they were another gift to Zakarbaal.

She laid herself down then, and embraced the ground as if her husband, her only husband, were just on the other side of where she lay, as if she could reach through the soil and feel his face and know again the love she was so desperate for. She ached to join him, wherever his spirit had gone to without her. She had felt that ache ten years ago and smothered it with action. But she was so much heavier now, so much older and more exhausted. Perhaps that first instinct had been the right one. Perhaps everything since had only been a delay.

The spilled gory wine was on her skin, soaking into her black hair, but she did not hate the smell now. She lay still among the sighing trees until darkness hid her and a restless sleep crept in.

A dream. Zakarbaal stood before her, as real and as warm as he had ever been. His arms wrapped her into his chest, his hands ran through her hair. But as she bathed in his love, she felt him shake. Looking up, she saw that he was crying. She asked what was wrong, but he would not speak. He had no mouth at all.

A thought. She had been so long without love that she could not trust herself to recognise it. She had looked for every sign that Aeneas loved her, and turned away in every moment where she might see something different, closed her ears to all the ways he had told her he would not stay. She had always loathed to look failure in the eye.

A dream. Dido chased Aeneas through a sparse forest. He sprinted ahead of her before stopping and looking behind, staying long enough for her to almost touch him before he leapt away again. She ran and ran until she was bent over with fatigue, and looked up to find that he was out of sight.

A thought. Aeneas had loved her. In the cave. In their bed. In the hours they had spent watching Ascanius, their hands laced so tenderly. She had felt love then. But Aeneas did not love as she loved. His love did not stretch beyond convenience. It was not worth what she had paid for it.

A dream. She held Ascanius's small hand in hers, as they looked for polished stones together on the shore. The child ran into the sea, and she laughed to watch his smile bob above the waves, until the surf dropped over him like a curtain and he was gone.

A thought. She might never have loved Aeneas, if she had not first loved Ascanius.

A dream. She was on a long and narrow road, stretching out to where the land met the sky. This was a new land, a land where her Tyrians could be happy, except that she could not find them. She journeyed on and on, thinking always that they were just ahead of her, that if she could only make herself move faster, see further, she could join them.

A thought. Love and power would always be opposite weights on a scale. She could not add to one without upsetting the other. Now all she had built up was scattered.

These notions formed, reformed, circled, repeated. Until each was folded into the other, and Dido could not be sure whether she had slept at all, or only lived out the night in her anguished mind.

'Dido?'

The voice seemed to mock her. It came again, like a cruel echo, but she ignored it and dug back down into her thoughts.

'Dido.'

Something jolted her shoulder. When she opened her swollen eyes, Anna was crouching over her.

'I should have known this was where you would be. It was Piddaya who thought to look here.' Anna twisted her head, and Dido blinked at the silhouette of her former maid against the morning sky. 'You had us so worried, Elissa.'

It seemed to Dido as if her two friends were less real than the dreams that had tortured her all night. She swallowed, winced at the resistance from her parched throat, and pushed herself up from the dirt. Anna helped her to stand, and Piddaya threw a cloak over her shivering shoulders. Dido could see her friends surveying her face, and remembered that she had fallen asleep in the spilled wine. She could feel, too, that her hair was undone, but made no effort to tidy herself. Her collapsing heart had brought her to the grove because it was the place she felt most safe, the place where she could allow her mask to slip and her stately self to unravel. In life and in death, she knew that Zakarbaal would not judge her. And neither would her sisters. There was nothing more raw than what they had already seen of her. And she was almost glad that her appearance now should be as ragged as her soul.

'You know what has happened? What is going to happen?' Her voice was dry as tinder.

Anna nodded. 'Aeneas is leaving.' Her friend spoke simply, without sickly sympathy. Dido was grateful to her for that.

'Is his ship still in the harbour?'

'Yes.'

'But it is loaded?'

Anna hesitated. 'Yes.'

'There is still time to speak with him.' Piddaya's soft voice was like a breeze trying to shift a boulder.

'We have said all that we can say to one another. Words will not serve me.' Dido ached at the truth of it.

'Then what you will do?'

Despite her pain, Dido almost smiled. Even now, Piddaya expected her to have a plan. And didn't she? It seemed as if it had been forming as she dreamed.

'I will build a pyre.'

Anna's eyes flashed at her, but she went on.

'For sacrifices. We must ensure the Trojans begin their journey with the gods' favour.'

'Dido . . . ' Anna reached out to her as one might to an injured animal. 'No one expects that. You look exhausted. You need to rest, I think. Come back to the palace with us. Put away duty and piety. You only need to think of yourself today.'

'I am thinking of myself. What power do I have now, other than to show that I have not been beaten? Aeneas cannot be my enemy if I care for him as an ally. He cannot abandon me if I send him away with good wishes.'

She stared at Anna, willing her to be convinced. She looked to Piddaya, too, hoping that she could still rely on her oldest friend.

'As you say.' Piddaya nodded obediently, as if she were a young girl again. 'If that is your course, we will help you.'

Anna was quiet. She stepped forwards and brushed some of the dirt from Dido's cheek. Dido held her gaze firm.

'If that is what you want.' Anna nodded without breaking her eyes away. 'But first, you must clean yourself up. Remind your people that you are the queen they deserve.'

Few words were shared on the walk back to the city. Dido's throat was half closed with thirst and grief, and she kept her eyes on the moving patch of ground before her. She did not look at the Ausean camp, or the fine outline of her city. She allowed Anna and Piddaya to guide her through the gates and to the palace. The hour was still early, so there were no crowds to contend with, no great hum of speculation to rake at Dido's pride. She reached her chamber in a state of dislocated calm.

'I'll have a maid bring you some water to wash yourself,' Anna said, and Dido met her eye as if just realising that she was there.

She nodded. 'And the pyre. It must be built quickly. Before the Trojans set sail.'

Anna nodded awkwardly. 'I will take care of it. You just refresh yourself. There is no hurry.'

'Do not build it at the sanctuary. Build it up on the cliff, overlooking the harbour.'

Anna frowned with doubt and opened her mouth, but Dido went on.

'It is for the gods of the sea, is it not?'

Her friend's brow remained heavy.

'Do this for me, Anna. It is a small thing that I ask.'

Eventually, Anna's head bowed. 'Perhaps Piddaya should stay with you.'

'That is not necessary.'

'I'd like to stay,' Piddaya said. 'I can help you dress.'

The offer was so honest that Dido could not refuse. Once Anna had left and the water was brought, Piddaya helped her to wash her face and arms. As each of her limbs was lifted gently, and the sponge run over them, Dido felt almost as if she were not in possession of her body, as if it were some doll being manipulated. She watched as the wine and the dirt were washed away, listened to the trickle of the water as Piddaya soaked and squeezed the piece of sponge, but even these sounds and images seemed distant.

Her mind felt snapped, like an overpulled bow string. Her thoughts floated, untethered, and Dido could only endure each one as it passed through her. Aeneas's blank face as he had left. Ascanius jumping over the threshold into her hall. Her fingers clawing the wine-soaked dirt of the grove. The grove. *The grove.* A part of her was still there, caressing the earth that hid her husband, pressing herself against that so deep, so shallow layer that separated the realms of the living and the dead. She remembered the temptation she had felt as she lay there, to sink and be hidden with him. No, it was not a memory. It was a buzzing, like a fly trapped in her ear. Other thoughts flared and faded. But beneath them all, the buzzing went on.

When her limbs and face were washed, Dido summoned herself again to the present and gave Piddaya a smile of gratitude. In truth, she felt no different than she had before. A sponge could not wash the grit out of her heart.

Dido insisted on choosing the dress. She had to dig it out of her dowry chest, but her hands knew the fabric by touch. It was the red dress she had owned in Tyre, the one that Zakarbaal had always called his favourite. Its colour was faded now, the threads frayed in more than a few places, but as Piddaya draped the cloth and fixed the pins, Dido could almost imagine that she was back in her old home, that Zakarbaal might walk through the door and wrap her in his arms and kiss her from one ear to the other. The phantom of him made her tingle with warmth and shiver in sadness.

When the dress was pinned, Piddaya combed Dido's hair, and tied the ruby-studded fillet around her head without needing to be asked. She smiled at her former mistress in her soft, direct way.

'Thank you, Piddaya.'

'We can sit a while,' her old friend suggested. 'Perhaps the pyre is not ready yet.'

'No,' said Dido. 'There is something I must . . . ' Her words trailed in distraction as she glanced about the room. She started suddenly towards her dowry chest again, and pulled out the saf-fron-bordered dress that Aeneas had gifted her. 'This will make a worthy sacrifice, I think.' She held it up as if it were a captured hare.

'You would burn something so beautiful?' Piddaya's voice was thin with concern, but Dido ignored it. She went about the chamber, picking up the other gifts Aeneas had given her – the diadem of amethysts, the silver-cased dagger – and the clothes and belongings he had not packed on to his ship. Perhaps he had been too cowardly to return to the chamber and fetch them. Now they filled Dido's arms as if she were a cornucopia, and she smiled breathlessly at the weight of them.

'No god could despise such gifts.'

Piddaya was watching her warily. 'Let me carry some of them.'

Dido let her friend take a portion of the weight from her arms, but she kept the slender dagger tight in her hand. 'To the pyre, then.'

It was instinct that kept the cold texture of the silver case close to her palm. She had not planned to take it or to keep it – not as she planned so much in her life – but as soon as her eyes had caught upon it in the chamber, it had fallen in with her feelings as if she had sought it all along. As she walked with Piddaya through the palace, along the city streets, up towards the cliff, she could not stop thinking about the sharpness of the blade, the deadly simplicity of it. The tightness in her chest was agonising. It had been there ever since Aeneas had walked out of her chamber, and it gave her relief to imagine opening a hole to it, allowing her grief to flood out and leave her to rest.

When she saw the pyre, Dido sucked an involuntary breath into her lungs. The logs were piled like a great ziggurat, a stair-way into the sky. She felt a surge of pride at the industriousness of her people, and gratitude to Anna that she had ordered everything so swiftly. The sight felt as if it were a further per-mission, like the hooting owl or the gory wine: a sign that fate would allow her to break away from this world, and that it would be left in the hands of those who could bear it well enough without her.

Anna turned as they approached the pyre, and Dido saw the sweat on her brow.

'As you asked, my friend.' Anna's gaze fell to the beautiful things they were carrying. 'We have two rams,' she said uncertainly. 'We'll burn them whole, if that is what you think best. Enough for a fair wind and a calm sea. I . . . Is this still what you want, Dido?'

'Yes. Burn them. And these too.' She held Aeneas's gifts and fine clothes towards her friend. 'Or perhaps I should place them myself.'

'The gods delight in gifts,' Anna said, 'but they do not look well on excess. The burning of treasures will not please them.'

'It will please me.' Dido despised the crack in her voice, and gave Anna a solid look. 'Come, Piddaya. We will lay these down and save our arms.'

The two of them stepped forward and draped the cloths and jewels across the tiered logs. But the silver dagger Dido kept, slyly veiled in the folds of her dress.

'Perhaps you are right to burn these gifts,' Anna said more naturally as she came to stand beside them. 'They are only worth as much as the man who gave them. We are well to be rid of both.'

Dido nodded as if Anna's words were wise and satisfying. It would be easy to tell herself that they were true, to make Aeneas as worthless in her mind as simple insults could make him seem. But Dido knew that her pain burned more fiercely for the very fact that Aeneas was not a worthless man. He was dutiful and he was kind. He was brave, for all that she might call him a coward. He was stubborn and proud, but only as much as she was. He had been a good match for her. He had been her chance to love someone who was her equal in strength and in fragility. And now that was wasted.

It seemed to Dido as if everything were wasted now. All that was good in her life felt spoiled and broken. Her love for Aeneas, and her love for Ascanius, too. Her fidelity to Zakarbaal, her friendship to Iarbas. Her father's faith in her, that had driven her so far and so long. His trust that she would play her game well, that she would put her city and her people before her own desire. Who was she without these bonds that she had tattered?

Standing before the looming pyre, Dido was intensely aware of the crowds around her. Those who had helped to carry the logs, those who had gathered to see what was being built upon the cliff. Their eyes and their voices seemed to stick to her. It felt as if they had come to witness her defeat. Or perhaps to see what she would do to overcome it. What clever trick would the Wanderer perform? What new strength would she pull out of herself? She felt their expectation in every sound and movement, dragging at her from all directions.

How far could her strength be expected to stretch? It seemed to Dido that revealing her strength, in all those moments of her past when it had been forced out of her, only made people assume that she had more. As if there were an endless spool unravelling from her heart's pocket. But these people did not see the thread running out, pulling so thin that a careless tug might break it. For ten years, she had made sure that no hand would have that chance.

She should have continued to guard herself, she thought bitterly. To love cautiously, or not at all. She scolded herself as if it were a choice she could make, as if hearts could really be shaped and sealed, as if will alone were the driver of the soul. All the ways in which Dido had loved and been loved had marked her. They had cut their grooves across her heart, and conducted the flow of each new drop that fell there. No choice or denial could erase those courses.

She swallowed the sourness in her mouth, the anxious bile of scrutiny and regret. The sticky eyes of the crowd were on her still. She wished that she could cry out, but kept her tongue caged and put the silver case of the dagger against her wrist instead, pressing at her frustration, her humiliation, her reopened grief. They burned within her, burned as if she were already afire. And the silver felt so cool.

A fly buzzed in her ear.

'Are the torches ready?'

Anna's shout was like a call to action. Dido's limbs tensed, and suddenly it felt so unbearable to be still. Stillness was paralysing. It trapped her in her pain. She needed to move, to do, to keep ahead of fear and failure. *There is no standing still, Little Jackal.*

With the silver case pressed against her skin, the idea that had been forming grew sharper in her mind. A path to relief, to the end of pain and of expectation. She convinced herself in that moment that it was a victory. What bolder action was there? What surer way to seize control? It felt good to make a choice. To steer herself out of the storm rather than let herself be buffeted. If it was not a victory, it was at least an escape from defeat.

Dido braced her body and focused her mind on what she must do. She had to be quick. Her hand could not falter with nerves or with doubt. She gripped the ivory handle of the dagger and put her foot on to the first log.

A hand closed around her wrist. She looked down in surprise, and saw Anna's arm locked to hers.

'What are you doing? Let go of me.'

'I can't do that. I can't let you throw yourself away.'

'I don't . . . How did you . . . ?'

'You must have forgotten, my friend, that I am a liar and a cheat, and able to spot another.' Anna looked across with a spark in her eye, but no smile.

Piddaya must have heard their muttered words, for Dido felt her other wrist wrapped by gentle fingers. 'You would not put yourself on the pyre, would you?' Her voice was hurt, but Dido hardened herself against it. 'Not after everything you have survived.'

'What right do you have to stop me?' Dido wrenched both her arms, but neither woman would let go. 'Is Aeneas's ship still in the harbour?' Suddenly, she burned to know. 'Are its anchors drawn? Is it still in sight? If you are my true friends, either of you, then you will go and tell me that.' Her voice was strung out and desperate. 'I need him to see my pyre burn.'

'Why, Dido?'

'To hurt him. To heal myself.'

'Then let him see it,' Anna hissed. 'Burn the pyre. Burn his gifts and all that he has left behind him. And let him imagine that he sees you burning, too. If you want to hurt him, that is the way to do it. Do not waste your life for it.'

'There is nothing left to waste, Anna.' A tear welled and she let it go. Her dignity was lost. The fragile firmness that she had braced within her had cracked. She only wanted to stop the nauseating swell in her chest. 'Let me go. Please.'

'I have seen your despair before.' Piddaya pulled at her wrist, held her arm with tenderness. 'And I have seen it mended.'

'I . . . I cannot do it again. I cannot rebuild myself as I did before. Distract myself with being a queen and building a city. I am too tired for it, Piddaya. And I am too ashamed. How can my people trust my judgement when I do not trust it myself?'

'There is no shame in any of this,' Anna said. 'Not from us, not from your people. They would still follow you across the world if you asked them. And if you died, they would grieve for you as if you were their own mother.'

Dido shook her head bitterly. 'Hashmun has turned them against me. They doubt me, and they are right to.'

Anna spat at the ground. 'You will throw away your life for that poisonous man? He is nothing. He has done nothing. The people barely listen to his tired ramblings. We will drive him out of the city, if that is what must be done.'

Another face came into Dido's mind. A kinder one, though twisted with disappointment. 'And what of Iarbas? I cannot face him, nor drive him away and make the Auseans our enemy.'

'You think that Iarbas will hold you in shame?' Anna's face was painted with confusion, and she made her voice gentle. 'Iarbas loves you more than any of us, Elissa. He always has.'

Anna squeezed the hand that still held the dagger, and Piddaya the other. Slowly, Dido felt her fingers loosening.

'I don't know how to be now,' Dido croaked. 'How will I find myself again?'

'We'll help you,' said Piddaya.

'You don't need to be anything today,' said Anna. 'Just be with us.'

The torches were brought and the pyre was lit. The great logs blazed, and Dido watched them. She watched the beautiful diadem warp and blacken, the saffron dress disappear as if it had never been. Anna was right, she thought. The gods despise the wasting of precious things. But her own singular life had been spared from the flames. She let her sisters hold her, and allowed that which she had given up to mesh itself into the world again.

Her mind wandered, briefly, to the ship cutting its way towards the horizon. To Aeneas and his son. She could not know if they looked back, whether they saw love's funeral smoke. For Ascanius, she hoped that he did not. And for Aeneas, she wished little at all. Her thoughts were pulled to the Ausean camp instead. To her old friend, whom she longed so suddenly to see again. And she smiled to think that she would. She smiled to think that she might do so many things.

Author's Note

On Historical Setting

Queen Dido, if she existed as a real historical person, likely lived in the latter half of the 9th century BC. This is indicated by historical records and inscriptions relating to her royal family members, and aligns with the dates determined by ancient authors for Dido's flight from Tyre and the subsequent founding of Carthage (either 825 BC or 814 BC). It may seem obvious, then, that a historical fiction retelling of Dido's story would take the 9th century as its setting. And mine would have done so, if Dido's legend were not more complex than her history.

Stories have their own history. They change over time – in form, in proportion, in detail. They invite new characters, new episodes, new endings. Dido's story has a long history, beginning before a time where we can trace it. But the earliest versions of it that we know include no mention of Aeneas. It was the Roman poet Virgil who popularised the doomed love story between Carthaginian queen and Trojan prince in his epic poem the *Aeneid*. Though he was apparently not the first to introduce Aeneas into Dido's tale, Virgil's version is undoubtedly the most enduring and influential, and is the version that I encountered before any other. I could not erase Virgil from Dido's history, and I did not want to. But I realised very early on in my conception of this novel that, if I, like Virgil, wanted to collide Dido's story with that of Aeneas, I would have to make certain compromises.

Aeneas is a survivor of the Trojan War. As such, he brings his own sprawling context to Dido's story. The Trojan War lies at the centre of a rich web of myths, but it is also possible (and, in my opinion, probable) that some version of the war really took place toward the end of the Mediterranean Bronze Age. That would place the 'historical' Aeneas within the early 12th century BC – several hundred years away from the historical Dido. Even the use of alternative dates based on Aeneas' legendary founding of Rome cannot resolve this issue of synchronicity. Indeed, writers contemporary with Virgil and those who came later complained that his insertion of Aeneas into Dido's story was anachronistic. In short, there is no way to satisfactorily align the timelines of Dido and Aeneas, whether according to history or legend.

My solution, then, was this. Rather than bringing Aeneas forward into Dido's historical context, I elected to send Dido backwards into the Late Bronze Age. I had several reasons for this, not least of which was the fact that my first novel, *Daughters of Sparta*, had already taken the Trojan War as its setting, presenting it as an historical reality taking place at the close of the Bronze Age, and featuring Aeneas as a minor character. Though my novels stand alone, I like to imagine that they all tell stories set within the same historically authentic and consistent world, based on deep research and a desire to faithfully reimagine the Mediterranean Bronze Age context that may have originated these myths.

The Wandering Queen, then, is set around 1200 BC. However, as our evidence for the early history of Tyre is sparse, I have relied upon a broad range of sources to reimagine a culture which feels more complete. These sources, by necessity, often come from outside Tyre itself – e.g., from Egypt, from Ugarit, from biblical and classical texts – and in some cases from later periods in the city's history, stretching into the Iron Age period in which the historical Dido may really have lived. Just as Dido and her story defy consistent dating, my novel's setting has to some extent taken on an amalgamate form, though I have tried to the best of my ability to root it in the archaeological and textual evidence which is available to us.

It should be said that, while direct archaeological evidence of Bronze Age Tyre is very slim, for Bronze Age Carthage it is non-existent. The earliest archaeological traces of settlement at the site are dated to the late 8th century BC – making them even later than the supposed date that our 'historical' Dido would have settled there. The city which my Dido builds is therefore not based on any real settlement, but is an imagining of what she might have built had she existed in the Bronze Age and made it across the sea to North Africa. The real Carthage would, in fact, be founded and developed much later.

For these reasons, *The Wandering Queen* should be taken as an attempt to reimagine the legendary figure of Dido within an historical cultural setting, rather than as a reconstruction of the historical figure of Dido or her part in the true political history of Tyre and Carthage.

On the Two Didos

As well as the tension between Dido's legend and her history, this complicated figure holds another conflict. As mentioned above there is a version of Dido's story that far predates Virgil, which is preserved most fully by the Roman writer Justinus (*Epitome of the Philippic History of Pompeius Trogus*, 18.4–6) and likely had its origin in Phoenician tradition. This pre-Virgilian Dido, also known as Elissa, can be thought of as 'chaste' Dido, because in her version she never meets Prince Aeneas and instead is famous for her unwavering fidelity to her first husband, and her ultimate choice to die by suicide rather than remarry. This version also gives a much richer backstory to how Dido came to find herself at Carthage.

Virgil's Dido, by contrast, is largely framed by her impact upon Aeneas' own journey. She may be one of the most famous and vividly drawn characters of his *Aeneid*, but she is still in essence a side character, an obstacle for the true hero to overcome and, literally and narratively, leave behind. Virgil inspired criticism for turning the legendarily chaste queen into a tragically abandoned lover. Over time, though, this love-maddened Dido came to replace the original chaste Dido in the Western cultural consciousness, and has been the basis of countless plays, operas and other artworks over the past two millennia.

I wanted my own retelling to re-centre the pre-Virgilian Dido – voyager, trickster, leader, survivor – while also incorporating and responding to Virgil's narrative. I wanted to create a version of Dido that was true to both sides of her tradition, and to neither. Not a paragon of chaste feminine virtue, nor a helpless victim of desire and tragic fate. But a complex, flawed, vulnerable, extraordinary human being. The alternating structure used in the novel was one way to entwine Dido's original story with her later story, and to imagine her as a single realistic character whose choices always tug at the threads between past and present.

For readers who would like to learn more about the history and legacy of Dido's story, I recommend *A Woman Scorn'd: Responses to the Dido Myth* (1998), edited by Michael Burden.

On Names

Those who have read Virgil or any other literary account of Dido may have wondered about my choice for the name of Dido's first husband. In classical accounts he is named as either Sychaeus, Acerbas or Sycharbas. Since I did not want to choose between these variations, and since they are all likely to be

Latinised forms of the elsewhere attested Canaanite/Phoenician name of Zakarbaal, this choice felt more authentic.

In other cases, I chose not to deviate from the classical names traditionally used for the characters in Dido's story. For example, Pygmalion seems to be a Greek rendering of the Canaanite/Phoenician name Pumayyaton, but since Dido's brother is consistently known as Pygmalion I decided not to change this. I have endeavoured to give all invented characters names which are culturally and historically authentic.

I have used modern names for some general geographical locations such as Italy, Sicily and Cyprus, for ease of identification and in cases where no other term felt more appropriate. It is not clear how ancient Canaanites or Trojans might have referred to Italy, for example, and while Virgil uses the poetic name of Hesperia (Ancient Greek, meaning 'land in the west') this term felt more tied to his literary world than to the historical context of my characters. North Africa, as in my previous novel *The Shadow of Perseus*, is referred to by the classical name of Libya for the sake of consistency. Canaan is used for the region encompassing Tyre as it has a particular political significance in the Late Bronze Age and is the most historically appropriate name for the region (more so than Phoenicia).

In working with ancient stories such as that of Dido, which have complex histories and contexts, there are many creative decisions which must be made. I hope that these notes are helpful in explaining some of my choices, and that you have enjoyed this reimagining of the legendary queen of Carthage.

Acknowledgements

This novel was refined by the keen eyes and minds of several editors, and I give my sincere thanks to each of them for their contributions and perspective. Thank you to Kate Norman and Tallulah Lyons at Hodder, and to Lindsey Rose and Cassidy Sachs at Dutton. Thank you also to the wider teams at both Hodder and Dutton for their efforts in launching this book into the world. Great thanks are owed also to my agent Sara Keane, for her early enthusiasm and feedback upon the novel's first draft and for her consistent support.

Thank you, as always, to my partner Andrew, who supports me in all things and who so frequently acts as my sounding board. Thank you to my family and friends for their love and encouragement. And thank you, reader, for spending your time with my book. It is always appreciated and never taken for granted.

'Heywood's wondrous retelling of the lives of two ancient princesses struggling for independence and agency in a patriarchal society resonates deeply in today's imperfect world. Required reading for fans of Circe, and a remarkable, thrilling debut'

Fiona Davis
New York Times bestselling author of *The Lions of Fifth Avenue*

'Heywood triumphantly reclaims the stories of three of Greek mythology's most deserving women. With brilliant, confident writing, *The Shadow of Perseus* has illuminated the stories of ladies too often relegated to the role of villain or damsel'

Claire M. Andrews
Acclaimed author of *The Daughter of Sparta* and *Blood of Troy*

RAISING READERS
Books Build Bright Futures

Dear Reader,

We'd love your attention for one more page to tell you about the crisis in children's reading, and what we can all do.

Studies have shown that reading for fun is the **single biggest predictor of a child's future life chances** – more than family circumstance, parents' educational background or income. It improves academic results, mental health, wealth, communication skills, ambition and happiness.[1]

The number of children reading for fun is in rapid decline. Young people have a lot of competition for their time. In 2024, 1 in 10 children and young people in the UK aged 5 to 18 did not own a single book at home.[2]

Hachette works extensively with schools, libraries and literacy charities, but here are some ways we can all raise more readers:

- Reading to children for just 10 minutes a day makes a difference
- Don't give up if children aren't regular readers – there will be books for them!
- Visit bookshops and libraries to get recommendations
- Encourage them to listen to audiobooks
- Support school libraries
- Give books as gifts

There's a lot more information about how to encourage children to read on our website: **www.RaisingReaders.co.uk**

Thank you for reading.

[1] OECD, '21st-Century Readers: Developing Literacy Skills in a Digital World', 2021, https://www.oecd.org/en/publications/21st-century-readers_a83d84cb-en.html

[2] National Literacy Trust, 'Book Ownership in 2024', November 2024, https://literacytrust.org.uk/research-services/research-reports/book-ownership-in-2024

RAISING READERS

Dear Reader

We hope that from time to time this page helps you remember the reasons behind reading and what we can all do.

Studies have shown that reading to children in their early years is a predictor of a child's future life chances – more than their socioeconomic status, education background or ethnicity. It impacts significantly on their language skills with consequences on both education and language.

The number of children reading for fun has dropped, with young people twice as likely to do so during lockdowns. One in six children aged 16 to 24 do not have a single book in their home.

Children suffer enormously if we take books away, and there's plenty we can do. But there are subtle ways we can all help more to nurture readers.

- Reading to children for just 10 minutes a day makes a difference.
- Don't give up on children who struggle to read. Persevere, listen, or share.
- Visit libraries and theatres to instil imagination.
- Encourage children to write or draw.
- Support school libraries.
- Be a role model.

For more information about how to encourage children to read, visit our website: www.RaisingReaders.co.uk

With all my thanks